Advance Praise for *The Thief of Auschwitz*

"Jon Clinch's *The Thief of Auschwitz* is the intensely dramatic and moving story of how a remarkable painting enables two doomed parents to save their beloved teenage son from the gas chambers of Nazi Germany. Abounding with richly developed, surprising characters, *The Thief of Auschwitz* is itself a stunning portrait of how love of family, of freedom, and of art can triumph over pure, relentless evil. *The Thief of Auschwitz,* for my money, is the best and most powerful work of fiction ever written about the Holocaust"

— Howard Frank Mosher, author of *Walking to Gatlinburg*
and *Where The Rivers Flow North*

"There is a painting of a child that figures throughout Jon Clinch's moving and fierce new book, one of many indelible and haunting images he paints in this story of one family's fight to keep love alive in a landscape filled with death. That painting will remain, like the story itself, in your heart forever."

— Robert Goolrick, author of *A Reliable Wife*
and *Heading Out to Wonderful*

Acclaim for Jon Clinch's *Finn*

Named a best book of the year by the *Washington Post*, the *Chicago Tribune*, and the *Christian Science Monitor.*

Named a *Notable Book* by the *American Library Association.*

Winner of the *Philadelphia Athenaeum Literary Award.*

Shortlisted for the *Sargent First Novel Prize.*

"A brave and ambitious debut novel… It stands on its own while giving new life and meaning to Twain's novel, which has been stirring passions and debates since 1885… triumph of imagination and graceful writing…. Bookstores and libraries shelve novels alphabetically by authors' names. That leaves Clinch a long way from Twain. But on my bookshelves, they'll lean against each other. I'd like to think that the cantankerous Twain would welcome the company."

— *USA Today*

"Ravishing…In the saga of this tormented human being, Clinch brings us a radical (and endlessly debatable) new take on Twain's classic, and a stand-alone marvel of a novel. Grade: A."

— Entertainment Weekly

"Haunting…Clinch reimagines Finn in a strikingly original way, replacing Huck's voice with his own magisterial vision—one that's nothing short of revelatory…Spellbinding."

— Washington Post

"His models may include Cormac McCarthy, and Charles Frazier, whose *Cold Mountain* also has a voice that sounds like 19th-century American (both formal and colloquial) but has a contemporary spikiness. This voice couldn't be better suited to a historical novel with a modernist sensibility: Clinch's riverbank Missouri feels post-apocalyptic, and his Pap Finn is a crazed yet wily survivor in a polluted landscape…Clinch's Pap is a convincingly nightmarish extrapolation of Twain's. He's the mad, lost and dangerous center of a world we'd hate to live in—or do we still live there?—and crave to revisit as soon as we close the book."

— Newsweek

"I haven't been swallowed whole by a work of fiction in some time. Jon Clinch's first novel has done it: sucked me under like I was a rag doll thrown into the wake of a Mississippi steamboat…Jon Clinch has turned in a nearly perfect first book, a creative response that matches *The Adventures of Huckleberry Finn* in intensity and tenacious soul-searching about racism."

— Bookslut

"An inspired riff on one of literature's all-time great villains…This tale of fathers and sons, slavery and freedom, better angels at war with dark demons, is filled with passages of brilliant description, violence that is close-up and terrifying…Everything in this novel could have happened, and we believe it…"

— New Orleans Times-Picayune

"Finn brims with tension, fueled by sentences as taut as a cane pole wrestling a catfish in muddy waters. Considering the heady literary terrain Clinch hopes to master, the novel succeeds better than anyone but its author could have hoped. It offers a jolting companion to the mischievous antics of *Huckleberry Finn*."

— Christian Science Monitor

"Shocking and charming. Clinch creates a folk-art masterpiece that will delight, beguile and entertain as it does justice to its predecessor...In *Finn,* Clinch expands the bloodlines and scope of the original story and casts new light on the troubled legacy of our country's infamous past."

— *New York Post*

"In Clinch's retelling, Pap Finn comes vibrantly to life as a complex, mysterious, strangely likable figure...Clinch includes many sharply realized, sometimes harrowing, even gruesome scenes...*Finn* should appeal not only to scholars of 19th century literature but to anyone who cares to sample a forceful debut novel inspired by a now-mythic American story."

— *Atlanta Journal-Constitution*

"What makes bearable this river voyage that never ventures far beyond the banks is the compelling narrative Clinch has created. He writes exceedingly well, not with the immediacy Twain imbued to Huck's voice, but with an impersonal narrator's voice that almost perversely refuses to take sides. Masterful."

— *Fredericksburg Freelance-Star*

"Disturbing and darkly compelling...Clinch displays impressive imagination and descriptiveness...anyone who encounters *Finn* will long be haunted by this dark and bloody tale."

— *Hartford Courant*

"Every fan of Twain's masterpiece will want to read this inspired spin-off, which could become an unofficial companion volume."

— *Library Journal* (Starred)

"An important work that would be regarded as a major novel, even if *Adventures of Huckleberry Finn* didn't exist."

— Kent Rasmussen, author of *Mark Twain A To Z*

Acclaim for Jon Clinch's *Kings of the Earth*

Named a best book of the year by the *Washington Post.*

"In his masterful and compassionate new novel, *Kings of the Earth*, Clinch borrows from a true-life case of possible fratricide. Three elderly, semiliterate brothers live in squalor on a ramshackle dairy farm in central New York state. The prismatic narrative shifts time and point of view, and Clinch easily slips into the voices of his diverse cast of characters—a nosy, good-hearted neighbor, a police investigator struggling to do the right thing, and the brothers' drug-dealing nephew. Through evocative descriptions of the landscape—'a countryside full of that same old homegrown desolation'—and by imbuing these odd men with a gentle nobility and an 'antique strangeness,' Clinch has created a haunting, suspenseful story."

— *O, The Oprah Magazine* (Lead Title, Summer Reading List)

"True feeling seems to be out of fashion in contemporary fiction, and fiction is the poorer for it. Disaffection and irony may be the tenor of the times, but too much of it can leave you estranged and lonely. Then along comes Clinch, and we are once again safe at home, in the hands of a master. *Kings of the Earth* recalls the finest work of John Gardner, and Bruce Chatwin's *On the Black Hill.* It becomes a story that is not told but lived, a cry from the heart of the heart of the country, in William Gass's phrase, unsentimental but deeply felt, unschooled but never less than lucid. Never mawkish, Clinch's voice never fails to elucidate and, finally, to forgive, even as it mourns."

— *Washington Post*

"Clinch's literary alchemy results in a stunning book. Because each chapter releases essential information, the book moves easily toward closure, but an intricate knot of story lines plays out through them. Recalling William Faulkner's *As I Lay Dying*, each short chapter is broken into a section that is told in the first person. Not only do we get the brothers' voices, we hear an entire rural chorus: the dead father and mother, neighbors, the sister, brother-in-law, lawyers and the police."

— *Dallas Morning News*

"The power of *Kings of the Earth* lies in the intricacies of the relationships among the Proctors; neighbor and childhood friend Preston, who serves as something of a guardian angel; the drug-dealing nephew, and the police. Clinch is canny enough to move his characters through their own understated lives, hinting where he needs to as he skirts the obvious, and refusing to overlay a sense of morality on their actions. The landscape informs the story as much as the internal terrain of the characters does, giving *Kings of the Earth* a grounding that is missing from many modern novels. We know the events that lie behind Clinch's novel were real, and that the novel is not. But the realism here is no less, with writing so vibrant that you feel the bite of a northern wind, smell the rankness of dissipated lives and experience the heart-tug of watching tenuous lives play out their last inches of thread."

— *Los Angeles Times*

"It's the sort of book you race through then read again more slowly, savoring each voice. Preston, the kindly neighbor who cheerfully admits he doesn't entirely understand the Proctors, says, 'Where a man comes from isn't enough. You've got to go all the way back to the seed of a man and the planting of it, and a person can't go back that far ever I don't think.' Clinch goes back to that seed and that planting, and readers will eagerly go with him."

— *Seattle Times*

"This is a gritty but warm-hearted and beautifully realized novel about three old unmarried brothers who live together on a rundown dairy farm in upstate New York. Clinch addresses one of Faulkner's favorite themes in this novel—our ability to endure—and explores it in ways that are inspiring and poignant. Enthusiastically recommended for readers of literary fiction."

— *Library Journal* (Starred)

"In Clinch's multilayered, pastoral second novel (after *Finn)*, a death among three elderly, illiterate brothers living together on an upstate New York farm raises suspicions and accusations in the surrounding community. Family histories and troubles are divulged in short chapters by a cacophony of characters speaking in first person. Alongside the police troopers' investigation, each player contributes his own personal perspectives and motivations. Clinch explores family dynamics in this quiet storm of a novel that will stun readers with its power."

— *Publishers Weekly* (Starred)

THE *Thief* OF AUSCHWITZ

A Novel

Jon Clinch

unmediated ink™

Visit jonclinch.com
to download a Reading Group Guide.

ISBN: 1479236667
ISBN-13: 978-1479236664

Version 1.1

For Wendy, as always.
And for the actual Sam.

"Things happened there—love and death, mostly death."

— Helena Citrónová

Auschwitz: A New History

Laurence Rees

"And I only am escaped alone to tell thee."

— Job 16:1

THE THIEF OF AUSCHWITZ

BOOK ONE:

Shadow and Light

Max

THE CAMP AT AUSCHWITZ TOOK one year of my life, and of my own free will I gave it another four.

This was 1942. I was fourteen years old but tall for my age, and I'd spent a lot of time outdoors, so I lied and I got away with it. My father and I passed through that barbed wire gate and presto, I was eighteen. It was his idea, and if I hadn't followed through on it they'd have been done with me in an hour, not a year. Maybe less than that. I was just a boy, after all. I was too young to be of any use.

That little white lie makes me eighty-eight years old now. I don't mind. My Social Security card lies and so does my driver's license, not that I drive anymore. You don't drive in New York unless you're some kind of a nut.

The last time one of the art magazines came around and asked me what I thought about some young Turk—it doesn't matter who; I don't even remember myself—what showed up in print sounded a whole lot like *you ought to forgive old Rosen, since he'll be turning ninety in a couple of years after all. Maybe he's going blind.*

Old Max Rosen.

Sympathetic, cantankerous, worn-out old Max.

King of the old-school representationalists.

The last believer in looking at things the way they are, and reporting back.

One

THE CLOCK BUILT HIGH INTO the station wall is painted on, a clumsy and heartless *trompe-l'oeil* that under ordinary circumstances wouldn't fool a soul, but those who pass beneath it have too much on their minds to look closely. If any one of them so much as glances up, some mother raising her eyes above the scuffle and the crowd for just an instant, she sees an ordinary railroad station clock and is reassured by it—reassured the same way that she is reassured by the crisply lettered signs hanging overhead and by the gaily painted flower boxes bursting with pansies beneath each station window. Reassured that all is well. That the train has stopped at an ordinary station and that she and her family have arrived at an ordinary village. That the rumors she has heard can't possibly be true.

Those who actually check the time are men, mainly. Two or three of them per car and no more, individuals who pride themselves on leading lives of regularity and precision. Shipping agents and clerks and shopkeepers, men of commerce, each fingering his vest pocket or raising his wrist to compare this public information with his own private store. *Half past three* says the station clock. Half past three will have to do, for these orderly men are surprised once again to remember that they've bartered away their watches in recent weeks or sewn them into the linings of their overcoats or otherwise set them aside. They shake their heads— *what slow learners they've become!*—and they move on. Keeping up. The clock says half past three. There is no time to waste.

Among those who don't look up at all are the four members of the

Rosen family. The parents, Jacob and Eidel. The children, Max and Lydia. Like everyone else in their car, they've been under way for three days or perhaps four. Not really traveling so much as waiting to travel, locked in the cars and anticipating movement and dreading it at the same time, for with each lurch forward the train has taken them another step toward a destination known only to itself.

*

Their journey began eighteen months prior and barely a hundred miles away, high among the highest ranges of the Carpathian mountains, in the resort town of Zakopane. It was the place of Jacob's birth, which meant that he'd be a long time seeing how very beautiful it was. He'd need help, in fact. The help of a girl, which is often the way these things go. Beauty of any sort had never been much in his line to begin with. He'd been a hiker during his youth and early manhood, but strictly for the exercise. Although his friends knew the name of every peak and the song of every bird and the chatter of every squirrel, Jacob Rosen cataloged only the most difficult routes from one destination to the next. It was never a walk in the woods for him. It was always a test.

At home he'd stand in the corner of his father's shop, drinking the last of the water from his canteen and watching the old man's hands as he trimmed the hair of a vacationer from Warsaw or Krakow. Listening to the stranger rhapsodize about the fields of undulating crocuses that he and his wife had discovered blooming in some alpine valley just this very morning. Thinking that this great lump of a tourist, sitting beneath a crisp white sheet as if masquerading as a mountain himself, sounded like a man who'd never seen a crocus before. Worse than that. Like the man who'd invented them.

As years went by, Jacob's father taught him what he needed to know about running the shop, including how best to endure men like these. He said *you don't want word getting out that young Rosen has no respect for the people who constitute his trade.* A reputation like that would be trouble enough right there in the town, but imagine if people began telling tales back in Warsaw. Saying, *visit Zakopane if you must, but get your hair trimmed before you go! Young Rosen would just as soon take your ears off!* It would be the end of everything that his father had built in this life.

More years had gone by and the old man had passed away and the shop was in Jacob's hands when Eidel arrived, Eidel Mankowicz from Warsaw, here for a month's skiing with her parents and her three younger sisters. She'd never seen a place even half so beautiful. She couldn't get enough of it. The truth was that she could barely bring herself to come indoors, and late one afternoon as Jacob trimmed her father's hair she waited outside the shop, utterly rapt and completely indifferent to what was going on inside, caught up in the gathering of clouds over the high peaks, her face illuminated by the last rays of the fading light.

Inside, Jacob slipped and nicked her father's cheek and Mankowicz said, "Perhaps you ought to turn on a light, the evening comes so early here in the mountains." He was a hard man by the look of him, worldly but tough-minded, a lawyer perhaps. Someone with the means to bring a large family here to the limits of the Carpathians on an extended holiday. He was a hard man but he could see that this barber wasn't going to turn on a lamp until the last possible minute, not while pretty young Eidel was standing outside his window with her face tilted up into the dying light. Not as long as he could still see her. Mankowicz was a man who understood the world, and he resigned himself to enduring another nick or two.

What was the harm? They were children. They wouldn't be young forever.

*

She didn't go home to Warsaw. When the month was over she stayed on in Zakopane, and she acquired her own apartment with money from her father, and she sent home for her paints and brushes. She skied or hiked each morning and she painted each afternoon and she let Jacob court her for two years altogether, although they both knew from the beginning exactly how it was going to end. They'd both known it from the moment her father had emerged into the starlit street outside the barber shop and she had looked past him, through the open door, and let her eyes fall upon the young man within. But here in the mountains the turn of every season was a fresh delight and twenty-four months seemed a reasonable interval and after the earth had gone twice around the sun she confessed what she'd known at the outset. That this was how she must spend the rest of her days. Here and with him. They took a train to Warsaw for the wedding, and then they hurried back to the mountains to set up housekeeping in the rooms over the shop.

Eidel claimed the attic as her studio and Jacob emptied it out and she washed the windows to let in the warm southern light. She could have spent every single one of the endless days ahead painting the changing face of Mount Rysy, registering its subtle changes without ceasing, if there had not been so many other subjects at hand. The beautiful and sturdy children of the town. The throngs of happy tourists in their holiday clothing. The steaming windows of the neighborhood *cukiernia*, jammed with pastries and marzipan. Her own husband.

On days that dawned particularly fine she would beg Jacob to close

5

the shop and come with her to the mountains, and if it weren't Monday (when the rabbi came at ten-fifteen sharp), or Thursday (when the cantor arrived at nine), he might consider it. The Sabbath was theirs either way. Eidel wasn't religious by nature, a condition as unremarkable in Warsaw as it was scandalous in the country. Even the Catholics raised their eyebrows to see her leading her husband down the main street toward the mountains, bundled for skiing or dressed for the trail, in the light of a perfect and God-given Saturday morning.

Through her eyes he learned to see all over again, both the things she painted and the things she didn't. Just the simple fact of her *looking*—whether at a larch tree or an angle of light, at a sunrise or a mossy cobblestone—made the thing that had fallen within her vision worth looking at. The gift of Eidel's attention to the world became his gift as well.

By and by the children arrived, Max entirely by accident and Lydia because Max had brought the two of them more happiness than they could possibly keep to themselves. By that reckoning, they realized only afterward, there might have been no end of it.

Max was like his father. Intense, constantly in motion, tearing through the world but in certain ways oblivious to it. Jacob himself, older now and wiser, prayed that some day, when Max was sufficiently mature to handle the shock, he would find someone like Eidel to change everything for him—someone to open his eyes and slow him down—although in his heart he doubted that it was possible. Lightning might strike twice, but not love. Not that kind.

As for Lydia, she was like neither of them. She was unworldly, ethereal. She talked late and she walked late and she was in no hurry for anything whatsoever, content to let the world come to her if it should come at all. About the time she was ready to start school, the synagogue got her attention. It was the other children, really, the line of them filing toward *shul* each morning, filtering one by one and two by two from the doorways of houses and cottages. They joined with one another and flowed down the streets like water, as if they had no will of their own and didn't require any. Her mother had never cared for the synagogue and her father had quit attending altogether, except on the holiest of holy days when he crept in later than the last of the shuffling old men and felt even more guilt than was necessary. But Lydia drew them back. She reminded her father of where he had come from, and she opened her mother's eyes to the invisible.

Men and women sat apart in the synagogue, the women in a balcony and the men below. The separation was meant to focus attention on the everlasting, but for Eidel it had the opposite effect. The absence of her husband and son was a powerful distraction. It set her on edge and kept her mind from settling. She was certain that if only she were able to sit alongside them she would be able to pray, although she couldn't decide if this was a failing on her part or a failing on the part of the synagogue or something else. In any event it was vexing in the extreme. She found herself trying to single out their voices during the prayers, Max's high and Jacob's low, entwining around the rote mutterings of the old men and enclosing them. This, the faithful and patient act of listening for her son and her husband, became of necessity her one and only prayer. It was enough.

At least she had Lydia by her side. Lydia whose idea this had been in the first place.

Early in the morning they would climb the thirty-six steps to the balcony with their coats still on and take their seats with the last of the snow still melting from the soles of their shoes, and from that chill and elevated place—an aerie itself—they would look out over the town through a high window and be the first to see the sun rising over the mountains. The men murmured below in the dark, and the Catholics were still asleep in their beds, and for just that one moment, the day was their secret.

*

The children grew, and Eidel painted them at every age. As a rule her paintings of Max captured him either in motion or in recovery. Playing some game or setting off along a mountain path or resting afterward. In the summertime she would catch him at the kitchen table with a glass of cold milk and the alpine breeze lifting the lace curtain, in the wintertime before the fire with a mug of tea, his cheeks ruddy, bending forward to massage the life back into his toes. She had to work fast when she painted her son, and she had to see him clearly and completely in the space of an instant, for soon he would be just a blur.

To paint her daughter, on the other hand, she had to learn patience. She needed to be watchful, for she might find Lydia anywhere, pensive or wide-eyed, with a book or a toy or just an open window, dreaming. But the trick was to capture her stillness, the moment of the painting and the moment before it and the moment after it all come together into one. Alone with Lydia for the hours it took, she sometimes felt as if she were entering into the child's dream herself. That was when the work went well. When the effort fell away and all that remained was love.

One such painting was her favorite. It showed the attic studio, shot through with light. In the window was Lydia, seated at a wooden table in profile, hands folded, the sun gleaming upon her auburn hair and burnishing it into surprising gold. Upon her small rapt face was a pink glow of anticipation for what might lie beyond the window. For what might lie ahead in the world. And behind her in a shadowy corner, barely visible but rendered with the same intensity of observation and care as all the rest, lay a castoff toy, a stuffed gray rabbit worn down to almost nothing, left there only the week prior but left perhaps for good.

The more she painted the children the less she painted her husband, not only because there were only so many hours in the day but because Jacob was usually busy in the shop downstairs. Thinking of the future, building up his trade, setting aside such treasure as he could for the days when the children would need it most. A university education. A wedding.

"But papa already has a fortune," Eidel would say, which only made him work harder. Max and Lydia were *his* children, not his father-in-law's, and their future required a fortune of his own making.

He hung a clock over the big plate-glass mirror and he put a sign in the window promising to cut any man's hair in five minutes and shave his face in five minutes more—a banker on a schedule or a busy shop-keeper with customers waiting could be spruced up and on his way in no time at all—and as the children grew his trade grew as well. No longer just the rabbi at ten-fifteen on Monday and the cantor on Thursday at nine, but the mayor and the chief of police and for a while even the monsignor from the Church of the Holy Family on Krupowki Street. On some days there was a line.

The line began dwindling with the Occupation. It didn't take long to peter out altogether, although during the first weeks Zakopane seemed almost immune, remote as it was from the great centers of population, the cities like Warsaw and Krakow where Jews lived in higher concentrations and made easier targets. But the glories of the Carpathian peaks appealed to the Nazis as irresistibly as to anyone else, and soon enough there were security police in the streets. *Sicherheitspolizei,* along with uniformed SS officers and grim-looking Hungarians and Slovaks and Ukrainians very different from those who typically visited this mountain town on holiday. These serious visitors were all men, for one thing, pale men with dark looks. Even their smiles looked hungry.

Rather than draw attention to himself, Jacob removed the sign from his window. The fortune he'd been laying up began to diminish.

The SS commandeered the Palace Hotel, the grandest building in town, a place known for luxury and opulence, although no one dared imagine now what kind of pleasures the new management might be indulging there. Now and then a Jewish family would receive word that they were to appear at headquarters for questioning, and sometimes they returned to the village untouched or apparently so and sometimes they did not, but under no circumstances did any of them ever speak a word of what had transpired. In the end they all vanished one way or another, either immediately into the bowels of the hotel or afterward into the mists of the mountains like mist themselves. Before long Jacob decided that taking down his sign wasn't enough in the way of self-defense.

And so, toward the end of 1939, they abandoned Zakopane for good. With their clothing packed in steamer trunks and Eidel's paintings boxed up in square wooden crates and Jacob's barbering tools tucked into a modest little folding leather case, they boarded a train and returned to Eidel's childhood home in Warsaw. Leaving, like any family at the close of their time in the mountains, with mingled sadness and anticipation.

*

Warsaw granted them fourteen months. Eidel's father had connections in the courts, and they served him just that long but no longer. So much for the illusion of immunity. So much for having faith that conditions would improve, that the occupation would end or that they would be somehow passed over. So much for going from the fire into the frying pan. Her father and mother packed a pair of small bags and set out for Sweden, begging Eidel and her family to come along as well, but what can you do with children, even grown ones? They have minds of their own. Jacob and Eidel took Max and Lydia and went to Krakow, on their second involuntary rail journey of the war years and the first of many that would serve to whittle them and their possessions down into kindling.

1941 was telescopic, their world collapsing upon itself at a rate that only increased. They stayed in Krakow for six or eight weeks, time enough to hang some of Eidel's paintings on the walls and time enough to barter some of them away for things that were more necessary. As if the paintings themselves were not necessities. After Krakow they lived in no one place for more than a month, then no more than two weeks, then no more than a week, and finally no more than a few days. Each apartment was smaller and meaner than the last, each village more crowded and less hospitable.

Along the way Eidel gave up painting entirely. One morning she looked out the window of a wretched apartment in a woebegone village and said to Jacob, *There's nothing here that I can stand looking at for long enough,* and that was the end of it. She abandoned her paints and brushes in a cupboard behind some earlier tenant's castoffs, and she used her last clean scraps of canvas to wrap food that would have lasted long enough only if her family had been living in some fairy tale, and they moved on.

She bartered away more paintings. Sometimes she stripped out the canvases and sold the bare frames. As time went by the wood became more valuable as fuel than as decoration, and the paintings themselves became worthless altogether. Jacob put a sign in whatever window was visible from whatever street they looked out on and cut hair for whatever he could get. For money, of course, until every coin in every village had been sewn into the hem of a dress or concealed in the false bottom of a traveling bag. Then for the things that coins represented, since translation of real goods into negotiable currency was no longer required or even possible.

Food. Coal. A tattered scrap of a blanket.

In one particularly dark and narrow village they shared an apartment with two other families, separated by not so much as a curtain, and when the time came to move on they left just about everything behind. Everything being almost nothing. They had the clothes on their backs and one battered valise holding a change of underclothing and not much else. Jacob's barbering tools. A book. A washrag hastily wrung out and hung to dry over the coal stove and stinking now of their provisional past.

They opened the door onto the warm spring day and flung their wool coats over their shoulders like capes, young Max deciding at the last moment to leave his hat behind since the weather was so fine, and Lydia carrying that stuffed rabbit under her arm and a silk handkerchief in her fist. The rabbit had left Zakopane on the train to Warsaw and had never been out of her sight since. As for the handkerchief, she'd been battling a cold for weeks and this was the only weapon remaining to her. Like everything else, it stank of coalsmoke.

Just inside the door was the very last of Eidel's paintings, standing on the mantle above the dead fireplace. It was the picture of Lydia in the attic, the room full of light, the child full of promise. Eidel took it down and measured it against the valise and saw that fitting it in was hopeless. She worked the canvas from the frame, rolled it up gently, folded it over and put it in her coat. Then she smashed the frame on the stones of the hearth, and put the pieces in her husband's valise.

Jacob snapped the valise shut and gave her such comfort as he could. He said the time had come to content themselves with the girl herself, and never mind the painting.

Something—a sliver of wood, a rusted coil of picture wire, a stubborn staple—had pricked her finger, and she put the tip of it in her mouth, tasting iron.

The four of them set out for the train.

*

The day is bright at the Auschwitz station as well, and they squint into it as they move forward. As a rule people on a boarding platform move with energy and purpose, but here they shuffle. Stopping and going and stopping again. There are too many of them. They pass low entrances lettered *Men* and *Women,* but the restrooms are occupied or at least the doors are locked. Lines of travelers form in front of them and slowly disperse in frustration and then reform from new constituents.

Everyone is impatient. Lydia asks her father where they're going, and he can't say. Max has learned not to ask. It's enough to be moving. Anyplace might be an improvement. There's always hope.

Eventually they reach a wire fence with a sign separating men from women. Eidel gives her husband a pained look, and he angles his head down and smiles the best smile he can assemble out of nothing and says, "Pretend we're in the synagogue."

"I've always hated that about the synagogue."

"I know."

"Hated it."

"I know." But there's no choice. He says, "We'll meet again on the other side."

Eidel wonders if today in fact might be the Sabbath. How long have they been on the train? What day was it when they boarded? Time has lost its grip and she can't say for certain, so she keeps the thought to herself. She leans toward her husband seeking one more touch, perhaps even a kiss, but a smiling individual with a death's-head on his collar intervenes. "There'll be plenty of time for that," he says. He seems kindly enough. He seems to understand their impulse. They separate, Jacob and Max going left and Eidel and Lydia going right. They walk on, along opposite sides of the fence, losing themselves in the crush. Into the sun.

*

A gravel roadway runs alongside the path, separated from it by a second wire fence and a low wall of stone, and urgent white vans bearing the Red Cross insignia come and go along it at breakneck speed, raising great windblown clouds of grainy gray dust. Lydia watches the vans rumble back and forth and reflects for a moment and asks her mother if the path they're walking leads to a hospital or a clinic of some kind, and her mother says she doesn't believe so but she can't be certain. Lydia squints into the sun and says she hopes that it might, with this cough of hers, with this runny nose. She picked them up in one of those apartments, and the dust of the vans' passage only makes them worse.

Her mother stops and lowers herself to one knee and takes the handkerchief and shakes it out and holds it to her nose and says *blow*, the women behind making angry noises at the holdup, grumbling and complaining in three or four different languages. It's an international convention of disapproval. They will tolerate no delay, for they seem to be bound somewhere at last.

*

The men's line snakes toward another officer wearing the death's-head. Unlike the first, who stood with his hands behind his back and showed his nicotine-brown teeth and spoke freely, this one stands at attention to a degree that is nearly supernatural. He's barely disturbed by his own breathing. His gray-green uniform is spotless and he wears tall boots that gleam despite the dust rising all around. A pair of black miracles.

Jacob smiles at him from a distance in case he should happen to glance his way, but the officer only looks straight ahead. He stands at attention with the thumb of his left hand parallel to the seam in his trousers and his right elbow cocked and his right hand lifted up to a point beneath his chin, suspended there as steadily as if it were hung from a wire. As each individual passes beneath his gaze, the index finger of that one hand makes a single tiny movement. It's the only part of him that stirs, the one component of a broken machine still functional. The finger points by five or ten degrees either to the left or to the right, apparently independent of anything but its own volition, not even seeming to consult with the officer himself, who stands at attention and makes no other movement while the line of men approaching him becomes two lines. Two streams of weary travelers parting around him like water.

To the right go the strong ones. Healthy full-grown men. To the left go the rest. The weak and the sick, the aged and the young. Those with

15

canes or crutches or even the slightest trace of peculiarity to their gaits.

Jacob grits his teeth and takes his son by the arm, and they stop dead. The man behind them in line stumbles and curses.

Jacob whispers in the boy's ear, "The gas is to the left."

Max says, "No. The Red Cross trucks are going that way."

Jacob says, "No. It's the gas. The rumors are true." They move forward again.

"There's no gas," Max says. "It's a clinic."

"You must go to the right. You must come with me."

"He'll send me to the right anyhow. I'm not sick and I'm not a child."

"You're fourteen."

"So?"

"Fourteen is a child. Children go to the left. Today, you're eighteen." He studies the SS officer as a cornered man would study a wolf.

"He isn't asking anyone's age, Papa. He isn't asking anything."

"He asks. Now and then he asks." For he does. From time to time the officer violates the rule of his own posture and tips his head forward just the slightest, no more than the five or ten degrees that his finger moves, and lifts an eyebrow by way of inquiry. He does so now, and Jacob grunts. "See? You see? Tell him eighteen."

"I will if he asks."

"Even if he doesn't. Just tell him."

"What if telling him makes him angry?"

"Do as I say."

"He looks like the type who might get angry."

"If he's going to get angry, we're already lost."

Max looks up at his father. "But what if it's just a clinic after all?"

"It's no clinic."

"It might be."

"It's not."

"Then what about Lydia?"

Jacob stops, and the man behind him stumbles into him once more, and the cursing starts up again. "Perhaps it's a clinic after all," he says. "Still, you come with me."

The boy doesn't argue.

*

Eidel is adrift.

Alone and adrift with nothing but an old silk handkerchief for comfort. A silk handkerchief and a rolled-up painting, although soon enough the painting will be gone too since a person can't hold onto anything for long. Everything falls away.

She's glad to have the handkerchief to cling to, but at the same time she wishes she had managed to return it to Lydia, for her daughter needs it more than she does.

Max

WYETH HAD HIS HELGA. Surprise, surprise, surprise. As if one single thinking person in the whole wide world was shocked to learn that straitlaced old Andy had been hiding nudie pictures in the barn.

Somebody else's barn, at that.

It was the secretiveness that made the whole thing dirty, and it was the dirt that got people's attention. How he never told his wife what he was up to, I mean. How Helga never told her husband. Crafty old Uncle Andy made two hundred and fifty-some paintings of that woman, give or take, over ten or fifteen years. Two hundred and fifty-some paintings of her in every possible state of dress and undress.

In my book, that's called an unhealthy obsession.

He didn't just dash them off, either. He didn't work fast. You can't work fast. Not and get things right, or however close to right Andy was capable of getting things, which is another question.

Helga herself, though. She's the main thing.

When people asked what it was that drew his eye to her—as if he needed a reason; as if he weren't entitled to paint whatever he pleased; as if the paintings themselves, plainspoken and flatfooted as they were, weren't explanation enough—when people asked, do you know what he said?

Her Germanic qualities. That's right. As if, once again, anyone could possibly have been surprised. The sturdy Prussian marching across the winter fields in her braids and her long loden coat. The homely Prussian undressed in a homely country farmhouse of the sort that Andy had reduced to some kind of trademark years and years before.

Helga. Uncle Andy's Helga.

You never know who's going to reveal himself to be a monster at heart, and you never know how.

No wonder he kept her a secret.

Two

THEY ARE TRAVELERS NO MORE. They're prisoners now, stripped of everything, their clothing abandoned inside the door along with whatever private treasures were hidden within it. Rings and gems and coinage from a dozen countries. Lockets and pearl buttons and pocket combs of ivory. Mementos meaningless to anyone but the bearer.

They've been shorn and shaven raw with razors whose edges have seen a hundred times a hundred men since last they were stropped and will see a hundred times a hundred more before they're stropped again. Their skin has been rubbed white with calcium chloride and they stagger forward into the light as pale as fish in their uniforms of striped burlap, ill-fitting trousers and jackets that stink powerfully and unmistakably of gas.

Don't breathe, they think. And yet they breathe.

One by one and two by two they emerge into the same bright day that they left not an hour before. The sky is still blue and the clouds are still white and the wind still blows. The river, for the camp is built alongside a river—*how could they have failed to notice this? what were they thinking? what other precious elements of the ordinary world have they neglected to see until now?*—the river still flows. Everything in the world is exactly as it has been, with the exception of these stunned men moving like the dead into a kind of parade ground to await whatever will happen to them next. Standing on tiptoe and craning their necks to look toward the other side of the building, where the women must surely be, and failing to see them. Walls and chains and crosses of heavy timber wrapped in barbed wire block the view.

Everything is the same and nothing is the same.

Max is wearing a pair of trousers at least five sizes too large. His father found them in the pile of uniforms and insisted that he take them because who knows when he'll get another chance. He'll grow into them by and by. Max is almost as tall as any grown man already, and he rolls up the cuffs thinking there must be a naked giant hiding in the camp somewhere. Or a naked giant lying dead, which is more likely.

He pulls back his left sleeve and watches the seepage of blood and ink on the outside of his arm. His father does the same—every man here does, as if they've decided one after another to consult their missing wristwatches—studying his serialized tattoo and taking the permanence of it as a good sign. With as much reassurance as he can muster up he says to Max, "I suppose they wouldn't have bothered if we were bound straight for the gas."

Max nods. looking around at the rest of the men. They're a sturdy and fit enough crowd, considering. Not a weakling or an old-timer among them. Not a bent back and not a crutch. Certainly not a child anywhere.

Max's father must make the same observation at the same time, for he is on his knees when the guards step forward to round them up.

Lydia. Lydia.

*

The women's camp is bursting, but all of the camps at Auschwitz are bursting. They were designed to be overcrowded, housing for rats or not even rats, and temporary housing at that.

Eidel doesn't mind the conditions. She doesn't even register the crowding and the filth and the hunger. She lies on her side each night in a wooden bunk with another woman pressed against her back and another one against her chest, the bunk itself barely tall enough to slide into, barely a grave, barely large enough to contain the women and the air they need to live through the summer night. Light leaks in from the outside in quivering arcs, searchlights in motion.

Some of the women curse and some of them pray. Eidel does neither. She only clutches the silk handkerchief in her fist and waits. She waits for sleep to come or not to come. It makes no difference to her, for tomorrow will be tomorrow either way.

Tomorrow she will still have lost her daughter and her son, and she will still possess the handkerchief. It's all she has of Lydia. All she has of anything.

She remembers the days of looking forward. When it was possible and when she could permit herself. She remembers summers past, walking on a mountain path or along the bank of an alpine lake with the children, alive to them and to their vitality, alert to the landscape, aware that at any moment she could choose to set up her easel and get it all down. All of it forever.

She remembers her husband's barber shop. The bright oily smell of hair tonic, and the warm round scent of shaving cream, and above it all the high astringent tang of witch hazel, hovering in the air like a sung note.

But she doesn't speak of these things. Not even to Zofia Kohen, who lives in the same block and sleeps in the same bunk and works in the same place she does, day after day. Eidel is lucky to have been assigned to the kitchen, although it's caused her to forget almost everything that she once knew about cooking. Not that she ever cared much for cooking or was much skilled at it—in her father's house a woman from Krakow had presided over the kitchen, a woman who'd studied in France, so it wasn't until she'd married Jacob and come to Zakopane that she'd even tried her hand—but then again this isn't exactly cooking, not by any definition. Potato soup that's little more than hot water, or turnip soup or pea soup or carrot soup that isn't any better. Looking down into one of the great boiling vats is like looking down into a deep and cloudy stream. Just a hint of something lurking near the bottom.

The heat in the kitchen is ungodly as well. She keeps the silk handkerchief in her pocket, and as she mops her brow she thinks of Lydia and Max.

In addition to the soup they bake bread, using flour that arrives three or four times a week in a wagon drawn by horses. The same wagon brings coal on alternate days, and the same men deliver it. A two-man *commando,* a work crew. Handling flour or coal they use the same short-handled shovels and the same wheelbarrow with the same broken axle, the alternation of their labor turning them white one day and black the next. The bread is gray and it weighs nothing. It tastes of combustion.

Wonder of wonders, though: as time goes by, the men of the delivery commando prove to be incorrigible flirts. Imagine that. This pair of ragged scarecrows, thin as sticks, worn down by work and woe to a condition beyond any determinable level of vitality or even age, behaving like youngsters at a country dance. Who could have foreseen such a thing? They are shy at the outset, though. Shy as Eidel's own son was and forever will be, God rest his soul. They communicate with sidelong looks and diffident postures. They linger by the door and whisper to each other, secretive as field mice, glancing up timidly from beneath the brims of their low-slung caps. But they are full-grown men after all, and their reserve can't last. Certainly not here in the camp, where time is both compressed and nonexistent. Where all things must occur at once or never occur at all. Where whatever happens will happen again and again without ceasing, as everything must always happen in the mind of God.

*

Most of the men in Jacob's block work on a water project, digging trenches for the new women's camp. It's dry work in the hot sun. The *capo*—the individual in charge of the work and in charge of the block too—is Slazak, pot-bellied Slazak from Lodz, denizen and product of one ghetto after another. He is both a Jew and a disgrace to Jews, and if Jacob had encountered him back when he was a free man freely at work in his father's barber shop in Zakopane, he wouldn't have stooped to cut his hair. Even six months ago, working for a couple of apples at a time, he would have turned his back. But six months ago Slazak was already ensconced here at Auschwitz, already proving himself the sort that the SS could depend on, clawing his way up toward that subtle meniscus where the prisoner begins to confuse himself with those who have imprisoned him. The role of the capo is an essential position but a tenuous one, because in order to earn the job and the green patch that goes with it a man must demonstrate a capacity for cunning and brutality that will surely doom him one day. For certain men, though, the dream is irresistible. No one believes in the future anyhow.

No one believes in the future, and yet the work proceeds. Progress occurs. The men dig trenches and lay water pipes and bury them again, inch by inch. Jacob and Max work like Percherons and eat like monks. A daily slice of bread and a partial bowl of thin soup, and in the evening a scrap of fatty meat or moldy cheese. It pares them down and it builds them up, at least for a little while. It builds them up out of nothing but the will to go on. Each of them has spent sufficient time in the mountains, traversing from peak to peak with never quite enough in the way of food and water, to have labored long on an empty belly before. But it was nothing compared to this.

They work through hunger and they work through pain and they work through broken hearts. They work through visions of Eidel and memories of Lydia, Max with his back bent and his gaze down and his father keeping a watchful eye on him for all the good it might do, here in this place that has already cost him one child.

Among the things that keep them both going is the idea of a new women's camp. It floats before them like a mirage. For if there is to be such a thing as a new women's camp, then the SS must be planning to move women into it—one of whom might be Eidel. So when Jacob's legs can support him no more and Max's hands are too bloody to hold the shovel, they think of her—they think of how this very trench will come to hold pipes that will come to hold water that one day she might come to drink—and they carry on.

For her, if not for Lydia. They can do nothing for Lydia.

Each morning, well before dawn, the men rise to the clanging of three alarm bells and drag themselves out to the yard to be counted. Slazak is always first. Slazak is everywhere first. A couple of old fellows from the country, as alike as a pair of skeletons, are always the last. One of them is named Schuler, Ernst Schuler, and the other one has no name at all that Jacob or Max has ever heard. The men call him *Schuler's Twin* because he models himself so closely on the other man and sticks to him as if they've been fused together, but they're probably no relation. Schuler has an airy manner about him in spite of everything. He stands upright in his rags like royalty and he never lowers himself to complain. Not about the sleeping accommodations and not about the rising heat and not about the awful rations. The reason is that he doesn't work on the water project, although his twin does. Schuler works in the sorting facility, out by the train platform, going through the belongings of new arrivals in search of whatever treasures they might have abandoned in pockets and handbags and the linings of coats.

It doesn't take long for Jacob and Max to understand how this sets him apart. Schuler's feet give him away. He owns an extraordinary pair of shoes, gum-soled and comfortable-looking as the pillows on which some sultan might recline, and one of them is tied with regular laces instead of salvaged wire or baling twine or nothing at all. Jacob considers his own shoes, poor burst things never meant for the abuse they take each day on the water project, and he works his way over to where Schuler stands to ask him where he happened to come by such a pair of marvels.

"Canada," whispers Schuler.

"Canada?"

"Oh, yes. Canada." Nodding imperceptibly. Keeping an eye on Slazak. "It's the land of plenty."

Schuler's twin explains. Canada is what they call the sorting facility. In Canada, a man with sufficient cunning can get his hands on practically anything at all. Sometimes even food. Particularly food. Cheese from every country in Europe. Chocolate wrapped in golden foil. Foods that keep well, foods that uprooted people will bring with them on a long journey, foods that even the starving will permit themselves to eat only sparingly because they're so precious and because they remind them of home.

No wonder Schuler doesn't complain about the rations.

*

For a while, Eidel believes that she might kill herself. She thinks of it night and day, lying breathless in her bunk or sitting at the big table in the kitchen slicing potatoes for soup. A knife in her hand. Once she slips the blade along the flesh inside her left wrist, just opposite the tattoo, and presses to see if she can draw blood. Just to find out if it's possible. It is.

Suicide would be a way of cementing that endless present in which she tries to exist, and the idea of it is comforting in a way. It doesn't clear her mind, but it does give her something to think about other than the obvious. It crowds out Lydia, at least for a moment or two, but soon she returns—Lydia and Max too, for Max was a child as well and he must have been doomed to the same fate as his sister—and all thoughts of saving herself by bringing about her own end vanish.

I have no right, she tells herself. No right to choose her own fate when Lydia and Max were given no say in theirs. No right even to distract herself with the idea of it. Such faithlessness is unbecoming of a mother. It's a betrayal of her family.

And so she goes on. Thinking that as long as she keeps her two children in her heart they are alive at least somewhere. Unwilling to extinguish that light from the world.

One morning, one of the deliverymen asks her name. It happens on a day when the wagon is loaded with flour, and he and his partner are white from head to toe. Later she'll realize that there's a reason for the haphazard haste with which they go about their work—at the end of the day there'll be a few ounces of coal or flour in their pockets and cuffs—but for now she sighs and gives not her name but her number. The number tattooed onto her wrist and sewn onto her uniform.

The deliveryman is persistent, though. He says his name is Oskar

Wirtz, and he's from Witnica by way of Barlinek by way of Krakow, and he's pretty certain that he's seen her somewhere before, no doubt under better circumstances. He leans there in the doorway like a scrawny ghost in his pale rags, smiling at Eidel with a kind of punch-drunk optimism, proving that some things never change. Even under conditions as hopeless as these.

"Come on," he says. "I've told you mine. Now you have to tell me yours."

"Eidel. Eidel Rosen."

"Eidel," he says.

"You can call me Mrs. Rosen."

"What happened to your Mister?"

"He's around here someplace."

"Are you sure?"

"I'm sure."

"Lucky you," says the ghost in the doorway, crestfallen. "My own Missus ran into some difficulty. I'm sure you understand."

"I'm sorry," she says.

The female capo who runs the kitchen, a gigantic Pole whose last name is Rolak and whose first name no one has dared speak in so long that it has entered into the realm of myth, hurries past in pursuit of some prisoner who isn't where she's supposed to be. Eidel puts her head down. *Don't draw attention.* The deliveryman smiles brightly at Rolak, though, and doffs his whitened cap to her, and she smiles back. They have some kind of understanding. "Don't be flirting with these women," she says, tossing the words back over her shoulder. "They don't have time for your nonsense."

Eidel has never seen the capo talk to an ordinary prisoner this way. Like a human being. Rolak is a great fat woman, astonishingly so for as long as she's been confined here in Auschwitz, but Eidel has never seen her eat so much as a bite. It must happen elsewhere. There are rumors. Rumors of imported delicacies consumed in secret. Eidel pictures her alone in one of the storerooms, shoving aside bushel baskets of turnips and beans to reach such rare foods as she might keep hidden in the darkness behind them; she pictures her in her little boarded-off room within the block, the private quarters behind whose padlocked door she might keep hidden anything at all. She pictures her luxuriating on the bed—*a bed with a mattress! think of it!*—her mouth crammed full of chocolate or sausage or cheese. Drowning herself in food.

"The capo," she says to the junkman. "Do you get food for her?"

"I can get anything." He smiles and takes one step toward the table where she sits. "A fellow in my position moves pretty freely around the camp. I know lots of people." It's true. For a junkman from Witnica, he's come up in the world.

Eidel hardly even knows what she is asking when she asks it. "Can you get information?" she says.

He cocks an eyebrow, putting his knuckles on the table. "Information? Of course!"

"I need to know just one thing."

"One thing," he nods—slowly, again and again, like the handle of a pump—leaning forward. "Everyone wants to know one thing. Remember, though: I'm not a fortune teller. I can't predict your future."

"I know you can't."

"For that, you'd need a gypsy." He smiles, all teeth.

"I don't want to know my future."

He shrugs. "Why not? It's the one thing we all want to know."

"I've already seen my future," she says. And she's right. There's no denying it. Not even for him.

"All right, then," says the deliveryman. "What'll it be?"

"My husband. Jacob Rosen. I need to know if he's alive."

"But you told me he was around here someplace."

"I was lying. I don't know for sure."

Again he looks crestfallen. Now that he's quit feigning shyness, this seems to be one of his two modes of communication. He looks either disappointed or predatory, depending. "You were lying," he says, shaking his head from side to side, heartbroken. "You were lying, to *me.*" Straightening up. His knuckles leaving white rings on the rough wood of the table.

"His name is Jacob Rosen. Jacob Rosen from Zakopane."

"Zakopane!" he says, all smiles once more. *"That's* where I've seen you!" The junkman from Witnica never gives up hope.

*

Schuler says that he can't work properly without adequate shoes.

They're walking now, Jacob's commando on its way to the excavation and Schuler about to split off toward Canada. He tells Jacob he needs the gum-soled shoes because he isn't on his hands and knees sorting through castoffs seven days a week. Oh, no. Not at all. On Fridays he's on his feet for the whole day, a man of his age, and he's working under a kind of crippling pressure that someone like Jacob can't possibly imagine. One false move and it's all over. He drags a finger across his own neck.

A young SS officer comes pedaling past on a bicycle. Schuler inclines his head toward him. Very softly he says, "He's one of them."

"One of what."

"One of the sons of bitches I'm required to keep looking sharp." The

SS man's hat falls off in the breeze and he stops the bicycle to retrieve it. "Every Friday," Schuler says, "I cut the officers' hair."

"No."

"Yes."

Jacob hasn't given this kind of thing any thought. The only barbering he's seen around here has been so brutal—his own occasional passage, for example, under the rusty razors of the commando of sadists and mental defectives in the shed out by the train platform—that it's never occurred to him that his skills might have any real use around the camp. Use of the sort that might get him away from digging trenches now and then. As a rule, keeping out of sight is a good idea; dealing with the capo is a terrible enough fate, without exposing himself directly to the SS. But on the other hand, the work doesn't seem to be doing Schuler any harm. He seems to be thriving on it.

"What came first?" he asks the old man. "The barbering business, or Canada?"

"Oh, the barbering. I was transferred to lighter work once they'd seen how valuable I was." He walks along, puffed up by more than his gum-soled shoes.

The SS officer with the bicycle is beating the dust out of his hat and watching the commando march past, smiling as if he finds the very sight of them amusing. The way they stumble over the rocky path in their ruined shoes and their bare feet. Jacob hazards a quick look in his direction, and notes a cowlick pointing straight up from the crown of his head. That's not all. His sideburns are uneven as well. Jacob decides that old man Schuler might not be quite as valuable as he thinks he is.

*

"Everything has a price," says the junkman.

"But all I need is to *know* something," says Eidel. "I'm not after food or anything else like that. Not like—you know." Puffing out her cheeks, doing her best impression of the capo.

"Information has a price, too," says the man in white. But before he has a chance to suggest what that price might be, the capo has come back and is shooing him out the door. Seriously this time. Vehemently. Her fat face is red and she has a rag wrapped around her fist and a piece of ice from the icebox is melting inside the rag. She's injured her hand in some way. Eidel can guess how. That stray prisoner she'd been running down. And sure enough, as the capo stands rubbing her fist and watching water trail along her arm and drip from her elbow onto the dusting of flour that the deliveryman has tracked in, she vows that next time she'll use a stick of kindling or maybe a poker. One of those big rusty soup ladles if nothing else. Letting it be known. Next time.

The deliveryman may have outworn his welcome for this morning, but there will be a next time for him as well. In a world where nothing changes, there's always a next time.

Max

MY MOTHER WAS A WONDERFUL PAINTER, I can tell you that.

Even then, you see, I had an eye. Even as a boy. You wouldn't have imagined it to look at me, but how could it have been otherwise? With a mother like mine?

The most remarkable thing about her work is that she was completely unschooled—by which I mean she schooled herself. She trained her eye by studying good work. How you can tell good work from bad when you don't have anybody around to educate you is the mystery, but it's the first indicator of a gift. It's where the gift begins.

She loved Vermeer, and you could see it everywhere in her work. She used to poke fun, calling herself *the third-rate Vermeer of the shtetl,* but there was nothing third-rate about what she did. And she'd never lived in the shtetl, for that matter. She grew up in Warsaw, under conditions of comfort if not opulence. Her father was an attorney. And then she met my father and they got married and set up housekeeping in Zakopane. Zakopane was a resort town then, just as it is now. They were privileged to live there. We were all privileged.

The only time she spent in the shtetl was toward the end, and it was then that she finally gave up painting. Nineteen-forty, nineteen-forty-one.

She'd never dressed things up. As beautiful as her work always was—and her paintings *were* beautiful, whether or not you happen to believe that beauty has anything to do with art—it wasn't because she was actively making it that way. Pushing things around, consciously or unconsciously. I suppose that's why she stopped when the going got bad; she'd never gilded the lily and she wasn't about to start. She was entering into a difficult period where everything around her was changing for the worse, and she didn't have any desire to document it. You have to respect that.

My mother was one hell of a painter, though. That's the main thing. Take my word for it.

Three

EIDEL MAKES NO DISTINCTIONS AMONG her fellow prisoners. She plays no favorites and she bears no grudges, and this sets her apart. It makes her inscrutable. When the women line up for their ration of bread and soup, she sinks the ladle to a point exactly halfway down into the pot for every one of them. Halfway and no more. Halfway and no less. There is always someone who will beg her to go a little deeper just this once, please—either for her own bowl, or for the bowl of a friend whose vitality is dangerously waning—hoping that down on the bottom of the pot the ladle will dredge up a couple of beans or a thin slice of carrot in addition to the filmy water that constitutes their usual undoctored portion.

But no. She never even looks up to dignify such a request.

She also makes a point of giving the soup one complete stir with the ladle after a certain number of portions served, keeping a strict count in her head. The number varies. It might be five one day and it might be three the next and it might be nine the day after that. A certain Mathilde Kessler, one of the older denizens of the block and one of the more cunning, has observed this, and as the women line up for each meal she hangs back and watches for the number. Once she's discovered it she counts the women in the line and positions herself to be holding up her bowl just after Eidel has stirred the pot, her theory being that whatever scraps of vegetables are in the soup will be highest in the suspension at that instant and most likely to be ladled up. There is risk to her system, as there is risk to everything. Wait a little too long and the vegetables will have been filtered out into other women's bowls. Wait too long entirely and there'll be nothing left. Not even water. For there's never enough soup.

This is how Eidel has endured, though. By establishing and maintaining utter equanimity. By concentrating on nothing but the present moment. By walking a middle path where there is no real path at all.

Five bowls of soup. Stir. Five bowls of soup. Stir. Five bowls of soup.

And this is how others endure, others like Mathilde Kessler, by keeping watch on the tiniest of details and turning them to their advantage if they can.

Five bowls it is, then. Count off by fives and your chances will improve.

But now the junkman has spoken, and a door has opened up in Eidel's mind, and the possibility of learning her husband's fate has changed everything. It fires her heart and it sets her on edge and it gives her hope and fear where she has taught herself to have neither.

The question—*I need to know if my husband is alive*—came out of nowhere. She certainly hadn't known she'd ask it; she hadn't known she'd ever have the chance to ask anything again. But now she does have the chance, and now the world has shifted or shown the potential to shift, and now she stands in the kitchen ladling soup with Jacob on her mind and she loses count of the women she's served. She curses herself for it.

Kessler is standing toward the end of the line and she sees what's gone wrong and tries to rectify it. Stepping out of line and letting two women pass her by and thinking halfway better of that after a moment and trying to edge up again by one place. But the capo catches her at it.

"If you can't stay in line," she says, "you'll have no rations at all."

"I'm sorry," says Kessler. She bows her head.

"You'll be sorrier," says the capo, reaching to confiscate the woman's bowl. Kessler hands it over and shuffles all of a half step back before the capo strikes her over the head. The gray crockery bowl is heavy as stone and Rolak puts her considerable weight behind it and Kessler goes down. The bowl breaks in half.

The line moves forward. The woman behind will find three tiny peas awash in her soup today. The discovery—if not the peas them-selves—will give her the strength to go on. Lucky her.

*

Edmund Vollmer, the deputy commandant, is responsible only to the commandant himself and perhaps to God. Few of the men have ever seen him in the flesh. Fewer still have seen the commandant, of course, and none have seen the Almighty. Many, but by no means all, have given up hope in that department.

Setting eyes on Vollmer at the edge of the yard during the morning roll call is therefore like sighting one element of the Holy Trinity. A murmur passes through the moving crowd of men like something alive and dangerous. Any interruption to the routine is dangerous. Everyone looks but tries not to be caught looking. Everyone stops but tries not to stop. *It's Vollmer himself. See if you can, but don't be seen.*

Jacob and Max have learned to take places near the middle of the middle row at the twice-daily roll call. It's the eye of whatever hurricane might ensue. This principal applies when they're in motion as well, en route to the dig or to a selection lineup or anywhere else. *Stay in the middle of the pack, where it's safest.* The roll call is a capricious thing, sometimes an actual counting of the men and sometimes not. It can last ten minutes or it can last an hour. In the mornings, when there's work to be done, it's generally a brisk affair. At day's end, when the only thing at risk is the men's sleep, it can go on forever. There are those who claim to remember counts that lasted twelve hours. Eighteen. Longer, entire days spent standing at attention in the yard in summer heat and winter snow. Men were reported to have crumpled over in the ranks during such periods, to have passed out on the ground and spasmed and died, with the only consequence being the need to begin the roll call over again. But who can say?

The *sturmbannführer* doesn't look like a man with time to waste. This is a good sign. He's on a small platform speaking with another SS officer—the young one who rides the bicycle—in a manner that permits no interruption. He is brusque but not hurried, intense but not urgent. The sun has risen over the low tarpaper blocks, and up on the platform its rays gleam from his hat and his belt and his boots.

Physically he's compact and sturdy and immaculate. If the Germans have set out to demonstrate their status as the master race, Vollmer would seem to be as good an argument as any, although every man standing here with his eyes on him knows that in a fair fight things would be different. Their strength has been sapped now, and their will has been destroyed. They have been weakened and wounded and worn down. But once upon a time a man like Vollmer would have been beneath their particular notice. Just another customer, just another head to trim, forgotten as soon as he'd left the chair. But not now.

Among them all, Max is an exception. It's his youth that makes the difference. Even here in the camp his strength has increased over the last couple of months, in spite of thin rations and backbreaking work or perhaps because of them. He is still fourteen but the lie has come true and he looks eighteen or older, for some chemical switch inside of him has not yet been thrown, and he can still turn almost any kind of nourishment into power. It's a condition that won't last.

But now he looks at Vollmer and turns his head a few degrees toward his father and whispers low, "I could take him."

"And you could get every last one of us shot."

Both of which are true.

Vollmer leaves off conferring with the other officer and steps down from the platform and takes a stroll along the lines of assembled men, almost as if he has overheard Max's challenge and seeks to draw him out. Down here on ground level he seems even smaller. Just a little man in a gray-green uniform among this ragged assembly of dust-brown stick figures, assessing them like crops. He looks satisfied, even happy, with what he sees. Down the line he goes, toward Jacob and Max, strutting in the way of his superiors, and the father hears the son draw breath. Jacob draws breath too, shifting his weight and turning his chin toward Max so very slightly that no one other than his own flesh and blood could possibly begin to perceive it. But it's enough. Max exhales. They both exhale. Vollmer nears and moves on without noticing either one of them. They're just two more scarecrows, neither one of whom dares to look at Vollmer's face. No one does.

It's the back of Vollmer's head that Jacob notices. The back of his neck, specifically. It's an area in which he still takes a professional interest, and the hair at Vollmer's nape is simply a disgrace. Ragged and asymmetrical and roughly chopped off, it could be the sign of an acceptable haircut gone too long between trimmings except that the skin below it looks red and angry and scraped raw. Jacob consults the calendar in his head and can't decide what day it is until he remembers that yesterday morning Schuler didn't walk with the rest of them toward his usual rendezvous with Canada. Today must be Saturday, then. Yesterday was Friday, the day the officers get their hair cut.

Butchery for the butchers. The irony of it rises up in him and makes him laugh for the first time since he's been here. Not loudly, though. Not loudly enough to be heard down the line.

Hours later, shoveling alongside his son, he still can't get over it. He says, "Did you get a look at Vollmer's neck?"

"No," says Max.

"It's a disgrace."

Shoveling away as they are, and under the observation of that pot-bellied pig Slazak, their conversation is telegraphic.

"Really?"

"Really. It's a disgrace to the Nazi party." Another shovelful. "Which takes some doing."

"How so?"

"Bad haircut. *Lousy* haircut."

Max just shakes his head. After all they've been through. That father of his.

Jacob shovels and goes on. "It's our friend Schuler," he says.

They work. The trench is deep but not deep enough. They've been edging toward a road that they must dig beneath in order to reach the plot of ground that will be the new women's camp. All month long the men have complained quietly to one another about the depth of the excavation, as if it's been just a whim on Slazak's part, but now they see. A German technician with a graduated pole stands on this side of the road and another one with a transit stands on the other side, and they shake their heads gravely at Slazak whenever he looks their way. *Not deep enough.*

Slazak walks along the berm of raw earth piled up on one side of the ditch and kicks some of it down onto the prisoners. Max stops to dig it out of his shirt collar and Slazak hollers at him to keep working. "I can move more dirt with the toe of my boot than you can move with that goddamned shovel," he says, demonstrating the truth of his claim with another kick. Clods pelt the prisoners and they labor on in silence, like men digging their way out of a hailstorm. Max grumbles and Slazak cocks his head to listen but his father hushes him. Slazak walks forward a couple of steps and kicks down some more dirt on more prisoners and spits after it for good measure—Slazak who began here as one of their own but has gone crooked now, Slazak spoiling for a fight, Slazak in league with the enemy and enjoying it, jamming his thumbs into his belt and leaning forward with his jaw jutting to make the men under his command a promise: if they fail to reach the road by the end of the day, they can lie right down where they are. The guards will draw their machine guns and a commando of fresh men will shovel the dirt back into the ditch and no one will be the wiser. There is always another path to the women's camp. There are always more prisoners.

Jacob looks up over the rim of the ditch to see the guards themselves, a couple of Ukrainians with dead eyes and thin lips, pass a look back and forth. It's hard to say what the look might mean, but he gets the feeling that they would just as soon Slazak joined the others in the ditch before they started in with the guns.

The surveyor laughs and steadies his pole.

*

In the end, Mathilde Kessler stands up and walks under her own power—but only after a certain amount of encouragement from the capo. Her head swims and she's unsteady on her feet and her kidneys hurt from Rolak's blows of encouragement, but she staggers to the hospital block without any help, pausing only now and then to lean against a wall or a railing. No one so much as watches her go, not even the guards, for what trouble could a woman in her condition get into? They could open the main gates wide, and she wouldn't have the strength to leave.

She isn't in the block when the lights go out, and she isn't at work the next day, and the rumors start. They're all variations on the same theme. *She's dead from a broken skull* or *She's dead from the fall to the concrete floor* or *She's dead from the blows to her stomach.*

Eidel tries not to listen. It doesn't occur to her that she might have had anything to do with Kessler's fate, whatever it is. That her tiny failure to keep to the middle path has cost this other woman so much. She has other things on her mind.

Night falls and Kessler is still missing. The rumors metastasize. *She's dead from internal bleeding* or *She's dead from an injection given to her by one of the doctors* or *She's dead because she's been selected for the gas.*

Eidel would cover her ears if she could move, but the bunk is too crowded. She can't so much as free her arms.

If by some miracle Kessler were to appear here in the darkness among them they would leap as if they'd seen a ghost, so sure are they that she must have become one by now. Her black fate spreads like oil. One woman claims that Kessler had a twin sister in another block, and that that same sister was spirited away during the roll call this morning. Spirited away never to be heard from again. The doctors have a special fascination with twins, after all.

Eidel can't bear it. She has her own torments. She lies on her side in the crowded bunk, feeling the pressure of women breathing on both sides of her, and she thinks of Jacob and the children. She sheds tears for both of them, unable even to reach the silk handkerchief she keeps jammed into her pocket as a memento. She wonders if Jacob might be thinking these same thoughts in some place more or less identical to this, and she resolves that she must find out. She must know for certain, now that she can.

Which means, of course, that she must resign herself to sleeping with the junkman. What else could he possibly want from her? She's not blind. People are forever pairing off around the camp, whether desiring one another or desiring something from one another no one can say. Even here, where the conditions are constant, the reasons vary. It's impossible to explain how lust endures, but there's no denying the fact of it.

She has seen how he looks at her. She has seen how he looks at every woman in the kitchen, even little Zofia Kohen, the most wasted and wan of them all, a pale mouse before she came here and a pale mouse now, Zofia who first suggested that in exchange for putting Eidel's mind at rest the junkman will surely demand the gift of her body. The truth of it is that Zofia has taken a shine to him herself. She adores the rakish tilt of his hat and she admires his freedom to wander the farthest corners of the camp, imagining for him a life as varied and exotic as the journeys of Marco Polo. That cocky little junkman from Witnica, out navigating the spice routes. She doesn't like to admit it, but it's true. Anyone can see. So when she suggested to Eidel that the only way she'd learn anything about her husband was to submit to the deliveryman's carnal requirements, Eidel said that she was imagining things. "You may dream of that for yourself," she said, "but don't go bringing me into it."

"I wouldn't," said Zofia, "and I'm not."

"You would, and you did." She leaned hard against her knife, driving it through a turnip.

But that was yesterday. Now she lies awake wondering what she'll have to endure if she wants the truth. Wondering what kind of an agreement she can reach. A scheme leaps up into her mind at one point—she will agree to do the deliveryman's bidding only if the news is good—but instantly she realizes such a system's shortcoming. He'll tell her anything to get what he wants.

On the other hand, he might tell her anything anyhow. Of what value is the truth to him?

No. She adjusts her position on the hard bunk. *No.* If she's to proceed, she must have faith. Faith in Jacob and faith in herself. And faith in a cunning little junkman from a backwoods village, trotting around this death camp in his motley black and white, making deals and carrying secrets and bearing God knows what contagion from door to door and bed to bed. Carrying worse than contagion. Perhaps even the makings of a child. Which would be the death of her.

*

"You need to be more careful," Jacob tells his son, the two of them jammed into a bunk no more than a quarter of a mile distant from Eidel but nonetheless at the other end of the world. "You need to be on your guard. You mustn't let them rile you."

"I don't."

"You do. It's instinctive. You're young."

"I'm not that young."

"You're young. And you won't get much older if you don't learn a little self-control." Other men are murmuring in the dark as well, and as of yet Slazak hasn't charged out from his little chamber to quiet them down. "You got riled at Slazak today. Over a little dirt."

"So?"

"So where does that lead? What would you have done if I hadn't shushed you?"

"Nothing."

"That's right," says Jacob. "You would have done nothing. So why start?"

"I didn't start."

"You wanted to start. You very nearly did."

Max doesn't deny it. He doesn't say anything at all. Jacob might be persuaded that his son has actually fallen asleep, if his chest weren't pressed so tightly against the boy's back. But Max is awake and his father can feel it in the beating of his heart. Nothing can be concealed under these conditions. Not from him. He breathes as deeply as he can under the circumstances and feels the pressure of his son's body against his, flesh of his flesh, not just the boy himself but the woman of whom the boy is the last trace. Eidel. Eidel who is all alone in the world if she is in the world at all, Eidel who has done nothing to deserve that fate, Eidel who ought to have a child of her own by her side if anyone should. At least Jacob has someone to look after.

Other men are still talking, a handful of them complaining about the heat and the food and the work, until Slazak finally bursts through his little door. "Quiet," he snarls, "unless you're rested enough to start digging again." Which is a threat on which he'd follow through if he weren't so exhausted himself. But the prisoners don't know that—they don't know *what* he's capable of, for not one man among them is foolish enough to believe that he's seen Slazak's limits—so they close their eyes and clear their throats and lie subdued, as still as firewood or fish.

Some of them sleep and some of them even dream, the lucky ones of freedom and family and sumptuous meals, the rest of torment and hunger and pain, and come morning the three bells awaken them all.

They all rise but one. Schuler, it would seem at first, judging from the position of his body in the usual spot on the usual bunk, but it's not Schuler. Schuler is in the latrine, and the body lying motionless on the boards is his nameless twin. A younger prisoner just then making his way down the line between the bunks, seeing the prone figure and spying Slazak on his way to rouse him and eager to gain a little favor, perhaps even aspiring to become a capo himself one day, reaches down and twists the twin's ankle and curses him in the vilest terms available in two languages or maybe three. Saying it's time to start pulling his own weight.

But Schuler's twin just groans. He hardly groans, come to that. It's just a sigh with a harsh trailing edge of resignation. The other prisoner turns his ankle again, more roughly this time and in the other direction—mainly for the benefit of Slazak, who's getting nearer and beginning to toss men out of his way in order to see what's going on in the dimness of that bunk—and Schuler's twin stirs. Pulling his ankle free and drawing it up toward his buttocks. Curling in on himself. Drawing breath and rolling over on his back and inching toward the light. Just in time.

As punishment for his weakness, he goes without rations. When they head out for the excavation he limps along pitifully, leaning on Schuler and reluctant to let go of him at the place where he needs to break off for Canada. It hardly seems fair that Schuler—relatively upright and more or less energetic, his every step cushioned by those gum-soled shoes of his—should head off to a soft job under the shade of a roof while his twin must hurl himself again into the ditch. The twin complains. Watching Schuler go, he lays out his grievances before the other prisoners and before God Himself, and although he's correct in every particular there will be no redress.

Jacob commiserates. He says that injustice strikes each man here in his own particular way. Consider his own situation. A skilled barber, a man who with his own hands has trimmed the hair of the monsignor of the Church of the Holy Family on Krupowki Street in Zakopane, he's condemned to digging ditches while every Friday morning, just like clockwork, Schuler goes off to commit his butchery. Talk about fairness, will you?

Slazak overhears. He laughs at first—*the nerve of these animals!*—and then he stops laughing.

Max

ARTISTS ARE COMBATIVE BY NATURE. Civilians don't realize that. You have to be pleasant and you have to smile nicely in the direction of other people's work and you have to say things that are suitable for quoting in family publications when critics ask you what you think, but that doesn't mean you're not combative.

It's Darwinism at work. Pure Darwinism.

How many people can rise to the top, after all? This isn't like business, where you have thousands of companies with thousands of big shots running them. It's not like medicine or law, where you're your own boss and nobody other than your CPA can see how well or how poorly you're doing. Have a bad year? Take out another loan and buy yourself the latest German car. Nobody will be the wiser.

It's not like that. It's more like education—college, I mean, *the groves of academe*—where the rewards are lousy and the egos are big.

By the time you're as old as I am, you'll have had it with pretty much everybody. Yourself included. After all, you're the one who fell into the trap. You didn't have to take it that far. You could have painted for the love of it. For the love of the things you painted. Like my mother.

Once you've reached this point, though, the only people you're going to be comfortable around are the ones who've achieved less than you have. And since they can't stand to be around you, what's the use? So you take up golf maybe. Find a foursome at the gym if you're a fitness nut which I'm not or at the synagogue if you're a religious nut which I'm not either. Some other guys you can talk to about anything other than art. Go chase a little ball around. Get drunk at the nineteenth hole every now and then. Have a little fun in the autumn of your years.

The alternative is to spend every minute either working or thinking about work.

Which means you go out there in the world and you smile and you nod and you wish the whole time that everybody but you would go straight to hell. And then you head home and sit down in front of your easel or your whatever, and you do your best to make that happen.

To save yourself with your own two hands.

That's art.

Four

THE DELIVERYMAN DOESN'T WANT HER after all. He wants something else. Something negotiable. There's a great sack of radishes in one of the storerooms. He knows about it because he was here when it was delivered a few weeks before, and he's watched Eidel and Zofia and the other women dice up the usual turnips and potatoes and carrots in the meantime, but it's been a rare day when he's seen a radish. There are surely some left.

"We're sparing of them," says Eidel.

"I'm sure. A radish is a rare thing."

"It adds flavor," she says. "There's little enough."

"Exactly," The deliveryman rubs his hands together. "That's why I need a couple of kilos."

"Two kilos of radishes." She's kneading dough for bread. Pushing at it with whatever strength she has.

"Just two. That's not much."

"It's a month's worth."

"For you, maybe, but not for a certain guard I happen to know. He eats them like candy."

It's unimaginable. The rumors that her own capo grows fat on bratwurst and chocolate are bad enough. Those things come from the outside, arriving in Red Cross packages for the Russians and turning up inside the suitcases of new prisoners who've come by train. They circulate in a black market so remote as not to exist at all from Eidel's point of view. But *radishes*. Radishes aren't imaginary like chocolate or sausage.

They're real, like potatoes or carrots. Two kilos of radishes could mean life or death for someone on the verge. A woman in her commando, her block, even her own bunk.

"I can't do it," she says.

"It's risky, I know. That capo of yours—"

"It's not the capo."

"What, then?"

He'll never understand, so she doesn't bother explaining. "I just can't do it."

"No matter. I'll find somebody who will." He laughs, shaking his head. Today is a coal day, and almost every part of him is black.

"I hope you don't. These women need the nourishment."

The deliveryman chuckles at the futility of everything. "You don't understand," he says. "That guard of mine will get his radishes one way or another. He's a Slovak. Cruel as they come. And if he doesn't get what he wants, bad things will happen."

"To you," says Eidel. "They'll happen to you."

"No, no," he reassures her. "Not to me. He relies on me."

Eidel lifts the dough and throws it down.

"The bad things will happen to the men he oversees." He raises up his shovel and squints along the length of it as down the barrel of a gun. *"Pop pop pop,"* he says. "No skin off my nose."

Eidel leans into the dough.

The deliveryman watches her, gauging everything. "So you see how it is. A radish less here, a bullet more there."

"I can't help you," she says. "I have to look out for my own."

The little misplaced junkman from Witnica leans on his shovel. "Too bad," he says. "You see, I've been making some inquiries as to your husband, after all."

*

The men are waiting in the yard for their rations, sitting on rocks and squatting in the dirt and speculating about what has happened to Schuler's twin—exactly when he disappeared, who in particular was the last to see him, where he might be and whether or not they'll ever see him again—when word comes down that Slazak wants to see Jacob in his quarters. He enters that little rough-hewn square the way he'd enter a mineshaft, tentatively, poking his head through the door to find the capo in a hard chair by the bed, a cigarette burning in his fist and a glass of vodka on a lace doily in the center of the table. The doily is the whitest thing in the room, the whitest thing in the block, and the incongruous sight of it is disorienting. It's something from another world.

"Come in, come in," says Slazak. He speaks through smoke.

"Yes, sir," says Jacob. He's left Max out in the yard. Better there than here in the lion's den, but the separation makes him uncomfortable.

"You say you're something of a barber."

So it's true. Slazak does hear everything. "Yes, sir. I was a barber."

"You were? *Were?*"

"Yes, sir."

"Have you forgotten how to cut a man's hair, then?"

"No, sir."

Slazak keeps on. "Was this all just *talk?*" He draws on the cigarette and his face glows red.

"No, sir. It wasn't just talk. I—"

"Fine, then. Fine." Slazak lets out smoke and laughs as the gray cloud of it emerges into the little room. He chuckles as if they're just friends here. Comrades. "That's all fine," he says. "I just don't want to be found wanting when I make my recommendations."

"Recommendations?"

"Even a fellow in *my* position has to look out when he makes recommendations."

"Recommendations?"

"For a new barber. Upstairs." He looks heavenward, as if the men he reports to live in that direction.

"A new barber."

"Schuler isn't long for this world. Look at what happened to that brother of his."

"Is that his brother?"

"Who knows? We'll never know now. They're old men, in any event. We can't have Schuler passing out in the commandant's villa, can we?"

"I suppose not."

The cigarette has gone dead, and Slazak lights it again, grunting into the flame. "I'm doing him a favor by finding his replacement."

Jacob is dumbfounded.

"You'll have to prove yourself tomorrow morning. The administration building. Eight o'clock sharp. Some SS clerk."

"How will I know?"

"You'll know. They're expecting you."

At such a thought, Jacob nearly stops breathing.

"Speak to no one," Slazak says. "Got that?"

"Absolutely. I'll speak to no one."

Slazak turns his attention to his vodka.

"Forgive my asking," says Jacob before he turns to go, "and believe me, I'm flattered, but do they always come to you for advice in this area? The SS, I mean. Do you have some specialty?"

Slazak puts down the vodka and coughs into his fist and wipes the flat of his palm on his pantleg. "My specialty is what you see. But when I see a chance to improve a man's lot, I can't help but take it." The lot he's referring to is his own, of course. And if along the way he can heap extra woe upon one or two of the men in his charge, that's fine too.

Jacob will be up half the night figuring the angles.

To begin with, it will mean light work at least one day a week. Make that *seven* days a week, provided that, like Schuler before him, he gets moved to Canada.

Then again, he'll be exposed directly to the SS.

And not just to any SS, but to the commandant and the deputy commandant and who knows who else. The highest of the high, and by any reasonable logic surely the worst of the worst. If a person has to watch his step around Slazak, imagine the risks of working directly for such men.

Schuler has done it, though. He's done it for longer than anyone remembers, and he's thrived. Just consider those gum-soled shoes of his. Shoes like that boost a man's health and prolong his life. Every man in the camp lusts after them. Jacob himself has not been immune to their allure.

But on the other hand, Jacob is a father. Shoes even half that fine, were they to come into his possession, would have to go straight to Max. No question about it. To pass them on would be his duty and his joy. Other benefits would accrue to Max as well. Slazak mentioned the commandant's villa. God knows what delicacies such a place holds. In Jacob's imagination it's a kind of gingerbread house, crammed with riches. A prisoner would enter through the back door, and where would the back door lead? Straight into the kitchen, of course. A kitchen, if the rumors are true, presided over by a grandmotherly German with, they say, a kindly heart and a soft spot for the starving.

Consider Schuler! Consider his twin! Those two old men could not have survived this long without help.

He pictures himself leaving the villa, his leather case of barbering tools miraculously restored to him, a bit of bacon or a slice of good black German bread tucked into his pocket.

He decides that he owes it to his son.

Provided that Max can learn to watch his temper. Who knows what might happen, without his father around to keep an eye on him every single minute? Perhaps that's Slazak's plan. To get the protective father out of the picture, and have his way with the temperamental son. In such a case, all of the bacon and bread in the world won't help.

But why would he go to such lengths? He can already punish Max at the slightest whim for any offense, real or imaginary. Why dream up a plot to get rid of Jacob, when Jacob poses no barrier to the worst of his instincts? It could be that all he wants is to burnish his reputation with those higher up. That's the simplest explanation, and the simplest explanation is usually correct. Which means that Slazak is honestly putting his faith in Jacob, counting on him to do his best when the time comes. And why not? Failure means doom, not just for the barber but probably for his son, and the pot-bellied capo surely has some scheme for removing himself from the equation if he should fall short. In such an event Schuler will get to keep his job after all. Life will go on.

Schuler, though. If Jacob proves himself in the morning, and he surely will, what will become of Schuler?

It's almost dawn before he decides that he'll never figure it all out. It's almost dawn and he realizes that he doesn't have any choice in the matter anyhow. Any minute now the three bells will clang, and the work day will commence, and at eight o'clock he'll be due at the administration building.

*

It's not fair, but Eidel is long past expecting fairness. *I've been making some inquiries as to your husband,* the junkman had said, and her heart had leapt, so in the morning she asks. "What exactly have you heard of Jacob?"

"Not so much, just yet."

"Tell me."

"There are…reports." His voice trails off.

"Reports of what?"

"Reports."

"All right," she says. "You'll have the radishes."

"And you'll have the reports."

"Not *will have.* I want them now."

"First, the radishes."

"No."

"Yes." She turns her back on him and reaches up to an overhead shelf to pull down a stack of bread pans. She knocks a few of them free with the heel of her hand and greases them with just the tiniest thimbleful of lard and turns back toward him. "You'll tell me what you know right now, and I'll give you one kilo of radishes."

"Two kilos."

"One kilo to get started. One kilo, and then you'll take a message to my husband. If he's still alive."

"Oh, he's alive all right," says the deliveryman.

"Thank you for the report," she says.

He's unruffled. "Messages cost extra," he says.

"One kilo for taking a message to my husband," she says again, "and the other kilo when you bring a message from him back to me."

"That's two messages." He's holding up his fingers. "The going rate for two messages—"

Eidel takes a step toward him and bends to open the oven. The hinges scream and a cloud of heat crowds all the air from the room and the deliveryman winces. Eidel works on. "The going rate for me to betray the women in my commando by giving away their food," she says without even looking at him, "is two messages. Take it or leave it. Take it or go find your radishes somewhere else."

She slams the oven shut and the heat still chokes the room and the little junkman from Witnica says, "Fine. Two kilos, two messages." He pulls a ragged little sack from his pocket and tilts his head toward the storage room. "Now…while your capo's still nowhere to be seen?"

*

The administration building is out by the gates, near the train station. It's enormous and complex, containing on one hand the echoing halls and damp, foul-smelling chambers where prisoners are stripped and deloused, and on the other the offices and conference rooms where the men who manage such things spend their days—and although Jacob has seen it before he's never seen it from this angle. He reports to a low door just around the corner from the main entrance. It's the kind of door a mouse would use. SS vehicles are parked in a lot close by—trucks and vans, black cars and powerful motorcycles. The high fence of electrified barbed wire is only a few yards distant. He could walk over and touch it if he wanted to. Touch it and die. Or die from mere proximity, since on either side are guard towers bristling with machine guns.

He knocks at the door but no one answers. He steps close and looks through the window into a dim and unwelcoming space with hallways leading off in three directions. A radiator stands in one corner and he realizes that he hasn't seen such a thing in a long while. The weather is warm now, summer having begun, but how luxurious it will be for these Nazi murderers come winter, settled here in their comfortable offices, enjoying the benefits of steam heat! He imagines the clanking noises when the steam begins to flow, the dry smell of dust burning off hot iron, the rising warmth. He imagines himself coming in through this door every Friday morning all winter long, stamping snow from his shoes and closing the door behind him and going on to penetrate the warm depths of this place for an hour, two hours, an entire working day.

The idea overcomes him and draws him in, and once his eyes have adjusted he can see that there's a woman at a desk at the end of the hallway straight ahead. She sits in a pool of light provided by a goose-neck lamp, and she talks on a telephone, and she doesn't raise her eyes as other women and men in SS uniforms hurry past her. She must be the one expecting him. He scrapes his feet on a rough mat and moves down the hall. Daniel in the lion's den, treading toward apocalypse.

She keeps her eyes down and looks only from a calendar on the desk to a pad of paper on which she makes a mark now and then, but she looks up as Jacob approaches—as if among all of these individuals this Jew is the only one with the ability to attract her attention. She looks up smoothly and without emotion, the way one of the men in the guard towers would raise his gun.

If she knows his name, she doesn't use it. If she knows that he even has a name. She looks down to read his serial number aloud from her pad and she looks up again and Jacob nods. He shows the tattoo on his left arm in confirmation. This is the way it always goes. Your capo might use your name, but no one higher.

She stands. "The *scharführer* is waiting."

But the sergeant isn't waiting. Not really. He's on a telephone call, apparently with someone higher up, and Jacob has to wait outside the office where the receptionist leaves him. Standing at attention, not touching the wall, not touching anything. Just listening. Standing there as if he has no more sentience than a potted plant.

The sergeant's name is Drexler, and he's the commandant's senior clerk. Jacob watches him as he listens and consults a piece of paper and idly runs his finger down the pages of an enormous ledger. The ledger sits on top of another one just like it, and there are many more on a tall set of bookshelves just behind him, rank on rank of them like volumes of an encyclopedia. Jacob has seen ledgers like these before, elsewhere in this very building. His own name and serial number were recorded in one on the day he arrived.

"Already this week," says Drexler, into the telephone, "we have had twelve die of heart attacks, nine more of inflammation of the kidneys, and fifteen of bronchitis."

Murmurs from the other end.

"Yes, sir. Of course, sir. Pneumonia is always good, but in my opinion it's more credible in the cold weather."

Murmurs.

"Yes, sir. I have indeed requested a greater variety of diagnoses, but as you know, the doctor has many other things on his mind. Yes, sir. I have done so under your authority. But you know the doctor, sir." Drexler glances up. He flashes a reflexive smile at the figure in the doorway, a smile either submissive or predatory depending, and when the figure in the doorway proves to be only the Jewish barber he withdraws it.

"Very well, sir," he says, smiling at the telephone instead. "My thoughts exactly, sir. There is no need to carry on this charade any longer. We shall close the book on it, so to speak. Yes, sir. Very good, sir. *Heil Hitler.*" He hangs up and touches the tip of the pencil to his tongue and draws a line across the open page before him, and then he shuts the book and waves the barber in. There is a wooden chair in the corner, alongside a round table arrayed with towels and soap and the rest. An empty basin and a jug of steaming water. A hand mirror and a white linen sheet and a barbering kit which although not half so fine as the one that Jacob lost along the way is nonetheless immaculately maintained and sharp as weaponry.

"Hurry up," says Drexler in Polish, carrying the ledger with him to the chair. "I don't have all day." He takes his seat with the book in his lap, and reaches up to loosen his collar. Jacob approaches from the front and bows his head a little bit and Drexler looks right through him, so he goes about his business. He locates and unfolds the white linen drape, and as he sweeps it around Drexler's shoulders he takes note of the word inked onto the front of the ledger. *Totenbuch.*

The Registry of Death. His head spins. They must keep such records, after all. It's the German way: everything in its place, everything properly noted. Even murder. But to happen upon it is like happening upon Satan himself in some dark mountain pass, Satan with his endless scroll of the damned. And this Drexler is the devil who maintains it.

"*Schnell,*" he says, settling beneath that death-white sheet with the book in his lap. And then he speaks in Polish again, assuming that Jacob could not possibly understand even the simplest of commands in more than one language, "Just a little off the sides, and trim the nape while you're at it." He points with his finger.

Concentration is impossible. Jacob tries the scissors and brings the comb toward Drexler's hair. His hands shake. He withdraws, breathing irregularly, and Drexler turns his head in question. Without thinking, and strictly against orders, Jacob speaks: "Straight ahead, please," he says, in German. The words are a combination of reflex and self-defense, and Drexler's response is reflexive as well. He straightens his neck and looks forward, the conventions of the barber's chair and his military background combining to produce automatic obedience, even to one so low.

The establishment of a familiar rhythm soothes Jacob. His hands steady a bit. He tries the scissors again and puts the comb to Drexler's head and finds himself all at once back in his element. Click click. Snip snip. He works briskly and automatically and he tries not to look at the outline of the ledger in Drexler's lap. He wonders how long before his own name will be inscribed there, or Max's name. He wonders if Eidel's is there already, and he is certain that Lydia's must be.

"Watch the ear," says Drexler.

He watches. Barbering a man in an ordinary straight-backed chair is different from using the old mechanical chair he had in Zakopane, his father's overstuffed leather chair with its pedals and its levers and its million fine adjustments. As many haircuts as he's given in one ghetto after another, on benches and straightbacked chairs and milking stools, he has never quite accustomed himself to the difference. These last few months of digging ditches haven't refined his skills either. But he perseveres. He empties his mind and he straightens his back and he keeps on.

"That's better," says Drexler.

Jacob dares to breathe. He thinks perhaps he'll get this assignment after all. Every Friday he'll come here for a few hours, and on the other days of the week he'll be sent to a soft job like Schuler's in Canada, and as a further benefit he'll acquire the right to move around the camp with more freedom than any ordinary prisoner. He'll go from assignment to assignment by himself, at least on Fridays. On that day he'll even be able to go outside the fence, since the commandant's villa is known to be on a street just beyond the entrance. He wonders where such freedom will lead him. What he might discover and what he might learn. It's possible that he could even get word of Eidel, regardless of whether or not she's being transferred to the new women's camp.

How happy that would make him. How happy it would make Max.

He sinks into this reverie and lets his hands operate according to their own will, and they work a kind of small magic on Drexler's appearance. When Jacob holds up the mirror, the Nazi smiles. It's a smile directed only at himself, but it's a smile nonetheless. "Go ahead and give me a shave," he says, indicating the jug of hot water and drawing a hand across his chin.

Jacob shaves him carefully and well, for Eidel and for Max.

Moments later he's outside again, shading his eyes from the bright sun, beginning the long walk back to the excavation. All alone out here he feels vulnerable and exposed—there's no pack of men to work his way into the middle of, and no protection from whatever brutality some stranger may choose to inflict upon him—but the truth is that no one notices him at all. Not the prisoners standing in one of the yards enduring a roll call that began sometime the night before. Not the capo in charge of those men and not the guards. Not the SS officer who careens past on a motorcycle and not the two wasted prisoners standing like supplicants outside the door of the hospital. He may as well be invisible. He wonders if it will always be this way, should he get the job and be permitted to come and go alone. If he will always be beneath notice.

He's thought all along that exposure would be the worst thing, *safety in numbers* and so forth, but now he's not so certain. As long as he keeps moving, and as long as he stays clear of the fence, he seems entirely safe. To test this idea he turns down a passageway between two blocks, not knowing where he's headed, and wanders freely for a while. Turning one way and then another at intersections between the buildings, moving steadily, looking purposeful. Nothing happens. He emerges into the clear and turns again, this time back in the direction of the main gate instead of toward the excavation, and once more no one notices. Not a pair of guards smoking alongside the fence, not a woman looking down from a high window overhead, not a group of prisoners queued up in front of the block waiting for something.

All of this walking takes energy. He's getting tired, and he realizes that he ought to save his strength for the dig. A commando of prisoners passes by at double time, raising dust with their torn boots and their bare feet, and under the cover of their passing he turns back.

He looks down at the tattoo on his arm as he goes and he thinks of the ledgers where such things are recorded. He thinks of Drexler and his *Totenbuch*. The sergeant was talking on the phone to someone higher up—Vollmer, perhaps, or even the commandant himself—about the entries filling that infernal volume. Bronchitis. Inflammations of the kidneys. Heart attack after heart attack.

More diagnoses were required, he said, a greater variety.

Jacob stumbles and nearly falls but catches himself at the last second. A misstep will draw attention. A misstep will destroy his anonymity. So he takes a deep breath and keeps on, understanding at last that he of all people has just seen the end of the *Totenbuch*. It has been a compilation of lies all along—how many prisoners can die of heart attacks in a single day? in a single hour?—and the Nazis won't be bothered to keep it up anymore.

Anonymity indeed. When men and women die from now on, their names and numbers won't even go on the record.

He steadies himself and picks up the pace ever so slightly. Not enough to be noticed, but enough. He must get back to the excavation. He must return to his son.

Max

THIS RETROSPECTIVE CERTAINLY WASN'T my idea.

They could have waited and done it without me. After all, I'm pushing ninety or thereabouts, depending on who you ask. But no. The National Gallery is the National Gallery and they do what they want to do when they want to do it. They don't ask you what you think.

A person can't help being flattered, though. At least a little.

Wyeth had to put himself through all of that Helga business to get his day at the National Gallery. I mean it. Don't think he wasn't fishing for the attention, for the *Time* cover and the *Newsweek* cover and all the rest of it, one last hurrah in his declining years. A nice infusion of cash, too.

Once his wife found out, I figure the two of them cooked up the whole deal together. It must have been harder on Betsy than it was on him, but what else was she supposed to do? Her husband spends ten or fifteen years making naked pictures of this Helga and hiding them in his buddy's place down the road. His old buddy Frolic Weymouth. That's right. *Frolic.* A full-grown man named after a foxhound. That tells you everything you need to know, doesn't it?

So when Betsy finds the pictures, what's she supposed to do? Anybody could answer that question. Lemons into lemonade. It's the American way. She capitalizes on her own misfortune, picks up the phone, and the two of them ride their pathetic little homegrown scandal all the way down to Washington, D.C.

The important thing is this: even though the Helga show came toward the end of Andy's life, it wasn't a retrospective by any means. It was just Helga. Helga and the chance for every curiosity seeker in the world to have a peek into Uncle Andy's private little world.

I guess they'd had their fill of *Christina's World* by then. Everybody had.

This retrospective of mine they're mounting, though? It's the real deal.

Five

"HOW SHALL WE GO ON without Lydia and Max?"

That's the message the deliveryman carries to Jacob. He knows exactly where to find him. He knows his commando and he knows his block. There's no reaching Jacob during the workday, though, not with the Ukrainian guards keeping an eye on things. His commando has dug their way under the road and come out the other side with only a half-dozen men lost to Slazak's temper and the guards' eager trigger fingers, and the road presents an additional barrier even if it's not a physical one. The delivery commando has no obvious business over there, not with coal and definitely not with flour, and time has proven again and again, to the little junkman and to every other individual who has passed through his commando either to be reassigned elsewhere or to die of overwork or to be shot for one offense or another, that the minute you have to start explaining things it's already too late.

The delivery commando works long hours, though. Longer than most, impossible as it seems, for just this reason. A black market operation requires access and access requires opportunity and opportunity requires a flexible schedule. So they start work early and quit late, and they constantly adjust their route to accommodate certain ever-shifting exigencies.

Thus they arrive at Jacob's block when the men are done for the day. They're done working and done with the first evening roll call—the one that happens before they get their rations, the one that sometimes goes on forever and supersedes the meal altogether—and now they're lingering for a few precious moments in the yard. The junkman wipes his brow with the back of his wrist, adding black to black. The day is still warm and he's wearing his coat in spite of it, for the usual reasons. Bits of coal collect in every fold of it. He tore the flaps from the outside pockets long ago to help the process along, and then he sold the fabric for a couple of cigarettes. It's the pockets inside where he tucks whatever secret merchandise he's transporting on any given day, although at this moment the merchandise is strictly in his mind.

He looks around for Jacob, stretching his shoulders and taking a shovel from the wagon. His partner draws the horse nearer to the building and the junkman lets down the gate and they begin scraping coal into the bin. They're in no hurry. There's not a capo to be seen, no authority figures at all except for the guards scattered around the perimeter of the yard with their machine guns and their flat looks and their eyes like coin slots.

The junkman spies Jacob squatting in the dirt alongside the building, his head bent in conversation with a younger man. A boy almost, a boy who's big and strong enough but a boy all the same. He can't get Jacob's attention but he gets the boy's. He winks at him and jerks his head. The boy speaks to Jacob and Jacob looks over toward the junkman and the junkman does it all over again. Standing there pretending to work, going slow, dribbling coal onto the dirt and over his shoes and into his pockets.

Jacob looks away but the boy looks back. He says something to Jacob again, and Jacob shakes his head. The boy begins to stand but Jacob puts a hand on his knee. His touch doesn't stop the boy. He rises and slaps dust from his trousers—long, comical trousers doubled over at the cuffs and doubled over again—and then he approaches the wagon.

"I've got a message for Rosen," says the junkman.

"I'm Rosen," says the boy.

"Good for you," says the junkman. "But this is for the other Rosen."

"You mean my father."

The junkman almost stops shoveling, but not quite. One of the guards has turned his attention their way, so he keeps his eyes down and his hands busy.

"I'll go get him," says Max.

"No no no no no no," The junkman doesn't look up. "Not so fast. The guards."

By the way he's speaking not to him but to the ground, Max gets the picture. Slowly, slowly, hardly moving at all, he takes a half step away and leans his back against the green tarpaper wall of the block as if he isn't here to talk to the junkman at all. After a minute the guard has turned his attention elsewhere.

The junkman goes on. "You Max?"

"I am."

"Max Rosen?"

"Yes."

"You're sure?"

"I'm sure."

"Son of Jacob and Eidel Rosen?"

Max steadies himself. "What do you know about my mother?"

"I know she thinks you're dead is what I know." More coal goes onto the ground and he stoops to pick it up, slipping a few grams into his pocket along the way. "I take it Lydia would be your sister, then?"

That's enough. Max can't contain himself. He springs away from the wall and leans in toward the junkman, avid. "She is."

"Watch yourself. The guards."

But the guards haven't taken note.

"What do you know about Lydia?"

The junkman makes as if to wring his own neck. "Sorry, pal." The look on his face would suggest that he's sincere. It doesn't last, though, because the capo has materialized in the doorway. He stands on the top step surveying the yard and sniffing the air, on his way to see about rations. "Oops," says the junkman. "Slazak."

Poor Max is so overwhelmed with thoughts of his mother and his sister that he can hardly understand. *Slazak.* It's the name of some demon conjured from another realm, a word that suggests something not entirely real, and he can't quite grasp its meaning. He can't quite grasp anything. He has been raised up and stricken down all at once, brought low in a way that all of the ditch-digging and starvation he's endured have been unable to accomplish.

"*Slazak,*" hisses the junkman again.

Max falls back against the wall, leaning there like lumber, and the junkman finishes his work. Max hardly breathes. He closes his eyes and keeps them closed for a minute and then opens them again as if he expects the world to have changed in the meantime. To have gone back to the way it was before the junkman arrived. But it hasn't. The junkman throws his shovel in the wagon and raises the gate. He drags a chain across it and the clanking of the chain gets Max's attention the way a ghostly visitation might. "Tell your old man," he says to the boy.

Nothing. Slazak clomps down the steps and stalks toward the kitchen.

The junkman climbs back into the wagon. "Tell him she wants to know what they're going to do without you and your sister. And tell him I owe her a message back. He can give it to me next time."

Nothing from Max.

"Don't forget."

He won't.

*

"How shall we go on without Lydia and Max?"

It was a hopeful message, now that she thinks about it. She hadn't meant it that way. It had been a cry from the heart and nothing more, the first thing that had come into her mind. But she sees now that within its context of despair is the notion of moving forward, which is hopeful. She wonders if Jacob will understand it that way.

When the delivery commando arrives with the flour, she practically accosts the junkman. "Were you able to get to him?" she asks.

"I was."

"And he said?"

The junkman shrugs. "He didn't say anything. There wasn't time."

She glares up from her cutting.

"The capo, the guards, you know how it goes. This place isn't always conducive to a long talk."

"But he gave you a message."

"No ma'am, he didn't." Taking a step away, lifting the white shovel. "I'm sure he'll have one for you soon enough."

Eidel crumples forward in spite of herself. No word. No word from Jacob at all. It's not possible.

The junkman begins shoveling. He looks back at her over his shoulder and asks himself if he should tell her about Max. How he's seen him and talked to him. How he's all right. Alive, at least.

Eidel picks up her knife again and turns away. "No message?" she says, turning resolute. "In that case, you won't get your second kilo."

It's the junkman's turn to be aghast. God knows what he's promised that ravenous Slovak guard of his. He could be right on the verge of that old familiar *pop pop pop* that he was so quick to bring up a couple of days before.

"No message," she says, "no radishes," believing that he's up to something. That he has a message—surely Jacob wouldn't have permitted him to leave without one—but thinks he can extract a little bit more for delivering it.

The junkman hardly believes his ears, although he knows he has it coming. *No message, no radishes.* The idea of leaving empty-handed turns his face as pale as the flour that covers the rest of him. "Wait a minute," he says, lifting his hat and giving his shaven head a theatrical scratch, "I seem to remember that there might have been a message after all."

"Is that so?"

"Oh, yes."

"And you're just remembering now?"

"I have a lot on my mind." He screws the hat down. "But I think it's coming back."

She's still cutting. Rutabagas today, although there aren't many of them and they're softer than they should be. Nearly rotten. She keeps cutting, and she doesn't look up.

The junkman slaps himself on the side of the head. A white cloud blooms. "The boy," he says. "The boy is alive."

She drops the knife. "Max?"

"Yes! Max! I've seen him with my own eyes."

"My son?"

"None other." He stands there beaming. "Your husband pointed him out."

She can't believe the reality of anything so wonderful. It must be verified. "Tell me about him," she says. "Tell me what he looks like."

"Very much like his father," says the junkman.

"Good guess. Go on."

The junkman looks hurt. "I'm not guessing," he says. "Beyond the resemblance to his father, I must say he looks pretty much like the rest of us. No hair. Shabby clothing. Nothing but skin and bones."

"Anything else?" She doesn't want to lead him, but there must be something. There *is* something. And she knows what it is.

The junkman pulls at his lip. "He's tall for his age," he says. "At first I thought he was a fully grown man."

"Max," she says, clutching her throat and putting down the knife. She has run the tip of that blade down a vein before and she's told herself she'll never do it again, but now she knows for certain. Not with Max alive. She'd been convinced that her husband was enough—*dayenu*, she'd said—but now, wonder of wonders, she's found herself in a world that still has her son in it too.

*

Ever since the disappearance of his twin, Schuler has been weakening steadily. When he kneels to sort clothing in Canada, his bones crack like firewood. The pain in his joints dims his eyes and twists his mouth into a grimace. His walking pace has slowed to a shuffle, and officers waiting for their Friday trim grow peevish at his absence even though when he finally arrives his hands shake so badly that his work is worse than ever before. When the word circulates then that a new barber has passed Drexler's scrutiny, there's a general rejoicing among the highly placed.

Schuler doesn't rejoice. He says farewell to his freedom. He says farewell to Canada, with its soft work and its riches. He examines his

gum-soled shoes, calculating how well they'll hold up on the water project, and he studies his own soft hands, imagining them callused and
bleeding. He despairs.

The first day that he's back among the ordinary run of prisoners,
trudging off to the excavation, men begin asking him questions they
haven't asked before. It's as if he's a traveler come back at last from some
mysterious place even more exotic than Canada. As if he's tumbled back
to earth from the heavens. Max is the most curious of them all, since his
father has gone off this very morning to take the old barber's place and
he wonders about the conditions and the people he'll meet. He asks him
if the sorting facility is really the land of plenty that everyone has been
led to believe.

Schuler, like an old voluptuary who's drained his last bottle, sighs
and nods his head. He can't even speak to make a proper answer.

Max asks if it's true that the commandant's cook is a grandmotherly
old woman who might part now and then with a little something in the
way of food.

Schuler comes back to something approaching life, barking out a
derisive laugh. "The commandant's cook? I should say not. The commandant's cook is just back from service on a U-boat, and he's a squint-
eyed Nazi devil if there ever was one."

"But—"

"But nothing. The kindly old woman you've heard about is the
housekeeper. Except she isn't kindly either."

"No?"

"Definitely not. She is, however, deaf as a post."

Max sags.

"Buck up," says Schuler. "If your father uses his head, deaf is a thousand times better. *Kindly* depends on someone else, you see. But *deaf*

opens the way for a man's own cunning."

Slazak has a length of pipe he's been carrying around as a walking stick, and he jabs Schuler in the ribs to keep him quiet. "Save your wind," he says, and when Schuler stumbles but walks on he hits him harder, this time across the back of the knees. Schuler goes down and cries out and Max tries to lift him but Slazak won't permit it. He clouts Max across the shoulders and the boy goes down too. This time he's able to help Schuler up while acting as if he's only helping himself. "Good boy," says Schuler under his breath, and Slazak doesn't hear, so that's the end of it for now.

Max starts asking questions again when they break for noon rations, but this time the other men don't want to hear about food. They think about food enough, without having to dream about the delicacies that Rosen might be able to get his hands on for the exclusive benefit of himself and his son. The truth is that they are of two minds about the subject. Half of them gave up all thoughts of food the moment they entered the camp, in order to keep themselves from going mad; the rest believe in thinking of nothing else, in order to keep themselves from despairing entirely.

Never mind the temptations, they say, tell us about the commandant himself.

"He drinks," says Schuler, leaning back on a pile of black iron pipe.

No one looks surprised.

"And as far as I can tell, he believes that Jews are gorgons."

There are a few blank faces among the men, so he elucidates by holding his hands up alongside his head and wiggling his fingers.

"Like Medusa," he says. "He'll look at them only in the mirror. Under any other condition, the bastard averts his eyes." The stack of pipe is warm in the hot sun and he leans on it like a lizard, gathering heat into his old bones.

"Could be he's ashamed of himself," comes a voice.

"Hah," says Schuler. "An individual more puffed up with pride never set foot upon this earth." He stretches his fingers around a length of pipe, feeling the warmth sink in.

Another voice: "So why didn't you slit his throat when you had the chance?" No one seems to know exactly where the words come from, but they hang in the air like notes from a church bell. A couple of the men check to see if Slazak or perhaps even one of the Ukrainians has overheard, but no.

Schuler sits up. "Why didn't I slit the bastard's throat? I'll tell you why." He surveys them one by one. "I did it to save the worthless skins of idiots like you."

A muttering comes from the men. Of course. They hadn't thought it through. The dream of standing behind the commandant with a blade of sharp German steel in their hands is powerful enough to block out all logic, all reason. Kill the commandant and you kill not just yourself but your commando, your block, probably half the prisoners in the entire camp. Just like that. To say nothing of what the Nazis would do to every blood relative you had in all of Europe. They'd hunt them down and slaughter them one after another. And when the bloodshed was finished, they'd install another commandant just like the first one. Worse, if they could find such a creature.

So old Schuler, deposed barber and sorter of stolen goods, lounging there on his stack of pipe like a dragon on his treasure and smiling to himself in an ecstasy of satisfaction, was right. Hands off the commandant. Hands off every last one of them.

*

Partly indoors and partly out, Canada is a great open-air bazaar of the lost and the stolen. Treasures lurk everywhere: rare gems and glittering costume jewelry, wedding rings and coins of all nations; dark Belgian chocolates and rich French cheeses and fat fragrant sausages from every corner of Europe. The first lesson that Jacob learns is that you never know where you'll find such things, and the second lesson is that the first lesson is an illusion. There are, after all, only a limited number of places where desperate people might have hidden their valuables upon reaching the end of the line. The hems of coats and dresses. The toes of boots. False bottoms and secret compartments in trunks and suitcases.

The capo is Jankowski, a Pole with the manner and build of an armored tank. He trundles about slowly and methodically, grinding beneath his feet anything or anyone unlucky enough to get in his way, and his huge square head swivels from side to side as he makes one circuit of the perimeter after another. He misses nothing. Some men say they've never seen him so much as blink.

He was anything but happy with Schuler but he's less happy with Rosen, because someone will need to train him. Training means not just outlining what goes where—men's clothing in these piles, women's in these; coins here and jewels here and food over there out of the sun; every single yellow star thrown into this burn barrel—but reinforcing the dangers of trying to pocket so much as an atom of contraband. *Organizing,* the prisoners call it. Since these ignoramuses learn only by example, someone is going to have to suffer.

Ordinarily, that wouldn't bother Jankowski in the least. He'd see it as an opportunity. But the trains have been delivering prisoners night and day, and Canada is filling up with goods faster than his commando can sort them, and the officer in charge has the sympathy of a baboon and the forbearance of an emperor. What Jankowski needs is additional men, a dozen strong and vigorous backs to bend to the work, not just a replacement for that shiftless old layabout Schuler. Not another one to be dividing his time between here and the barber's chair, off every Friday currying favor among the officers and complaining about any work that might roughen his delicate hands.

For this, for the education of this new part-timer Rosen, he's going to have to sacrifice a perfectly good worker. It infuriates him, but there's no alternative. Making his slow transit around the edge of the yard, he assesses the men under his command with an eye to choosing the one most in need of a little salutary discipline. Ideally it will be one whose loss, whether temporary or permanent, will set back the commando's output as little as possible. He spies Wasserman. Wasserman is as innocent and harmless as they come, a timid and pigeon-chested weakling afraid of his own shadow. His work is cautious and slow but impeccable; he never makes a mistake and he's never been caught pocketing anything. Jankowski hates him for it.

Wasserman will do.

The capo grinds on past, his square mouth opening into a narrow black smile. It looks like something a gunner would fire through. He lowers himself step by step into the sorting area and veers toward a table piled high with coins. Jacob is there emptying a sack onto the tabletop, the coins tumbling out like water and singing like music. "Faster," says Jankowski, "and more carefully," although coins will only fall out of a canvas sack so fast, and no amount of caution will have any effect on the end result. It's just what he says.

"Wait," he says then, and Jacob waits. He picks up one of the fallen coins and assesses it, squinting at it from both sides, examining the marks around the edges, hefting it in his meaty hand. He pauses and thinks and dampens his thumb with his tongue and rubs it over the coin's face, poking out his wet lower lip and drawing down the corners of his mouth. An eyebrow lifted, he looks from the coin to Jacob and back again. He grunts and shakes his head, as if to suggest that he of all people—this capo Jankowski who before his brief heyday at Auschwitz was a farm laborer in the deepest reaches of the countryside, hauling silage and shoveling manure—as if to suggest that he has found this particular coin not entirely up to his standards.

Jacob stands at attention the entire time—waiting for a chance to explain that this coin has come from the same source as all of the others and that he doesn't know what on earth might have happened to it if anything happened to it at all but that whatever it was that happened most surely took place long before the coin fell into his hands; waiting for the more likely outcome, which is that Jankowski will abuse him in some way without hearing an explanation or wanting one; asking himself what old Schuler's secret was for thriving in this treacherous environment—but in the end not one of these things happens. Instead the capo calls out to the nearest of the guards and flips the coin and they both watch it as it soars upward into the sunlight. Everyone watches. The coin spins slowly and slowly, bright sun glinting from it. Time stops. At the top of its arc the coin rotates one last impossible time and the sunlight sparks and the descent begins. Jankowski holds out his hand, and as the guard watches, and as every man in the commando watches too, he catches the coin and slips it into the pocket of his shirt. Just like that.

Then, and only then, does he turn his attention to Jacob, holding out one meaty index finger like a sausage or the barrel of a gun and waggling it back and forth. *Don't you try that,* the gesture says, as if such a thing needs saying.

What follows is a perverse morality play. Jankowski goes to Was-serman's table. One end of it is piled high with men's shoes and the other end with women's. Children's shoes, of which there are many, go in a separate crate. No one knows what will happen to the children's shoes, there are so many of them left behind and so few feet to fill them up. None at all, really.

Narrow-chested Wasserman, stunned from watching Jankowski pocket the coin and on his guard for whatever terrible thing might hap-pen next, his arms laden with shoes, stumbles toward the table himself. He has half an impulse to speed up and half an impulse to slow down, but he does neither. He just keeps moving. Jankowski beats him to the table and begins examining his work. A thousand times a thousand shoes, lying one atop another like dogs and stinking in the heat. He rummages through the pile and comes up with a particular pair, wingtip brogues the color of oxblood, and he examines them like treasure.

"What's this?" he says as Wasserman reaches the table. "No laces?"

Wasserman dumps his load of shoes on the ground. "They came that way," he says.

The capo squints. "Empty your pockets," he says.

Wasserman complies. The pocket of his shirt holds a morsel of bread that he's been saving for two days now, and Jankowski grinds it to powder between his fingers and blows it away into the summer air. The pockets of his trousers are empty.

"Let's see *your* shoes, then," says the capo.

Wasserman lifts the cuffs of his trousers to display a pair of ancient workboots closed at the tops with tiny twists of wire.

"Reason enough," says the capo, lifting the wingtips, "for you to steal a proper pair of shoelaces."

"But I didn't," says Wasserman.

"You've hidden them somewhere, haven't you?"

"No, I haven't."

"We'll see." He orders Wasserman to take off his shirt and trousers and turn them inside out. Wasserman complies, standing there in Canada with the sun shining and the breeze blowing, clad in tattered woolen undershorts the color of mud. "Off with those too," says Jankowski, as if Wasserman might be hiding something within them other than his dignity.

Once they're off, one of the guards laughs and raises his machine gun, elbowing the fellow next to him, pretending that he can't sight accurately on a target so small.

"Hand those over," says Jankowski. He makes a show of trying to make as little contact as possible with Wasserman's filthy undershorts, and when he gives them back the gold coin falls out.

"What have we here?" he asks no one in particular. "It's not enough to steal shoelaces! Shoelaces I might be able to forgive! But this!"

Wasserman falls to his knees.

"You should know better."

"I *do* know better. I didn't—"

Jankowski tells Wasserman to bring him the coin. Wasserman does, naked on his knees in the naked dirt, lifting up the gold piece like an offering. The capo takes it and heaves it with all of his strength toward Jacob, who actually makes the catch. Poor Jacob, making himself Jankowski's accomplice in the process.

The capo steps away from the kneeling man. It's in the hands of the guards now. He can't take responsibility for how they might judge so terrible and daring a crime against the Reich. The one with the raised machine gun, the one who laughed, fires a single short burst. There's something offhand about it, and when it's over, perhaps half a second after it began, he lights a cigarette.

Jankowski hopes aloud that whoever is sent to replace Wasserman will be an improvement. Regardless, the new man has certainly learned how things go.

Wasserman's clothing goes straight to the sorting tables. His boots as well. And within moments, one stealthy prisoner or another has pocketed those two precious twists of wire.

Max

ANDY HAD FROLIC WEYMOUTH'S roomy old place down on the Brandywine River, attic and barn and all, but what do I have? Where would I
hide anything that I wanted to keep a secret? Space is precious in the
city, and I've been a creature of the city ever since I came to America.

People go around singing *O beautiful, for spacious skies* and that's fine
for them, but I say to hell with spacious skies. Spacious skies give me the
willies.

It's true enough that in the city you never know what's lurking
around the next corner, but in the wide open spaces you just never *know*,
period. Anything could happen. In the city you've got a fair chance, but
out in the open you could get struck by lightning or the earth could
open right up or you could just get lost without one single thing to help
you tell one cornfield from another.

Don't call it paranoia, either. It's not paranoia. It's an acquired response. It's one more souvenir I picked up at Auschwitz. Try working in
the sun and the wind for a year or two, with Ukrainians pointing machine guns at you the whole time—or try lining up in a big open square
every day for something that's ostensibly roll call but that's really a kind
of random selection process for who's going to get a bullet in his brain
this morning—and you'll decide that a blind alley with a broken street-
lamp is a pretty good alternative to the great outdoors. Try watching the
clouds race overhead when you can't go anywhere yourself. Try watching
the seasons change.

You'll end up like me.

Anyhow, there's a young girl working on the retrospective, an intern or an assistant or whatever who comes up from Washington and camps out in a hotel somewhere for a week at a time just to keep tabs on me, and she keeps asking if I've got any pieces I haven't shown. I keep saying where in hell would I keep them. I'm nice enough about it. At least I hope I am. She's just a girl, after all, just a child, and she keeps asking the same way a child would keep asking. As if there's a chance that I might have a cookie jar hidden on a high shelf somewhere.

You know what would make me blow my top? If she asked in the context of Helga. If she said, "Andrew Wyeth came up with those Helga paintings when he was 70 years old, you know, so I was wondering—"

She'd *never* see what I've got in the locker. Not after a question like that. Nobody would ever see it.

Six

TO KNOW THAT HER HUSBAND and son are alive changes things, but not entirely for the better. Such is the way of the camp. Like the river of the world it bears a certain fixed amount of everything there is—good and evil, love and hate, life and death—in proportions that are cruel but constant. Any gain here requires a loss there. The slightest disturbance ripples through everything.

Where once she worked at murdering time, at creating a perpetual present, at eradicating her memories and destroying her dreams, she is unmoored now. She can think of nothing but Jacob and Max. She certainly can't empty her mind entirely. There's no more counting bowls of soup and mechanically stirring the pot and sinking the ladle halfway regardless of the pleas of the women in the line. Each prisoner's woe speaks to her, and she would help every one of them if she could, for every one of them is an incarnation of her husband or her son.

Jacob and Max are here but not here, and the frustration of their proximity brings her back to Saturdays in the synagogue in Zakopane, sitting with Lydia in the balcony, trying to concentrate on her prayers but unable to—listening instead for the sound of their voices rising above the rest.

She sees the two of them everywhere. She sees Jacob back when they first met, stealing glances at her through the window of his father's barber shop in the fading alpine twilight; she sees Max charging through her house and her heart like some unstoppable force, the duplicate of his father in so many ways; she sees the two of them standing side by side in the line alongside the camp train station.

And in the midst of it all she sees Lydia. For such is the way of the camp too, with its precarious balance of life and death, and love and hate, and good and evil. If it should permit a heart to rise, it will just as surely strike it down.

*

"Canada is just like everywhere else."

Jacob has given Max half of his bread and a little bit of the gristly boiled beef that the cooks slid onto his plate. They sit side by side against the foundation of the block, on the shady side where the masonry is cooler against their backs. The day has been hot and their shirts and trousers are soaked through and this is the only pleasure to be had. This and companionship.

"Did you get any food there?" says Max, chewing and chewing on that tough scrap of beef.

"No," says his father. "There's food around, but they keep a tight rein on things. I don't think Schuler ever really got much from Canada."

Max reaches into his mouth and takes out the gray knot he's been working on. "I thought—"

"I know what you thought," says his father, holding up a hand. "I didn't get anything extra, but on the other hand I haven't worked as hard as you. I'm sure of that."

Max sits holding the meat between two fingers and a thumb, the knob of it like another filthy appendage and just as appetizing. "Papa—"

"Go on. You're a growing boy." He takes what remains of his own bread and scrapes the plate with it, soaking up the little bit of watery runoff that arrived with the beef. "Eat up," he says.

Max does.

"People die in Canada just like everywhere else. It's no paradise in that department." He tells Max about Wasserman and the gold piece. Wasserman and Jankowski and the gold piece and the machine gun.

"So there's really gold? There's really gold?"

Youth. It hasn't been wrung out of him yet.

"This fellow Wasserman," says Jacob, shaking his head, ignoring the question. "He was a weakling. A weakling even here among us weaklings. I'd thought that such a man could get by in Canada. Look at Schuler. He may not be as pathetic a creature as Wasserman was, but he's older by fifteen years. Maybe twenty."

"Schuler's dead."

"Dead?" Jacob is licking the damp spots on his plate, but he leaves off. It's only been one day that he's had the old man's duties. "Dead?"

"He committed suicide."

"How? Where?"

"At the excavation." Max lowers his voice to a whisper, and his father leans in. "Slazak didn't like the way he was digging. Schuler talked back, told him that his work was always good enough for the capo in Canada. Said that maybe Slazak should take a lesson from him instead of complaining." Max shakes his head and swallows. "We buried him where he fell. Those nice shoes and everything."

Perhaps the youth has been wrung out of him after all.

*

Zofia is standing outside the kitchen door, fending off the two *boulevardiers* of the delivery commando. One of them, not the junkman of Witnica but his partner, formerly a knife-sharpener and mender of pots from a village in the Carpathians, has brought her a couple of cigarettes. "Free of charge," he says, "no obligation on your part whatsoever." He smiles and shows teeth that he could have sharpened in an earlier life. Tilted incisors and long canines and molars like tombstones. Certain gaps where teeth have rotted and fallen out, and certain other gaps where gold teeth have been removed with a pair of pliers. He has a cigarette of his own jutting through one of those holes, just as if he'd intended it for that purpose.

Three cigarettes in total, then, one between his lips and two more peeking from his pocket, the Holy Trinity incarnate in pilfered tobacco. Three cigarettes, a treasure as great as Blackbeard's, possessed by a man—this being a coal delivery day—whose skin and clothing and facial stubble are as black as that very name. Call him Blackbeard, then. Blackbeard the sharpener of knives and mender of pots.

Zofia doesn't fancy Blackbeard the way she fancies the junkman, but he'll do. He has the cigarettes, after all. That helps. It more than helps. It's everything. The junkman has never offered her anything but a smile and a flattering remark, and she knows the value of those.

"You must want *something* in exchange," she says, lifting up a coy hand for her smile to hide behind. The capo, great fat Rolak, is busy somewhere else, probably in one of the storerooms either helping herself to whatever delicacies she has hidden there or enjoying a carrot or a stalk of celery that ought by rights to be going to the prisoners.

Blackbeard takes out his cigarette and purses his lips. "Have you any ideas?" he says.

"Nothing that you haven't thought of, I'm sure," says Zofia.

He shrugs. "There's nothing new under the sun."

"No," she says.

"Something conventional then," he says. "One of the old standbys."

As much as he hates putting off the inevitable, he's well accustomed to bargaining for everything, both here in the camp and in his prior life. *Always let the customer suggest a price,* is his belief, *because you never know what value he might place on something.*

Zofia reaches out and takes one of the cigarettes from his breast pocket. It's probably the most daring thing that this poor timid creature has ever done in all her life, a physical act of flirtation, even if it's only a carrying-forward of something already begun by Blackbeard himself. The cigarette is gray and bent and precious. "I'll take this one as a down payment," she says.

"A down payment on what?"

But Zofia has vanished, blushing furiously, tearing up the two or three steps into the kitchen and bending over the stove to transfer fire from a stick of kindling to the end of the cigarette. She can hardly breathe and it isn't the smoke or the exertion of running. Eidel looks over from the chopping block and sighs. "A down payment?" she says.

Zofia looks up. Her face is red and wreathed in smoke, and with laughter bursting from her she staggers to the chopping block to take up her own knife again. Eidel laughs too. Laughing is something that neither of them has done in a very long time. It seems as if they've never laughed before, and together they keep it up for a while, perhaps the better part of a minute, with Blackbeard down in the yard craning his neck and the junkman climbing back onto the wagon and the capo appearing out of nowhere. She trundles down the hallway from the storerooms like a battleship, wiping her mouth on her apron. She's still chewing something and when she begins to speak tiny bits of it explode from her lips like shrapnel.

Only the shame at being caught with her mouth full contains her ferocity. It's a close call, but Eidel and Zofia are both definitely working and the sack of rutabagas on the table alongside the chopping block is surely diminished so she clamps her mouth shut and shakes a finger at them and lets their laughter pass this time. She lets Zofia's cigarette pass as well, choosing not to ask how she came to be in possession of it. Those men in the delivery commando, no doubt. She wonders what she has given up for it but she thinks she knows. It's unforgivable, the way these people live.

*

Late Thursday, Jacob is given a new suit of clothes intended to make him more presentable for the senior SS officers he'll be visiting. His old uniform is taken away and in its place he's issued a relatively clean jacket and trousers made of a lighter weight fabric, closer to new than the uniform he's been wearing and showing signs of actually having been pressed at some point during their lifetime. Certain men in his block are envious. Certain men would be envious of anything, of any change, of any attention that doesn't result in injury or death. "Imagine," he tells Max, "coveting such a ridiculous thing—when the truth is that my old uniform was heavier and I'll miss it when the winter comes."

"Who believes in winter?" says Max.

The evening roll call is approaching and Jacob must sew his serial number into the new uniform in time, so he sits working furiously with a needle and thread. Clouds are moving in and the light is dying and he squints. Another prisoner comes by and watches him work, a prisoner named Rubin who claims to have been a tailor and who scoffs at Jacob's hurried work. "I could do that for you in a moment," he says as he walks away, "but you'd have to give me the jacket for my trouble." An ironist.

Jacob's fingers won't cooperate, and the roll call draws nearer, and he begins to wonder what this infernal new uniform will cost him in the end. Slazak walks past and gives him the resentful look he once reserved for Schuler. He walks past in the dirt and continues around the corner and then comes back and looks more carefully, clucking and stroking his chin. "It would be a shame to go to roll call without proper identification," he says.

"Yes, sir," says Jacob, not even looking up. He sticks himself with the needle and blood drips onto the patch he's sewing and Slazak clucks again. *Shame, shame, shame.* Sweat beads up on Jacob's forehead and he swipes at it, leaving behind a red streak. "Incredible," says Slazak. "A few days of soft work, and you've lost every bit of strength you once had. This won't go well."

"I'm doing my best," says Jacob.

"Perhaps you need a few extra minutes."

There is nothing more dangerous than Slazak in a solicitous mood. "Oh, no," says Jacob. "I'll be all right. I'll be finished in plenty of time."

"Perhaps we should put off the roll call until after rations."

Jacob looks up. "Rations first?" A few other men in the yard stir, like the first members of a pack of wolves picking up some fresh scent. Getting rations before lining up for roll call would be the rarest of delights—not just because the men would eat earlier, but because they would be guaranteed to eat at all. It has been a while since the first evening roll call stretched on into the blackest hours of the night, but you never know. Word spreads in some intangible and unknowable way, as if on chemical traces carried by the air itself. Footsteps stir within the block. Men poke their heads out the door.

Slazak makes the call, rations it is, and they start to line up. Rain begins, a soft rain that patters down on the dusty clay. Max stands and his father stands alongside him and Slazak says, "Oh, no. Not you two.

First you must finish the needlework on that fine new uniform."

So that's how it will be. Jacob hurries, working his fingers even more frantically than before, but by the time he finishes sewing and they've made their way to the back of the line the rations are gone. Slazak sees their disappointment and grins. Jacob merely turns and walks off toward the yard, but when they get a few steps away and the bell sounds for roll call he apologizes to Max, saying that this may be all of the punishment that Slazak feels comfortable meting out to him in his new position. They'll need to be careful, though. He can always punish Max instead.

They line up with their stomachs complaining. It's late and the sun is down and the yard is lit by searchlights. The soft rain keeps up. Slazak patrols the perimeter with a pair of other capos, one of them a German convicted of murder and rape before he was freed and sent to Auschwitz, although he has only gone downhill here. Behind them in the darkness are the guards with their machine guns, black guns carried by gray men in shadows that swim with rain. Two SS men stand on the platform looking straight ahead, one of them the young one who rides the bicycle and the other one the sergeant whose hair Jacob cut last week, Drexler. In Jacob's chest a kindly feeling toward him rises up unbidden, a feeling connected to the sergeant's approval of him as the new barber, but he fights it down. One personal kindness is nothing compared to the *Totenbuch*. He hears Max's stomach growl and knows himself responsible for it. So much for not calling attention to himself.

The sky opens and thunder rolls and the rain begins in earnest. It's a cold rain after a warm day, and although it refreshes the men and washes them clean it feels good for no more than a moment. If it felt good, the SS wouldn't let them stand out in it. Jacob watches Drexler adjust his hat and gather his coat around his shoulders and he thinks that he looks like a man prepared to stand in the driving rain for as long as it takes.

There's a sour look on his face, though, a look that says he would be happier filling the *Totenbuch* with lies than standing out here counting prisoners in a rainstorm. It's a clear look of regret, and Jacob thinks that perhaps Drexler has learned a lesson of his own. *Keep a low profile.*

The roll call proceeds. The men line up and count off, giving their serial numbers. Slazak and the other capos circulate and listen and make marks on paper as the count proceeds, and when it's over they compare their figures against other figures on other papers. Today's count versus yesterday's. They shake their heads and confer, standing in the rain, and after a few minutes they order the prisoners to count off once more. Drexler and the other officer watch without comment, without even showing frustration or disgust. On the second count the numbers come up short again, and once more the capos order another roll call.

This time, though, the figures seem to match, and the capos deliver their various papers to Drexler for review. He studies them under a flashlight's dull beam, frowning dramatically, looking like a man who's trying to persuade himself that this job—an enormous and soggy demotion from the clean, dry office work he once did—is not only important but worthy of him. He flips through the wet pages—cheap paper that clings to itself and tears and separates—and he scans the columns with the help of a gloved finger. Everyone holds his breath.

"No good," he says finally, stabbing at the tally sheets. "This one's missing."

The capos bend together in a little circle of dismay. Two of them add their pointing fingers to Drexler's. "That'll be one of Slazak's," says one. "Just look at the handwriting," says the other.

Slazak bows his head, beaten. "That's one of mine all right," he says.

Drexler tears the pages loose and thrusts them at Slazak and tells him to count again. The other capos risk smiles, and the young officer with the bicycle sees them and clears his throat, and Drexler says *every-one* must count again, not just Slazak. It's all or nothing.

They all step away, but Slazak stops. "Wait a minute," he says.

"Wait a minute?" Drexler looks as if he's never heard the words before.

"Just so. Another count will do no good, you see. I know the man."

"The missing man?"

"The missing man," says Slazak. "I know who he is. I know *where* he is."

"Are you quite certain?"

"Leave it to me."

"It will be my supreme pleasure," says Drexler.

Slazak leaves the platform and strides off down among the ranks of prisoners. No heads turn to track his progress, but each man he passes relaxes just a little as he goes by. *It's not me he wants,* their postures say. *He's after someone else.*

He slows as he draws near to Jacob. He stops and he folds his hands behind his back and he smiles, his face streaked with rain. "You" he says. "You know the missing man."

Jacob has no answer. He knows so many missing men, after all.

Slazak goes on. "Don't be coy," he says. "He would be right here among us if not for you."

So now it's twenty questions. "I don't—" says Jacob.

Slazak leans in toward him and spits out a mouthful of numbers.

Jacob shows the serial number sewn to his jacket. It's not a match.

"I'm not talking about *you,*" says Slazak. "I'm talking about Schuler. The man whose job you stole."

Of course. Everyone must be accounted for at roll call. Even the dead.

"Go get him," says Slazak. "We won't wait forever." He takes Jacob by the collar of his new uniform and heaves him down the line, from darkness into darkness.

Max calls after his father. "Three days," he says. "He's been in the ground for three days." It's a hint as to how far back in the excavation his father will find the body, and Slazak doesn't appreciate it. He steps back and clouts Max's jaw with the back of his hand and Max staggers backward but doesn't fall. It takes courage not to fall. The sweep of a searchlight freezes this instant and one of the guards raises his gun but Slazak lifts his hand. Perhaps he has other things in mind for the young man. The guard shifts his stance and aims instead at Jacob, tracking him as he moves down the line.

The men wait and the rain comes down and Jacob trudges off with a shovel over his shoulder and a guard at his back. There's no speaking to the guard and there's no telling what time it might be other than by his own weariness, and his weariness makes a poor indicator because he's always weary. They come to the course taken by the water project and they follow the line of the excavation to the road it passes beneath and then beyond that, the earth growing more disturbed as they go, more heaped up and less compacted. Jacob counts his paces. He casts back in his mind as to how many days ago it was that they tunneled underneath the road and he subtracts from that number the three days that Schuler has been dead, thinking that he can calculate an average number of paces per day and perhaps get close to the man's corpse on the first try.

The ground is soft enough where he sinks the shovel in, but it's heavy, mostly clay, and it's saturated with rain. He digs a channel perpendicular to the water line and not much wider than the blade of the shovel, pausing whenever he strikes something harder than the surrounding dirt and going down on his knees to see if he's located Schuler.

No. Not on the first pass anyhow. He digs all the way down to the iron pipes without finding a trace of him. All the way across to where the clay is solid and undisturbed and too hard for digging. The guard shakes his head and laughs. He would be out somewhere standing his watch in the rain anyhow, so this is nothing to him.

Jacob paces off a yard's distance further on and starts back across. "Not so fast," says the guard. "Fill in the first trench."

"I'll fill that one with the dirt from this one," says Jacob, daring to speak to the armed Ukrainian thanks to the darkness and the rain and his desperation, demonstrating his intent with the first shovelful. "It'll save time."

"And you'll dig ten more holes and find what you're after and then what?" says the guard. He lifts the gun and lets loose a fusillade of bullets into the ragged earth three feet from Jacob, showing him exactly where he wants the dirt restored. Jacob does as he's told.

So it goes until the fourth pass, when the shovel finds bone and the touch of it is unmistakable. It's no rock, no root, no iron pipe or bit of substrate from the road. Oh, no. He can feel a human being at the other end of the shovel the way you can feel a human being on the other end of a telephone connection, perhaps more so because of the unmediated physicality of it. Flesh to flesh and bone to bone. He goes to his knees and clears away the mud with his hands and sure enough, it's Schuler's pantleg and shin and ankle. A dead man in a dead man's shoes, buried no more than three feet down. It could be worse.

Jacob comes to his feet and begins excavating the spot, calculating the position of the body inch by inch, working the shovel as cautiously as he dares. He's conservative but within limits. Come too close, and he risks striking the dead man again, perhaps even taking off a finger. Give the corpse too wide a berth, on the other hand, and he'll do more work than is entirely necessary. The rain keeps up and the clay turns to mud and the mud runs. Schuler's striped uniform is saturated with it and Jacob's is saturated too. His hands slip on the wet handle of the shovel and he pitches forward onto the dead man in the ditch, embracing him. The corpse gives under his weight, limp, a couple of days past rigor mortis. Swollen and straining the wet burlap. Just something in a sack. He lifts it up.

The Ukrainian makes him fill in the hole before he goes, although when the time comes he will make him dig it open again and lay Schuler back down at the bottom of it and cover him up once more, but until then it's a matter of principle. Jacob labors on steadily, wet and cold. He pictures the men standing at attention in the yard waiting for his return. He pictures Max, standing there all night without a thing in his belly, a bruise growing on his jaw like a shadow from the blow of Slazak's hand. Fourteen years old. Then he takes up the body and hoists it onto his shoulder and drags it back, like some figure in a fairy tale bearing a burden that whispers its own well-known and wordless demands.

With the addition of Schuler's body, the count is complete. Everything adds up, so Slazak is happy and the other two capos are happy and the young officer is happy. Even Drexler is happy or at least satisfied. No one says a word more than is necessary. Conservation of energy is the order of the day.

The sodden men, prisoners and guards and SS alike, wait in the rain while Jacob drags Schuler's corpse back to the water project and buries it where he found it. It's another hour's work. Dawn would come soon if it could break through the cloud cover, but the rain keeps up and threatens to keep up forever. One more black day. He comes back staggering, supporting himself on his shovel, as unsteady on his feet as some golem conjured up. Drexler recognizes him at last. The barber. He calls to Slazak and asks how a man in such condition is supposed to present himself before officers of the SS in the administration building tomorrow, never mind the commandant's villa and the deputy commandant's apartment on the main street.

Slazak's eyes light up with complicity. He bobs his head and says that Drexler is correct. Such a figure is unfit to go on so elevated a series of errands.

Drexler says, "Then that makes two mistakes you've made."

"Two?" says Slazak.

"Two," says Drexler. "The body from the water project. It was three days old at least."

"Three days, sir," says Slazak. "That's correct, sir."

"And you certified the count this morning? And yesterday? And the day before that?"

"Yes sir," says Slazak. "All by the book."

Drexler shakes his head. "And all of it lies." He calls out Jacob's number, and Jacob comes to the front. "The two of you," he says, "exchange uniforms." Jacob swims in Slazak's, and Slazak's pot belly keeps Jacob's from buttoning up properly, but they accomplish it. "Now come close," says Drexler, and they do. He draws a folding knife from his pocket and leans down from the platform and cuts the green patch from the uniform that Jacob wears now, the patch denoting *capo*. Slazak puts out his hand to accept it, but Drexler crushes the little scrap with a muttered curse and jams it deep into the pocket of his overcoat. "Plenty of better men are waiting for your position," he says. "In the meantime, I have no doubt that these prisoners will do everything in their power to welcome you back among their ranks." A harsh murmur goes up among the scores of wet and weary men, a kind of animal hunger made audible.

"As for you," he says to Jacob, looking from his wet uniform up to the cloud cover that simply will not disperse, "hang those clothes up to dry. Make yourself presentable. The night won't last forever."

And thus they're dismissed.

Max

I'VE WALKED WITH A CANE ever since the days when I could pass it off as an affectation. One of those things that artistic types just *do,* like dressing in those diaphanous hand-dyed fabrics if you're a woman, or wearing a beret if you're a man. Like using a cigarette holder. Not that I've ever smoked, and not that I could ever see myself in a beret. Berets are for old Frenchmen, and as far as people of my background are concerned, an old Frenchmen is most likely a sympathizer.

I've sold them plenty of pictures, though, the French. They have a number of pretty fair museums, and their money's as good as anyone else's, although I do confess to having experienced a little shiver—I wouldn't call it a *frisson,* exactly, ha ha ha—when the euro kicked in and all of a sudden they started using the same currency as the Germans. Time was, you could make a distinction between a French franc and a Deutschmark. Not anymore.

I told my agent from that moment on I'd only accept payment in American dollars. I suppose I sounded like one of those jingoistic political hacks or oafish country musicians—Barry Goldwater or Merle Haggard or someone like that. *Love it or leave it.* Demagoguery and fiddle music. I hate that kind of thing, but on that one occasion I don't think anyone could have blamed me.

Anyhow, back to that cane of mine. For a time when I was young, people couldn't decide whether it was an affliction or just an affectation. That was fine with me. It was no concern of theirs. The leg was stiff and I'd have limped without the cane to lean on but I never complained, and when it hurt—which was most of the time even then—I never let it show. *Ever.* A rumor went around for a while that I'd had polio when I was younger. Polio was something that people got back then. You got it and it damaged you for good and even though it went away you never entirely got over it.

Maybe I should have told them I'd had polio after all.

The first cane I had came from an antique shop right here in Manhattan. I didn't have one when I came over from Europe. Everybody in Europe needed a cane then, or worse. A cane or a crutch or a wooden leg or a gurney. The whole continent was on its last legs, shot full of holes and staggering forward, trying with every last bit of strength not to fall into its own grave. The hospitals were packed with men whose needs were far greater than mine. Who could even think of depriving them? So I limped across Germany and I limped across France and I limped to the boat that took me across the channel to England. And then I limped to the ship that took me over the ocean blue, all the way to New York, New York.

Seven

"IF THE FIRST ONE WAS a down payment," Eidel asks, "then what would this one be?"

Zofia leans over her chopping block, slicing carrots, and in the pocket of her uniform Eidel can see the tip of a second cigarette. Who can say where or when she got it? The day is still early, the sun isn't even up, and the delivery commando isn't due for hours. Perhaps she met Blackbeard overnight somewhere, in an alcove between the blocks or against a wall lit only now and then by the searing arcs of the searchlights. Perhaps, in other words, out there somewhere in the black rain, she's already lived up to her end of the bargain. The more Eidel looks at her the more she decides that she looks flushed and content, or as flushed and content as a living corpse can be, She looks like a person keeping a gratifying secret.

Zofia leans into the knife.

"Paid in full, then?" says Eidel.

"You could say."

Rolak passes through, using an iron poker as a walking stick. She frowns to see that some of the carrots aren't quite transparent, and she growls at Zofia. *"You,"* she says. *"Thinner."* Zofia glances at the pale orange pyramid remaining to be whittled down slice by tiny slice, and she sighs and sets aside the knife. In the drawer is a whetstone. She locates it and takes it out and cleans the rust from it on her apron. "Don't fall behind," says the capo, for there's no satisfying her either way. Zofia permits herself a half-dozen rapid strokes on either side of the knife and puts the whetstone back and resumes cutting, faster than before. If an ideal round of sliced carrot has the qualities of a thick copper coin, these have the qualities of yellowish dappled sunlight on a woodland floor. Just try picking one up. Just try subsisting on a diet so ephemeral.

Eidel dabs her forehead with the silk handkerchief. The coal stove is roaring and no breeze stirs in the predawn gray. The capo watches the two women work and gives her head one abrupt nod to indicate that she's satisfied for now. Then she moves on.

Eidel indicates the pile of carrots. "At this rate," she says, "you won't have a free minute to smoke that cigarette you worked so hard for."

"Who said it was work?" says Zofia.

"My point exactly," says Eidel.

Zofia smiles and shakes her head, a naughty schoolgirl. She smiles and takes the cigarette from her pocket and says in that case maybe she'd better smoke this while she works, raising the knife in one hand and the cigarette in the other and stepping away from the chopping block in the general direction of the stove—until the specter of the capo materializes in the doorway again, and she freezes.

"What do you think you're doing?" Rolak raises the poker.

In an instant Zofia is back at work, the unlit cigarette jammed cold between her lips, one hand going for a carrot and the other raising the knife, but it makes no difference. It's too little, too late. The capo has been itching to use that poker and now she does, catching Zofia across the shoulders and buckling her forward over the block. The newly sharpened knife slices away two fingers at the first joint.

Rolak laughs. "Too thick," she says. "You'll never learn."

Without a moment's reflection, Eidel binds up Zofia's hand in the silk handkerchief. She would go with her to the hospital if she could— this will probably be the last time she will see her, since there's a selection at the hospital every other day, a few prisoners left behind and the rest sent on to the gas—but there are carrots to be sliced and she doesn't dare ask. Her work has doubled, at least for now.

She doesn't know which she wishes more: that she'll see Zofia alive again, or that she'll somehow regain the silk handkerchief that once belonged to her daughter. And she doesn't know which of these outcomes is the less likely.

*

The men stink like wet dogs. Jacob lies among them naked and shivering, waiting for the three bells to ring. He hasn't slept. He's too exhausted to sleep, too full of anticipation for what the day ahead might bring, so he's lain awake on the hard bunk unable to move and unable to breathe, locked in position with his face pointed toward the spot where Slazak's old uniform jacket hangs ghostly from a crossbeam. It occurs to him that just this once there is no capo in the block. He can't remember ever experiencing such a thing. There'll surely be a new one in the morning. Drexler has no doubt reported Slazak's demotion, and some individual or some mechanism has arranged for his replacement. Roll call will reveal his identity. Jacob wonders what kind of beast this new capo will be, what crimes he may have committed in the outside world and what crimes he will commit here.

His mind runs to Max. The boy is sleeping beside him now, but when he awakens he must tell him to be especially wary of the new overseer. To keep his eyes open and his mouth shut, because you never know. Any man taking Slazak's job will be particularly keen to make a good impression on the SS. There's no telling what such an individual might do.

He realizes that while he's at it he ought to tell Max to be wary of Slazak himself. After what happened last night, Slazak will be a wounded animal, angry and bitter and certain that he has nothing much to lose. Max, good boy that he is, might have an instinct to be kind to such a creature, but that instinct will not serve him well. Slazak has never liked Max and he'll like him less now. He'll pull him down to his level if he can.

There is so much he needs to tell Max. A lifetime's worth. He lies listening to his son breathe and he stares at the ghostly image of Slazak's hanging uniform and he wonders how much time he has left to pass on such knowledge as he's accumulated. Not enough. There is never enough.

The bell rings three times and the men rise, emerging from their wet tangle one after another. Moving perhaps a shade more slowly than usual, given Slazak's absence. There is no one here to threaten them, not even the guards who stand outside the door with their machine guns at the ready, welcoming them to the day. They stumble to their feet and they stretch and yawn like any gang of hard-pressed men anywhere, grumpy and tired and sore, and in low voices they speculate as to what roll call will bring. Half of them wish for another extended bout like last night's because it would mean a shorter workday, and the other half is certain that the SS will use last night's careful count as a means to get them out and on their way earlier.

"What could have gone wrong in the night?" asks one. "Particularly a night as short as this?"

"Just you wait and see," says another.

They don't need to wait long. The last men out see it: the dark, narrow slot of one of the bunks isn't entirely empty. It's a bunk that's seen some activity lately, the bunk where Schuler slept until last week and the bunk where his twin slept until a few weeks before that. The men assigned there have been luxuriating in the open spaces left behind by their absence. There's been sufficient room to roll over, sufficient room to breathe, so no wonder it was there that Slazak found a place to lie down the night before. He'd even asked their permission, as shocking as that was. It was the first time he'd been reduced to anything like common courtesy, but he'd asked and the men had acquiesced, shifting to one side and the other, complaining about the crowding and mocking his pot belly but accepting this alteration to their fate the same way they accepted everything else.

Now morning has come, and he's dead. Dead in the bunk on his first and last night back among the prisoners. Dead in Jacob Rosen's muddy uniform, stinking of Schuler's corpse.

The guards order the last men in line to carry him out and prop him up for the count. Someone reads off his number and the capo from the next block over makes a mark on a piece of paper, but beyond that no one looks very closely. Roll call takes almost no time. There is work to be done.

*

Another woman is in Zofia's place this morning, a young woman barely old enough to have passed the initial selection at the train station, a rail-thin and careworn creature all knuckles and bones. Just a girl. The capo has her scrubbing the chopping block with fine gravel from the yard and rinsing it with a bucketful of boiling water and scrubbing it again with coarsely ground salt. Rinsing it again. The girl's pale skin reddens and stays that way. She works without looking up. Eidel asks her name and she says "Gretel" and says no more. Eidel gives her her own name back, but Gretel seems not to register it. Eidel wonders what the poor child has been through, for although everyone's story is the same there are always variations.

Rolak comes by and sees that yesterday's stains on the chopping block are still visible and orders Gretel to begin again with more gravel from the yard. The girl sinks. Eidel says she'll go. She puts down her knife and picks up a crockery bowl and a heavy spoon for digging and steps outdoors.

There he is, past the fence that marks the women's camp, beyond the great crossed timbers wrapped in their tangles of barbed wire, hurrying along in another man's oversized uniform: Jacob. He looks nothing like himself—he's bristly and thin like the rest of them, and his eyes are sunken, and his old mountain-spanning stride has been replaced by a kind of furtive scuttle—but she would know him anywhere. She would know him in Hell itself.

He's twenty yards distant. The capo is scolding little Gretel right behind her, and guards are posted along the fenceline with machine guns. She can't call out to him but she does have the bowl and the spoon, so without even thinking she brings them together once, just as hard as she dares. Nothing. He walks on. It's useless. Just another sound in a place where the air is filled with sound, just one more noise beneath notice. Jacob doesn't even look up. He's nearly past her now. She realizes that this may be the last time that they will ever see each other, no matter how long they may live. She thinks of that and she doesn't think of anything else, certainly not of what the immediate future might bring. Once more thrust into a perpetual present where nothing else matters, she lets her fingers go slack and permits the crockery bowl to crash to the concrete walk. It smashes into a hundred pieces, and gets the attention of everyone.

Rolak leaves off scolding Gretel and comes to the door, arms akimbo like some furious old hausfrau, but Eidel doesn't see her. She's too busy looking at Jacob. He's too busy looking at her. He's stopped short by the fence, frozen in place and reaching out one hand as if to touch the barbed wire, by this unconscious act daring the guards and a passing SS officer and indeed the whole camp to take note of him and to do with him as they will, which would suit him utterly for he has seen at last the one thing that he has given up hope of ever seeing again in this life.

In that moment he looks like his old self. It's a miracle.

But the guards turn and shoo him along, and the capo reaches out to pull Eidel back into the kitchen, and the moment ends.

The capo rants for a while about two bowls broken this month—the first one over the crown of Mathilde Kessler's head, and now this one—as if the prisoners are plotting to overthrow the Reich by means of diminishing its supply of crockery. She says that Eidel would meet the same fate as Kessler herself if the commando weren't already short. She says that as worthless as Eidel is, at least she's a step up from this new girl they've sent to replace Zofia.

The capo sends her out to clean the walk with her bare hands—no broom and no dust pan, be quick about it and don't miss a single sharp fragment—and as she bends and works and bleeds she thinks of Zofia. Zofia and the missing silk handkerchief. Zofia and the missing silk handkerchief that was the last link to her own poor lost child.

*

Jacob takes it as a good sign. The image of his beloved there on the walk lingers in his mind like a holy vision, something sent down from heaven to inspire him and lift him and urge him on. Despite his lack of sleep, and despite the fear that goes with this being the first day on which he'll visit not just the full run of SS officers but the commandant himself, and in his own villa, that one instant of seeing Eidel very nearly puts a spring in his step. Everything else—the entire camp—falls away.

His work begins in the administration building, where he finds that he's been granted an assistant. An assistant! Imagine! His name is Chaim and he's just a child, younger than Max by three or four years. Where he's come from and where he lives and how he came to be here are questions that Jacob doesn't even bother asking himself. The world is full of mysteries. The more he looks at the boy the more the puzzle deepens, though, for he looks like the very embodiment of everything that the Nazis hate the most. Not only olive-skinned and dark-haired and almond-eyed, he's slight of build and perhaps even a little girlish. He's certainly unfit for any labor more demanding than this. But he proves to be cheerful, endlessly accommodating, and infinitely deferential, and Jacob decides that these qualities are the ones that have saved him.

In addition to an assistant, he actually has a parlor. Not a parlor exactly, but a sunlit corner of the kitchen where a counter has been laid out with the tools he'll need and a shelf has been filled with fresh white linens and water has been set to boiling in pot after pot. The officers will come to him, Chaim says, one every fifteen minutes starting at eight. If anything needs to be communicated, the boy will do the talking. The SS men think of him as a pet, he says, like a trained monkey or a talking bird. The fact that he can communicate at all is a marvel. They never tire of testing his abilities.

If not for the monsters coming in and out every quarter hour, this place would be paradise. The familiar scents of talcum powder and hair

tonic and rubbing alcohol bring him back to his father's shop in Zakopane. The gleaming tools on their bed of white linen are nearly sacra-
mental in their power to invoke a vanished way of life. Even the very
smallest of sounds—the snick of the scissors and the complaint of the
tap and the brushing of the broom on the hardwood floor—restore him.
But that's not half of it.

For beyond the window is a wide-open view of an unfenced and
boundless world. Cars and trucks come and go on the main road.
Commerce goes on. Old women and little children stroll on sidewalks
sharing treats from the *cukiernia,* as if the village of Auschwitz were still
a perfectly ordinary place. As if the whole world were still perfectly ordinary. And he can almost believe it.

The last man comes at noon, and after they have cleaned up and
packed away the tools for the afternoon's work, the cook points them
toward a little rough bench and a low table set up behind the washtub.
The table is laid out with rations fit for a czar. It's all Chaim's doing. He
knows all the angles. He's everyone's friend. He's the exception to every
rule there is. The platter of food—boiled potatoes with rosemary and
pepper and plenty of salt, the overcooked end of a pork loin all caramel-
ized and crusted, chewy bread that has actual caraway seeds on it and no
traces whatsoever of sawdust or coal—is mainly for the boy. Jacob is only
incidental. And when he whispers across the table that he means to tuck
some of this bounty into his pocket, Chaim makes certain that he understands their arrangement.

"My pleasure," he says with a twinkle in his eye. "Help yourself."

Jacob nods. He folds bread and pork into a little sandwich that won't
leak too much grease onto his uniform and tucks it away inside his
pocket, not for later but for Max. He watches the child on the opposite
side of the table gorging himself after a morning spent sweeping up hair

and fawning on SS officers, and he thinks that his own son deserves this much nourishment and more for the hard labor he's doing on the water project. For breaking his back under a new and unknown capo.

As they head out for the commandant's villa, they pass the woman at the desk with the gooseneck lamp and she stops them with word that he's unavailable today. That's all she says, looking up at Jacob as if daring him to question her further. As if willing him to pry into the commandant's business so that he might be punished for it.

But Chaim is her friend too, if not her pet, and he sidles up to the desk and bats his eyelashes and puts on his very sweetest voice to ask her straight out. "Tell me," he says, is the *obersturmbannführer* away on business, or did he just have too much to drink last night? Thursday is the *Skat* tournament in the Officers' Club, correct? *Skat* and schnapps have been Herr Liebehenschel's downfall before."

Jacob can't believe his ears. This saucy little villain will get them both shot. But he can't believe his eyes, either, for the woman at the desk just smiles down at the boy and gives her head a shake and clicks her tongue as she would at a naughty child of her own.

"I thought so," says Chaim, and as the woman at the desk raises her hand to stifle a laugh he drags Jacob off to the deputy commandant's apartment.

They go along the hall and out the door, trailing the rich aroma of roast pork like a flag. Jacob is certain that his theft will be detected just by the scent rising from his pocket, but they pass between the guards and out through the gate without incident. Further useful friends that the boy has cultivated. Jacob is completely terrified and so utterly amazed that he fails to appreciate the moment of release, and he's a free man out on the road before he even recognizes it.

They walk the access road and come to the end and turn onto the main street, not in the direction of the commandant's villa but the other way. According to Chaim the deputy's apartment building is a block farther from the center of town, and they hurry along the sidewalk as if they fear being caught out here. People stare. Jacob feels clownish in this big flapping suit of striped burlap, as if he and the boy are being presented as an act in a circus or a cabaret, the foolish adult and the wily child who outsmarts him at every turn.

"Tell me," he says to the boy as they hurry along the street. "Why don't you just run off?"

"Why don't *you?*" says the child, turning back the question.

"Because they'd kill my son. That's why."

"Good thinking." The boy stumbles along, a wooden box in his arms loaded with supplies in little drawers and compartments, fragrant towels stacked on the top.

"They'd kill my wife as well, if they could put the two of us together. If they haven't lost track of our marriage in all of those numbers they keep."

"Then let's hope they have," says Chaim.

"Besides," says Jacob, "this way I can bring back a little something for Max. To help him along." He smiles knowingly and pats the greasy bulge in his pocket, hungry for it already and ashamed by his own animal nature. Within the last hour he's eaten more than he's been eating in a typical month, and now he has the audacity to feel hungry. "It's a father's duty," he says, wondering if that remark is a step too far, wondering what's become of this poor boy's family, not daring to ask.

But Chaim isn't troubled. "Do you still want to know why *I* don't run off?" he asks.

"I do." They're drawing near what must be the deputy commandant's apartment building, the only one of its kind on this block, three stories of red brick with a little portico below. The building looks as if it would be more comfortable if it stood closer to the center of town. It looks as if whoever built it had hopes that the town might one day grow large enough to encompass it, but Auschwitz has grown in another way instead.

"I don't run off because they'd kill *you,*" says the boy. "They'd kill you for not stopping me." He says it with a little chirp in his voice, as if it's the most delightful thing in the world.

Jacob has to agree that he has a point, but as they turn down the walkway he wonders aloud, "Back to me, then. If I ran off would they punish you, in addition to my family?"

"Hardly," says Chaim, turning to put his back to the glass door. "I'm just a child. I can't help what a grown man might do." And he pushes his way through into a dim carpeted lobby, big as life.

Max

IN THE SAME WAY THAT VENICE is a city of canals, New York is a city of elevators. They reach everywhere, they come in all sizes and shapes, and everything travels by way of them. They run the gamut, from big gleaming jewel boxes in the grand hotels to dingy little closets in all but the most exclusive apartment buildings. It's shocking, really, to discover what shabby elevators people will ride to their multi-million-dollar penthouse co-ops. It's pathetic.

If you go to the right places and look hard enough, you'll see teensy little dumbwaiters, too, just big enough to hold a bottle of champagne. I've seen them. Plus those big freight elevators that rumble around all over the place—not just in warehouses and factories, but in concert halls and museums, the most sophisticated places in the world. Here in New York, whether you know it or not, Rembrandts ride around in the equivalent of freight cars. Rosens do too, and Warhols and Wyeths—although at least one of those two very different Andys would have said he didn't mind that kind of treatment a bit. He'd have been all *aw shucks* about it, the old phony.

He thought he could get away with hiding pictures in a barn, for God's sake. *In a barn.*

Anyhow, if it weren't for the elevator I'd never get down to the basement with this leg of mine. I'd have no access to my storage locker at all, never mind my apartment on the fourth floor. I'd be stranded at ground level. It's a studio apartment, in case you're wondering. Half studio, half apartment. You can smell the paint in the hallway, people tell me. You can smell it in the elevator. But who cares? New York smells like paint half the time anyway. Somebody's always painting something.

If anyone complained, I'd say it's the price of living alongside some-one who's about to have a retrospective at the National Gallery. But no-body asks. They already know. It's just urban living, really. I can't fling wide the windows and let the sweet summer breeze blow through from off the Brandywine, can I? No wonder my work is different from his. Darker and more cramped.

No wonder there's so much more packed into it.

Eight

THE *STURMBANNFÜHRER'S* APARTMENT IS ON the second floor, and he's busy when they knock. Vollmer walks home to have lunch with his children each noon, and since he hasn't spoken with the commandant today he doesn't know that *obersturmbannführer* Liebehenschel is lying face-down in his own villa sleeping off last night's schnapps. Otherwise he'd have adjusted his schedule by the required fifteen minutes—not to accommodate the Jewish barber, but to remove that vulgar little pest Chaim from the premises as quickly as possible. He hates that creature, even though he would seem to be the only one around who does. He hates exposing his children to him.

Jacob and Chaim wait in the entry hall, standing at attention and dead silent, listening through the dining room door as the family finishes lunch and talks together in their muted voices. When the housekeeper swings open the door to the kitchen, they jump like rabbits. "In here, quickly," she says, and no sooner has the kitchen door closed behind them than the dining room door creaks open onto the vacated hall and the children emerge on their way back to school. To Jacob they are nothing but voices and scuffling feet. A girl and a boy, he thinks, but he can't be certain. By the sound of it, their mother goes with them. That leaves Vollmer waiting alone in the dining room.

Chaim leads the way once the water has come to a boil. With white linen draped over his arms and a basin of water raised up before him, he could be a participant in some holy sacrament. This moment of entry into the dining room is the first time all day that Jacob has seen him subdued, however, the first time he's seen him subdued in the least, and there's a sudden and palpable tension in the air. It isn't just a matter of Vollmer's rank. The man simply doesn't look at the boy and the boy simply doesn't look at the man. Jacob watches as Vollmer pushes his chair away from the table and Chaim puts down the bowl and unfolds the drape and arranges it around the *sturmbannführer's* neck. Vollmer recoils at his touch, as if the boy has been dipped in poison.

"Begin," he says to Jacob, and Jacob begins.

The light here is good, pouring in from large windows on two sides and reflected by a broad mirror mounted high on one wall. He doesn't need to ask Vollmer to change position even once, which is good, since he's not certain that he ought to be speaking to him at all. Now and again Vollmer checks himself in the mirror with a sly look not intended for Jacob to see, and it's clear enough that he finds the work satisfactory. *It ought to be, after the butchery committed by Schuler.* Jacob catches the thought before it's halfway formed and reminds himself not to think ill of the dead, especially the dead with whom he's recently been so intimate. If he weren't wearing Slazak's uniform instead of his own, the deputy commandant would no doubt detect the stench of Schuler's corpse on him right now.

He's wearing one dead man's uniform so as not to smell like another one. All things considered, he's lucky to be alive.

Nearly finished, he steps back and slowly circles Vollmer in the chair, the comb upraised in his left hand and the scissors upraised in his right, narrowing his eyes and permitting the scissors to dart in exactly once for a final microscopic snip. *There.* Perfection and relief in one quick movement. He puts down the comb and the scissors and takes up a little whisk broom to tidy Vollmer's neck, and that's when he finally looks up and sees the painting.

It hangs right over the fireplace. He doesn't know how he could have missed it, and yet he does know. In the presence of a cobra, a rabbit wouldn't take notice of a da Vinci.

It's Lydia. Lydia in Eidel's attic studio in Zakopane, lit by that alpine sunlight and caught by that loving hand and preserved by both of them forever. Lydia lost and Lydia found.

Vollmer can't possibly *know*. He can't have any idea as to where the painting has come from or what sort of child it represents. The mountain light falling like gold upon Lydia's hair has surely persuaded him that the image represents one of his own, an Aryan child. Damn him for his blind stupidity. Only an imbecile would be so persuaded, an idiot lacking any ability whatsoever to perceive the world before him. Why, the deputy's hair itself has shifted color and tone and texture a million times as Jacob has circled around him during the past ten minutes, changing with the changing light from the north window and the east window and the mirror hung high on the opposite wall. It's the simplest thing in the world, a matter of physics, a matter of geometry. Shadow and light.

Damn his pigheaded stupidity, then, but be thankful for it too, because it has saved this painting—and with it this child—from at least one kind of oblivion.

The painting is matted in alpine greens and browns and mounted in a grand gilded frame carved all over with oak leaves and acorns. Jacob can't stop looking at it, looking at it the way a parched hiker would look at a mountain stream. Thank God, then, for the reliability of old professional habits. He sweeps the long white drape from around Vollmer's body, and with the skill of a stage magician he vanishes it into the wooden supply box. Chaim moves in with the broom and Vollmer lifts up his feet with a cringe that suggests aversion more than accommodation. But meanwhile the deputy has noticed the failure of Jacob's concentration, the drift of his eyes even as he packs away his tools, and he pats absently at a cowlick that has never before stayed down and turns toward him in the chair and says, "Isn't she lovely?"

The painting. The child. Lydia.

"Without question, sir. She is." Lovely enough to enchant a monster.

Perhaps this is why they kill the children. To keep themselves from falling in love.

BOOK TWO:

Testament

Nine

ON THEIR WAY BACK TO the camp, Jacob asks the boy what he knows about the painting. How long it's been hanging there. Where it came from.

Chaim knows everything. "Believe it or not," he says, "it came through Canada. Which means I've got news for you: That kid? She's no *shiksa.*"

"Never mind that. Never mind the girl. Tell me about the painting."

"It's a pretty good joke on Vollmer, don't you think?"

"Never mind the joke."

"A Jewish kid on his wall?"

"Never mind his wall. Never mind Vollmer. Tell me about the painting."

"What's the difference? You some kind of artist yourself?"

"Let's say I have an interest."

Chaim stops and puts down the box and picks it up again and they go on. "Word is that Jankowski got his mitts on it and traded it to one of the Ukrainians for a whole pile of cigarettes and then the Ukrainian sold it to an antique dealer in town. The dealer was the one who put it in the frame. Dressed it up so when Vollmer's wife saw it looking so nice, she just had to have it." Chaim shakes his head. "Women."

"Women. Right."

"Plus even the wife could tell it wasn't a genuine antique, so she got it for next to nothing."

"Really?"

"Really. She practically stole it. Frame included."

For the first time all day, Jacob laughs. "And they talk about Jews," he says.

"Exactly," says the boy. "And they talk about Jews."

*

It's just a bottle. A long tall narrow glass bottle that once held vinegar. Gretel has discovered it beneath one of the big coal stoves, glinting there in a dusty black corner, and one of these days when no one is looking she'll take the poker or a stick of wood and risk whatever burns might be necessary in order to get her hands on it. In the meantime she'll wait and keep her own counsel and perfect her plans.

How will she get it out of the kitchen?

In her sleeve, her own arm being so thin as to take up no room at all.

Where will she take it?

Home to the block, where she'll hide it in the rafters above her bunk.

What will she do with it once she's claimed it for her own?

She'll fill it up with stories, and then she'll bury it. She already has a spot in mind, a place she knows behind the block where water runs down from the roofline and disturbs the earth, churning up mud around the foundation and exposing loose gravel. It will be safe there, safe until the day when some historian excavates this place and finds it.

The bottle is everything she knows of hope. That and the scraps of paper and the tattered bits of gauze bandage and whatever else she can find upon which to scratch out the history of Auschwitz. She has the stub of a pencil that must have fallen from an officer's pocket—she keeps it in the hem of her jacket by day and jammed into a crack in the wall of her bunk by night—an irreplaceable stub that was the catalyst of her campaign. When she came upon the single bitter inch of it scuffed down hard between the floorboards, it was like discovering a passageway to a new continent. A whole world bloomed before her, a world in which someone would someday know what she and the rest have endured here. She marks time not from the date of her birth or from the date of her arrival at the camp, but from that transformational morning.

The bottle under the stove seems to have a paper label on it, the idea of which thrills her. She'll peel it off and write carefully around the printing and then turn it over and write on the back, for she must let nothing go to waste. Any inch left unfilled is a story untold, a cry unheard. Search as she might she can never find scraps to write on as quickly as the testimony piles up, but she does her best. The tip of the pencil is blunt, and she makes her letters as tiny and precise as she can.

Eidel finds her squinting down at such a project one day, a charred curl of cigarette paper pressed down flat on the chopping block and a look of utter concentration on her face. Eidel clears her throat and Gretel jumps. She's prepared to swallow the evidence, pencil and all.

"Drawing," asks Eidel, "or writing?"

"Writing." Gretel smiles and rolls the paper up around the pencil. "Just getting some things down," she says, tucking everything into a hole in the hem of her jacket.

"I understand," says Eidel. "I was a painter, once upon a time. I was forever getting things down."

Gretel nods, picking up a rag with one hand and worrying the pencil deeper with the other.

"It seemed so important when I was doing it," Eidel says, "but now I don't know. The paintings are all gone, everything's gone, so maybe it was just wasted time. Maybe I should have been doing something else instead. Living instead of looking."

"I'll get that down too," says Gretel. "If you want me to. If there's room. There's already so much."

"What do you mean?" She moves toward the oven with a rag in her hand and opens the door and checks on the bread.

"I'll write down how you lost your paintings." Gretel moves closer to the oven's radiant heat and puts a finger to her lips. "I'm writing down everything that happens here, so people will know." She goes on to tell Eidel about the vinegar bottle she's discovered beneath the stove, and about her plan for filling it up with words and burying it as evidence. A message set out upon the sea of time.

She says that she has scraps hidden away in every corner of the camp. She's jammed them under clapboards and pushed them into gaps in masonry. She's stuck them beneath washtubs with a paste made of water and mud and rolled them tight enough to slide into the little tunnels eaten into her bunk by worms. She's spread them around everywhere, her own furtive infestation of truths too precious to be concentrated in one place until now. It's entirely possible that she has enough scraps to fill the vinegar bottle already, she won't know until she tries, but if that's so then she'll cap it with a plug of wood or stone and bury it where it will come to light one day, and then she'll keep her eye out for another bottle. Perhaps Eidel will help.

"On the other hand," Eidel says, "you could trade that bottle for something better. Food. Cigarettes if you must. A favor of some kind." For bottles are notoriously hard to come by. They can contain anything, for purposes ranging from safekeeping to transport. Even when broken they can be put to use. Perhaps especially when broken. So it seems a shame to bury one. Eidel comes to her feet and closes the oven door and takes her by the arm. "You're so *thin.*"

Gretel pulls free, her mind on other things. "I could never be that selfish."

"It's not selfishness. It's self-preservation."

"For what? You and I won't live to see the end of this place. The bottle will be all that's left of us."

Eidel puts down her rag and walks to the doorway and looks down the hall. The capo is down there but she's busy, seated at her worktable with her back turned. So she picks up the rag again in one hand and the poker in the other, and she dips the rag in cool water and wrings it out and goes to kneel down before the stove. "My arms are longer than yours," she says to Gretel, and then she stretches to reach underneath.

*

Wenzel is the new capo. He doesn't look like much—he's baldheaded and bookish and if he speaks at all he speaks with the methodical cadence of a man struggling to mask a painful stutter—and on the first day, Max finds working under him no trouble. "Wenzel's all business," he says to his father, and it's true. Where Slazak was a *provocateur* and a slave driver, the new capo picks no fights and makes no particularly unreasonable demands. Under his guidance the men work quickly and well and without incident. Their rations arrive on time. No one is hurt on the first day, and nobody dies.

Things go differently on the second day, but it's not Wenzel's fault. A man pushing a wheelbarrow overflowing with lime stumbles against a pile of black iron pipe, sending one eighteen-foot length of it into the ditch and crushing another man's skull. Wenzel looks irritated but not angry. He looks like a weary traveler who has just learned that a train he's been waiting for will be delayed. He makes some notes on paper—one day it will come out that he was a bookkeeper before he came to the camp, and that his crimes all involved being a little too handy with figures—and then he orders the fallen man brought up and covered over with a tarp.

The guards, those slit-eyed Ukrainians who've seen it all, haven't seen this. A dead Jew decently covered over. They light cigarettes and shake their heads, cradling their guns as the smoke rises. One of them comes over to Wenzel after a minute and makes a recommendation, pointing with the barrel of his gun, kicking at a shovel with his boot. Why not just bury the bastard where he fell?

Wenzel shakes his head. Oh, no. That might have happened under the other fellow—what was his name, Slazak?—but it's his commando now and he'll run it his way. It's all about motivation. Keep the men working and get the job done.

The Ukrainian laughs and grinds out his cigarette under his boot. He's still laughing when he gets back to where the other guard is waiting for him, and he's coughing from the cigarette, and it's all he can do to explain that the new man doesn't have the first idea as to what he's supposed to be doing. Wenzel thinks the job is to build a water line, when the job is actually to kill Jews.

"He's different," says Max to his father at the end of the day. They're resting in the yard under the eyes of the Ukrainians. The late afternoon is hot and still and the place is dead silent except for the dry and distant sound of a train creaking into the station. Black smoke from the high chimneys goes straight up. "He's not half as bad as Slazak," says Max, pointing toward the tarp beneath which the dead man lies. "There'll be a special burial detail tonight. Outside the fence. I'm on it."

"And what an honor *that* will be," says Jacob.

"You don't understand," says the boy.

"I understand that one of our brothers has died. That's all I need to understand."

"But it was an accident."

"An accident, fine. But an accident in the service of what?"

Max squirms. "At least he'll have a proper burial."

"That's cold comfort," says his father. But cold or otherwise it's all the comfort his son can find, and even as he says the words he feels guilty for depriving him of it. Still, he sees that as much as he's needed to protect the boy from Slazak's brutality, now he'll need to protect him from Wenzel's cunning. Enough, though. Enough for now. "Did I tell you," he says, "how beautiful your mother looked when I saw her through the fence?"

"You did."

"She looked beautiful to me, anyway."

"I'm sure she did."

"I wish you could have seen her."

"I do, too, Papa. I do, too."

*

Long after dark, when the men are all jammed tight into their bunks and struggling to sleep, Wenzel emerges from his compartment and slips through the darkness and awakens Max. Max and another young man, another boy really, a boy who has probably lied about his age as well. Such is the advantage of those who are born with strength to spare. Both of them are reduced now, though, Max and the other boy. They've begun to look old in the way that anyone sufficiently ill or overworked looks old. Their eyes are hollow, weary of witness.

All the same, having Wenzel confirm their selection for the burial detail cheers them up. No one in the block has seen this kind of operation before, two men and a corpse outside the fence unsupervised. There's a commonplace, assembly-line quality to the regular burial details. The men assigned to them—the ill-fated *Sonderkommando*, doomed by the repetition of their ugly work to haunt these premises like bodies whose souls have been scraped out—are anything but lucky. Sooner or later such an assignment always proves to be a one-way ticket. But this is different. Max and the other boy will be out there alone, past the line, within sight of the guards but beyond earshot. It will be a thing so close to freedom that if they work quickly they may have time to say a few words over the body before shoveling the dirt back down. They're just two boys, nothing like a *minyan*, but times are difficult. You make do.

Wenzel stays behind, watching from the doorway as they move toward the fence in the company of a guard. The moon is a vague sliver behind a high overcast and the stars are invisible and down on the ground the beams of the searchlights rake at everything. The three men stop at the place where the fallen man lies alone under a tarp, the guard shooing away a curious dog with the barrel of his gun and the two prisoners stooping to lift the body. Max takes the corpse and the other boy takes the shovels and they move along, four of them now.

Soon they're out of Wenzel's sight, across the yard and down behind another block, so the capo goes back in and makes his rounds. Satisfied, he lets himself into his little chamber. Everything is quiet.

When they come to the fence they turn and go along the barbed wire searching for a hidden gate—the guard is certain it's here somewhere—and when they find it he opens the padlock and stands back while Max hauls on the chain. The gate swings open. Without lowering his machine gun, a little penlight propped in his mouth, the guard checks the serial number on the dead man's coat against a number he's written on the palm of his own hand. Then he shoos the boys and the dead man on through, standing at a kind of lazy attention in the open gate. They go as far out as they dare, even farther, the dead man's shoes dragging trails in the clay, until the guard calls out to them that they've gone far enough. That will do. The searchlights claw the ground and they dig.

Thank God for their youth, because they're not entirely too winded to offer a blessing once the man is in his grave. And when they finally finish and reenter the camp and return to the block, they slip into their usual sleeping places with the belief that they've accomplished something worthwhile.

*

Somehow, the summer passes.

No longer reduced to counting bowls of soup, Eidel marks days instead and soon enough she realizes that her husband walks along the fenceline exactly once a week. On Fridays, at seven-thirty in the morning. So she manufactures reasons to be on the step outside the kitchen at the right time, tossing soapy water into the yard from a dishpan or wringing out a mop, and they become like mechanical figures on a cuckoo clock, Jacob passing by on his rounds and Eidel poking her head out through the door, synchronized but doomed never to meet. It keeps them going.

Fridays for Jacob begin on a high note, with that brief glimpse of

Eidel, but for every moment he spends anticipating that vision and thrilling to it and reflecting on it he spends another dreading the instant when he must step into Vollmer's dining room, the instant when he must face the painting once more.

Chaim asks him about it as they make their way toward the apartment building. "So Vollmer rubs you the wrong way, too?" he says, for he's noticed the pattern. He's seen how Jacob's mood worsens as the day goes on. He's caught the final profound downward shift of it when they leave the commandant's villa and head for Vollmer's apartment.

"It's not Vollmer," says Jacob.

"Don't kid me," says Chaim. "I know people. I can tell. You don't like him any better than I do."

"I don't like any of them."

"Aww, they're not so bad." He walks along munching a crisp red apple that the commandant's housekeeper pressed into his pocket on his way out the door. A little gray boy walking along in a little gray uniform with a big bright red apple raised up in his hand like a target.

"Maybe they're not so bad to *you*, but that's a different story. In any event, it's not Vollmer. It's something else." He can't take his eyes away from the apple.

"So I was right," says Chaim

"You were wrong about Vollmer."

"I was right about it being something."

"Fine," says Jacob, salivating over the apple but unwilling to ask for a bite. "You were right. It was something."

"What kind of something?"

"The painting," he says.

"The painting of the girl?"

"The painting of the girl."

"It's a nice painting."

"I know. It's a very nice painting."

"So?"

"So?" Jacob stops on the sidewalk and the boy stops alongside him, taking another bite of the apple and wiping his chin with the back of his hand. "So?" He draws breath and looks up at the sky and looks down at the boy again. "So it's a picture of my daughter."

"I didn't know you had a daughter."

"I don't. Not anymore."

Chaim's face collapses. "I'm sorry. I didn't know."

"That's all right." He starts up again but the boy doesn't move.

"I thought you just had Max."

"It's all right."

"That picture must break your heart."

"It does. Every time." He stands looking down at the boy and assessing the sympathetic look on his face and wondering what it might mean. Wondering if it means anything at all, or if it's just a look on the face of a boy who's taught himself how to respond to almost anything. Deciding in the end that it doesn't matter. "The thing that makes it all worse," he says, "is that my wife painted it."

"No."

"Yes."

"*Your wife painted that picture?*" he says. An old woman with a child in tow and another one bundled up in a carriage passes them by and clears her throat and gives a hard look back over her shoulder. Time to move along. But Chaim isn't going. "Your wife in the camp?"

Jacob watches the old woman go. "My wife in the camp," he says. "I suppose she would be happy that it wasn't destroyed with everything else. But she'd be heartbroken to think of it hanging where it does."

The old woman has come to the corner and is speaking to a policeman there, a policeman who nods his head and presses his lips together and looks their way. Jacob takes the apple from the boy's hand and jams it into his pocket, and then he takes the boy by the shoulder and together they hurry along the street again, their steps furtive, their eyes downcast. A couple of mice. The policeman loses interest only when they turn down the walk leading to Vollmer's apartment building, because they certainly can't get into any trouble there.

Max

"MAX ROSEN'S HUMAN FIGURES, rare as they are, have turned their backs upon you by the time you take notice of them."

That was Edgar Mudd, writing in the *Times of London* in the spring of 1958, and it was probably the only defensible line of criticism that he ever delivered.

Mudd, you'll remember, was a great booster of Calder and those big toys of his that the museums were all fighting over at the time. The most respected museums in the world, bidding against shopping malls and office parks and what have you. Airports. Frankly, I think every airport in the world should have a Calder. They're too big to miss, even if you're running past with a suitcase in tow, which means everybody gets the impression that he's been exposed to something important—and yet they don't require or even reward any actual thought. That makes them just about perfect for a culture on the move.

Besides, putting the damned things in airports would keep them out of the museums.

Back to Mudd, though, God rest his soul. In a rare moment of illumination, poor blind Edgar noticed that if there are any people at all in my paintings, they seem to have rejected the viewer and whatever interest he might have in them. They might even be hiding, concealing themselves among the planes and angles of the closed-in spaces that have always fascinated me so. For once he was right.

As I believe I've already said, spacious skies give me the willies. The critics have never known exactly what to make of that. It would be politically incorrect to blame it on my being an East Coast Jew, a New Yorker, a city boy. It would be philosophically taboo to blame it on my history in the camp. Heaven forbid. People act as if you make everything up out of whole cloth, as if you could possibly help the way you're built and the things you've gone through and the way your work comes out. As if you could choose to overrule your own nature and experience.

They're wrong. I've tried.

You can't paint someone else's paintings. You can only paint your own, with greater or lesser degrees of success.

Does this mean I've been too hard on Andy, after all? Andy and his fields and his farmhouses? Andy and his beloved teutonic Helga? I don't suppose he could help himself any more than I can.

Calder, though. There's no excusing Calder. Never mind what I said about airports. His kind of nonsense belongs underneath a circus tent.

Ten

THEY NEVER REALLY SEE VOLLMER'S CHILDREN. Not in the apartment, at least. There is one occasion when they spot them going back to school in the company of their mother, hurrying toward them down the sidewalk and crossing over at the last minute even though the school is on this side. According to Chaim it is, anyway, and he knows everything.

Aside from that one moment, the boy and the girl are just voices through a closed door, footsteps on hardwood. The day when they finally do get a chance to see the two of them is cold, bitter and blowing with the windy change of the seasons, and the children are too bundled up to be entirely visible. Jacob and Chaim shiver in their thin burlap, thinking of how they'll want to race between buildings when the winter comes, too distracted to look closely.

"There they go," says Chaim, and they're gone. Jacob shoots a look across the street, over his shoulder, but even looking is dangerous. That policeman on the corner has been keeping an eye on them ever since the day they paused with the apple. They can see he's waiting for them to make a single misstep. Just dying for his chance.

"They could have been anybody," says Jacob. "I didn't see."

Chaim sighs. "You didn't miss much," he says. "They're a couple of little piglets. Exactly as you'd imagine."

Jacob nods and hugs himself and they walk on.

The *sturmbannführer* wants to talk about the little piglets, though. With Chaim sequestered in his usual corner, he begins by rhapsodizing over the painting of Lydia as he has done so many times before. A person might think that Jacob would be accustomed to this by now, accustomed not just to seeing the painting each week but to hearing it analyzed in painstaking detail, but such a person could never have been a father. He tries not to listen as Vollmer keeps on about the angle of the light, the curve of the child's neck, the golden gleam of her hair. Enchanted as he may be he's no appreciator of art, since for the most part his response is not to the painting before him but to the girl it depicts, not to the rendering but to the flesh. He speaks as if she's right there before him. He goes on to say that even though the painting brings unspeakable joy to his narrow life in this dreary little town, there is one thing about it that troubles him.

Oh, no. Jacob guesses that someone's told him the child in the painting is a Jew.

But that isn't it. "Each time I study her," Vollmer says, referring to the painting by referring to the girl, "I wish that I could find a way to pair her with a similar painting of my own children. Perhaps the whole family. A formal portrait."

Jacob nods.

"The question is, where would I find an artist even half as accomplished as this one?"

In the corner, Chaim clears his throat.

"There's a fellow in town who does landscapes. Mountains and trees and that sort of thing. The occasional still life, I believe. A bowl of apples. A round of cheese."

Jacob chews his lip.

"But my children are not apples," says Vollmer. "They are not cheese."

Jacob sighs in a kind of abashed agreement.

138

"I can see you've learned nothing whatsoever about painting," says Vollmer, "despite all I've tried to teach you." He shifts in his chair, causing Jacob to recalibrate. "But whether you can understand or not, I simply cannot put my children in the hands of a landscape artist."

Jacob shrugs. Chaim clears his throat again. And nothing more gets said on the subject, not today. But on their way back to the camp, Chaim asks Jacob if he's lost his mind.

"No" he says. "No, I haven't."

"That was your big opportunity."

"So you say."

"So I *know.*"

"You're the expert in such things."

"I am. Vollmer likes you."

Jacob laughs. It makes quite a sight: a shaven Jew in striped burlap, laughing on an Auschwitz streetcorner. *"Vollmer likes me,"* he says, shaking his head.

"He does. And this is your chance to make him like you even more. To earn some favors for both yourself and your wife."

"Never. I could never send Eidel to that apartment. If she saw the painting, she would die on the spot."

"You didn't."

"I nearly did, the first time." He looks down at Chaim, indignant. "And what do you know? I very nearly die each time I set foot in that room."

"But that's in a manner of speaking."

"She would die, period. It would kill her."

"Maybe she's tougher than you think."

"She's an artist."

"A person can be tough and be an artist."

"She doesn't paint Nazis. She paints subjects of beauty."

"Leave the beauty to her," says Chaim. They turn and keep going, down the lane toward the gate in the barbed wire fence. "Next week, tell Vollmer that it was your wife who painted the girl. Don't forget: she'll get a soft job out of it. That's the main thing to keep in mind. A soft job."

"If she can endure the shock."

"She's endured worse."

Which Jacob can't deny.

Trucks come and go. A motorcycle or two and a couple of children chasing a ball, crying out, oblivious to the camp just a few yards distant. They walk on. Up ahead, the lane intersects a gravel road used by the familiar Red Cross vans on their way to and from the processing station. The man and boy watch them sail past raising gray dust.

"What if I were to go ahead with it?" says Jacob. "Should I take a step further, and tell him it's my daughter?"

"I wouldn't. He doesn't need to know that." Chaim lifts his shoulders a little straighter and walks a little more erect, having taken on the role of trusted counselor.

"I suppose you're right," says Jacob.

"Don't let pride get the better of common sense."

"I won't."

"Vollmer likes you, but there are limits."

"I know. And I'm not saying I've made up my mind to tell him at all."

"You should. You will. She'll get a soft job out of it. She'll get back to painting."

They stop at the edge of the gravel road to let Chaim adjust the weight he's carrying. A drawer in the wooden box slips open and a comb falls out followed by a small glass bottle of witch hazel, the comb skittering across the gravel and the bottle crashing on the stones but not breaking. The guards opposite, standing ranked on either side of the gate, hardly look. Another van careens by, its tires narrowly clearing the bottle. Jacob begins to reach down but stops himself just in time. The guards laugh. Chaim sets his box down by the side of the road and the towels tumble from it into the dirt and he picks them up and studies them with a look of disgust and the guards laugh again. They're putting on quite a show, these two.

The coast is clear for a moment—no vans—so Chaim ducks into the road and gets the bottle and the comb and restores them to their drawer. He and Jacob recover themselves and take a breath and prepare to cross, but the bunched towels are piled higher than usual and Chaim can't see where he's going and he steps out into the gravel road nearly into the path of one of the vans. Jacob catches him by the collar just in time.

The rear windows of the van are hung with black curtains, but the window on the driver's side is open and the window on the passenger's side is open as well, and both the driver and his passenger smoke furiously as the car tears past. Three streams of exhaust altogether. There was a time when Jacob would have raised a fist at so careless a driver, but that time is long gone. It doesn't even occur to him, certainly not in the presence of those guards on the other side of the road. "Some Red Cross they are," he says as he bends to straighten Chaim's load, and Chaim says, "Don't you know?"

"Don't I know what?" They cross and stop just outside the fence, waiting for the guards to swing open the gate and admit them. Jacob always enjoys this moment. It's the only time all week when somebody waits on him instead of the other way around. He figures that if he were to reach out and try to lend a hand, though, he'd be shot in an instant. He lowers his chin and speaks to the boy again, "Come come, you little villain. Don't I know what?"

Chaim bites his tongue until they're safely inside, well away from the guards. "Those wagons say Red Cross," he says, "but that's not what they are. They're full of bug powder. Only they don't use it on bugs."

*

For days, Gretel goes about the camp like a reverse Johnny Appleseed, picking up the seeds she's sown into every crack and crevice and jamming them into the pockets of her uniform and transferring them from there into the vinegar bottle. It fills up quickly. She's had no idea, she says to Eidel just before roll call one morning, no idea of how much evidence she's assembled already. The bottle is in the rafters over her bunk, lying on its side and spilling its contents like milk, and there are still a hundred more little scraps of paper and bark and cloth hidden in a hundred additional places that she knows of right off the top of her head, never mind how many she may have forgotten.

She dreams through the day half-dizzy, wondering where she'll get her hands on a second container, imagining the moment when the wickedness preserved beneath the clay of Auschwitz will rise to the surface as it must. Overcome with a vision of the bottle rising up from the mud like a corpse, unbalanced as any saint by the certainty of resurrection and rapture, she can think of nothing else.

Eidel struggles to keep her focused on the work before her. "The last girl," she says, "got careless with that same knife. Her name was Zofia, poor thing."

Gretel remembers spending her first morning scouring the chopping block, the blood soaked deep into the wood, and she does her best to concentrate. Rolak careens by. Gretel dares not look up. The capo opens the door and steps out into the wind and the wind slams the door shut behind her. The room goes quiet again. Gretel tries to remember all of the stories that she hasn't written down yet, linking them one after another into a single unforgettable narrative of which she'll remember every part long enough to get it all down. She finds a place for Eidel's story somewhere near the end, the story of the loss of her paintings and the loss of her daughter, a touching story to be sure but nothing special compared to the thousand other stories clamoring for their due.

She asks herself how much one person can remember, how much weight one person can carry—even if the weight is as small as a scrap of paper, as slight as someone else's memory. And she drifts off again, and the pace of her work slows, and Eidel worries. A person can think too much for her own good.

*

It's cold in Canada. Some men work inside and others out, and those lucky enough to be shielded from the high winds and the occasional burst of early snowfall are unlucky in a different way, for they are the ones who must endure the greater portion of Jankowski's presence. He doesn't like the cold any better than anyone else, so he stays inside for the most part, leaving the men in the covered yard under the supervision of the guards.

Jacob is among the outdoor men. He hates the cold but he likes the absence of the capo. Most of what's being sorted here is the dregs, material that's already passed once or even twice under the most watchful eyes that Jankowski can put on the job, castoffs among castoffs. Buttonless coats and laceless shoes and hats with the bands torn out of them in case they might have concealed something of value. Suitcases stripped of their linings and trunks jimmied apart into pieces that now resemble firewood more than luggage. The man alongside Jacob has somehow acquired a pair of gloves that are the envy of the commando. Dirty gray wool raveled and threadbare and thin as lacework, they'll be of only a little use against the coming winter, but a little is better than none. The prisoner wears them only on the coldest of days, and in between he keeps them hidden God knows where. They can't take up much room.

Jacob looks for a pair of his own. Everybody looks. But not just any gloves will do. There is one pair on a table among the exploded hats, shiny black leather gloves stuffed full of warm white fleece, worth their weight in gold but sadly untouchable. First, because Jankowski and the guards have already taken note of them. Second, because their color and thickness would stand out on a prisoner's hands. The ideal gloves, if you could find them, would be beneath notice. And so the prisoners' need for stealth drives them to police their own happiness.

Jacob shakes his head and tells himself that if he were working on an escape plan, an essential element of it would be stealing those marvelous gloves at the last minute. They would go a long way in the outside world. They would mark a man as a king. But he isn't planning an escape, so he sets his fantasies aside and proceeds according to the rules, shaking out shirts and jackets and going through pockets and cuffs and knife-split seams with a probing finger in case someone indoors has missed something. Usually he comes up short, but not always. In the waistband of one pair of trousers, he discovers a tooth. Not just any tooth, but a tooth capped with gold. Its crevices are tobacco-stained and its roots are red and rusty, and he contemplates how it might have come to be hidden here in this waistband. He imagines an old man arriving in one of the thousand train cars, a canny old figure experienced with the world and not easily fooled by anything or anyone, a banker or a lawyer or a doctor perhaps. Yes. A doctor. A doctor, for what must come next.

He pictures the doctor having set aside everything at various points along the tortuous journey to this place—his watch and his rings and his money, his practice and his dignity and his loved ones. And then he pictures him looking out the window and seeing the station, this final station, bedecked with its flower boxes and painted with that stalled *trompe-l'oeil* clock. Marked with the hanging sign that even now, not far from Canada and visible from where Jacob stands, is being touched up by a prisoner with a stepladder and a fine brush and a can of thick bright velvety paint. *Auschwitz.*

He sees how the old doctor's understanding grows, he sees it in the weariness and revulsion that pass over his fallen face—weariness, not fear; revulsion, not despair—and he sees him reach defiantly into his own mouth with two steady fingers and extract his own gold tooth. He lowers the prize to his lap and studies it furtively, swallowing blood, pushing his tongue into the welling socket, perhaps thinking of how much it cost him in the first place and when, and then he wipes it dry on the back of the seat ahead of him and works a few threads free in the seam of his waistband and slips it inside as far as he can. The Nazis can take the tooth from his trousers for all he cares, they'll take everything sooner or later, but they will never take it from his mouth. He's granted himself that much grace.

Good for him, thinks Jacob, holding the tooth. One of the guards sees its gleam and points with the barrel of his gun. Jacob stiffens. Lately he's found himself imagining stories like this one for every single thing he encounters in Canada, against his will dreaming up some sadly detailed narrative for every last stick of chewing gum, every last nail file, every last hair ribbon. The stories leap up in his mind unbidden and he catalogs them the same way that the system here catalogs the artifacts themselves. They weigh on him like curses, like stories from the Torah. Like anything with the sudden shocking incarnate power of the Word. He nods to the guard behind his gun, and he carries the gleaming tooth to the table where it belongs.

*

A change in the weather has been coming since sunup, a transformation unfolding itself. The wind has been howling nonstop and the clouds have been racing overhead like liquefied rock and Jacob has found himself ill at ease, troubled, more unsettled than usual even for a day in Auschwitz. He checks out of Canada in the gathering dark and wraps himself around himself, bone upon bone, and hurries along to reach the yard in front of his block just as the prisoners are filing back in from the dig. One or two of them pass him a look that he reads as pitying, but he could be wrong. Surely he's wrong. Pity is everywhere, moving freely from man to man, like a current in water. Pay it no attention.

Nobody speaks. Not even Wenzel, who waits before the coalescing grid of men with an unreadable look on his face and a pencil in his hand. He stands impassive, conserving his breath, looking ahead. The men will certainly not speed up, not after a day's work and not without rations, so why demand it. To ask the impossible is to fail. To fail is to weaken. So he waits. A sly one.

Jacob looks left and looks right, but Max is nowhere. He feels naked and alone, more alone than he has felt since he first arrived here so long ago. A lifetime, really; the only lifetime he knows anymore. The prisoner to his right looks in his direction and frowns. It's the sad apologetic look of an unwilling conspirator: *Don't blame me.* Then the man looks straight ahead again, toward Wenzel, who has coughed up something and noisily spat it out on the ground by way of getting everyone's attention.

The roll call begins. A million things go through Jacob's mind, racing like the clouds that have chased each other across the sky all day, chief among them certain garish images of the various dead men he's seen dragged to their feet for roll calls in the past. Schuler in particular, old man Schuler whose stink was on his uniform when Slazak lay down in it for his last rest. And then Slazak himself, the very next morning, propped up between two of his own murderers.

The count, like most counts under the businesslike Wenzel, goes mainly without incident. There's some confusion over a prisoner who's acquired a case of laryngitis and probably won't last out the week as a result of whatever's behind it, but he raises his hand to show the number on his wrist and another prisoner answers for him and all is well. Max, though. Max is the problem. His number isn't even called. It's as if he doesn't even exist. As if he's never existed. And yet he can't be dead, or else he'd be here. That's a hard fact for a father to take any comfort in.

Jacob's mind goes to his wife. He wonders how he'll let her know about Max if there turns out to be something she must know. Perhaps he can make contact the same way that she first did with him, through that fellow in the delivery commando. Perhaps Chaim can help. Chaim knows everyone. Yes. He'll ask Chaim.

He wonders further if he should take a lesson from whatever it is that's befallen his son—if he should sieze the day, make up his mind at last, and tell the deputy that his wife, Eidel Rosen of the women's camp, is the artist he's been seeking. The same one who painted the girl. *Absolutely,* he decides, he must do it as soon as possible, if only to give her one single day a week during which her body will be more or less safe from the violent predations of the camp. He must trust that her mind and heart are strong enough to endure the sight of the painting.

The roll call breaks up and the men proceed to their supper, squeezing together into one long line. Jacob asks the man who's given him the sad look if he knows what's become of Max, and the man says oh yes, he certainly does. Max is in the hospital. A broken leg. It happened this morning, when they were stacking pipe. Wenzel was furious over the interruption, he says, the little bookkeeper acting as if they were all participating in some kind of race together and now Max had spoiled their chances by coming up lame. This man himself had hauled him to the hospital in a wheelbarrow. The injured boy had made quite a load, and one of the guards had amused himself by firing at the ground near the man's feet just to see how fast he'd go.

"Max couldn't walk at all? Not even with a crutch?"

"It's a bad break. Your boy's a tough one, but it was a bad break. Compound, the doc said."

"What else did he say?"

The man shrugs. "I had to come right back. You know."

"Of course."

"I couldn't very well wait around."

"I understand."

"He gave me a little note for Wenzel. It's what excused your boy from the count this once."

"This once. Of course."

"You know how it goes."

"I do."

*

Wenzel grants him permission to visit Max, and in case the hospital proves to be only the first of the stops he needs to make he lights out as fast as his feet can carry him, scurrying over the cold clay like a bug, oblivious to the searchlights and intent on his mission. In his pocket he has his own concealed rations, along with a few crumbs of cheese scraped from the pocket of an overcoat in Canada earlier in the day, presents for Max, something to build up his strength. The best he can do.

The doctor is a prisoner himself, a bespectacled Frenchman. At least he claims to be a doctor, and the Germans believe him because belief costs nothing. He says that he specializes in women's complaints, but there are plenty of other doctors, good sound Nazi doctors, more qualified for such things, and so he has been pressed into service as a general practitioner, dealing with the usual run of burns and lacerations and broken bones. Ailments of the heart and the liver and the lungs. Puzzling accumulations of symptoms that when taken together point nowhere but the grave.

Max is in a cot, pale and unconscious, his leg bent at an odd angle. The doctor has stopped the bleeding with a tourniquet and he's packed the wound with some rags but he hasn't done anything about setting the bone and he surely hasn't given him anything for pain. Nor will he. There's nothing to give.

"Wenzel wanted him kept alive," the doctor says, "but I can't say why. It seems cruel."

Jacob hurries to the cot and kneels there, whispering in his son's ear, but his son doesn't respond. He wonders what to do with the rations and the crumbs of cheese in his pocket, thinking that he can't trust the doctor with them and aware of his own burning hunger and hating himself for letting his attention wander from his child to his stomach.

The doctor muses on aloud, since they're alone here except for Max and a handful of other men curled up in corners and sprawled on the floor, sleeping or unconscious or dead. The hospital is a way station, a kind of reverse purgatory located between the hell of the camp and the release of death. The selection might take place tomorrow or it might take place the next day, but either way most of the men here will be bound for the gas. "Perhaps it's one of their experiments," he says. "Perhaps they want to gauge how much a young person can endure—for the sake of the war effort, you know."

Max draws a ragged and shallow breath.

"He *is* young, isn't he? Fifteen? Fourteen?"

"Fourteen. Just a child."

The Frenchman's face lights up as if has discovered the cure for something. As if Max has risen from the bed and walked. "You see?" he says, beaming. "You can't fool a man of medicine." Guessing a patient's age is a mere parlor trick requiring nothing more than the sharp eye of a carnival operator, but in the absence of implements and diagnostic tools and drugs, it's all he has.

Jacob stands. "So what will you do for him?"

"Let him rest. Watch and wait."

"How long?"

"How long for a full recovery? It could take years, if all goes well." The doctor removes his glasses and rubs the lenses between his thumb and forefinger.

"No. Not a full recovery. I mean how long can he rest?"

"Who can say? The capo seems to place some value on him."

"That's no surprise. My son works hard. He does as he's told."

"Still," the doctor says, putting his glasses back on and squinting through them toward the single burning light bulb, "it's difficult to put much value on a cripple. A man who can't get out of bed. Even if that man happens to be a boy."

"Has Wenzel come to see about him? Have you filed a report?"

"Neither. Give it time, though. They'll decide when they decide."

Jacob puts his hand on Max's shoulder and Max winces in his sleep, recoiling from his father's touch into the realms of his own agony. He's so pale, so thin. His father can't believe that he has strength enough to cringe.

"I'll see what I can do," says Jacob. The folly of which brings a twinkle to the eye of the doctor, back behind his blurry lenses.

He steps out into the night and makes himself invisible, walking as purposefully as he can, neither hurrying nor making any attempt to conceal himself. But he doesn't return to the block. He goes the other way instead, toward the camp's main entrance. It's a walk he makes every Friday, and he hopes that those on guard duty will recognize him in some unconscious way and think nothing of his presence.

He wipes a tear from his eye and tells himself that it's the cold, even though he doesn't actually feel the temperature. He can't feel anything now but the urgent weight of Max. His mission can't wait until tomorrow, when he will visit Vollmer in his apartment and could beg for a favor, a deal, a compromise. Max could be dead by then, so he must go now. He walks on past the women's camp, all of it buttoned up tight, the kitchen door shut and the rooms behind it dark. He wishes that he could speak to Eidel, explain the bold thing that he's about to attempt, in case he should fail and leave her entirely bereft—her son taken by accident and her husband taken by his own love and daring. She would surely understand. She would surely approve now and tell him to go ahead, if only she knew. And so he goes.

The rear entrance to the administration building, the little low entrance through which he passes every Friday morning, is down a walkway at the head of which a solitary guard paces back and forth. Other walkways break off from there toward other destinations, most of them mythical or at least unknown, all of them off limits to prisoners except under special circumstances. The guard shuttles back and forth at a leisurely pace, speeding up only when his course and the course of the searchlight threaten to intersect. Jacob catches sight of him and slows a little in the darkness, not enough to be noticed, not enough to stand out, but enough to be ready to ascertain the guard's identity when the searchlight passes again. Sure enough: a familiar face. A Hungarian, he thinks, not one of the most fearsome of the guards but then again each one is fearsome in his own way. He wishes now that he'd found something better in Canada today than these crumbs of cheese. A bit of chocolate, perhaps, or a cigarette. But he has what he has, even if it's nothing but his wits, and he must make do.

He raises his hands in the symbol of surrender and approaches the guard big as life, confident. "I'm the prisoner they sent for," he says, wasting no time. "Rosen."

"No one's been sent for."

"Rosen the barber."

"I said no one's been sent for."

"They sent for *me*. Begging your pardon."

"Your number?"

Jacob gives it, turning his upraised left hand as if he could possibly make the tattoo visible in this light.

Concentrating and looking upward and moving his lips, the guard strains in the effort of committing the number to memory.

Jacob repeats it and lowers his arms to his sides, and the guard raises his machine gun a couple of inches.

"Who sent for you?"

"Vollmer."

"The *sturmbannführer*."

"The very same."

"And you're the barber."

"I am."

"Perhaps the *sturmbannführer* needs a trim just now? A shave?"

Jacob tilts his head a few degrees and gets to the heart of the matter: "I've learned not to question."

"Very well," says the guard, getting an idea that a prisoner might, just this once, have a point. He takes a penlight from his pocket and flicks it on and signals to another guard, down in the grayblack chiaroscuro past the administration building. Nothing happens for the longest time. Nothing but the clawing of the searchlights. The clawing of the searchlights and the beginnings of a little snowfall sifting downward through their arcs.

"I was told to report to the Officers' Club," Jacob says.

"Then you were told correctly," says the guard, still waiting, tapping his foot. The other guard signals back with a single quick flash, but otherwise the night holds nothing. "Every Thursday night they play *Skat*. The whole lot of them. Just like clockwork."

The other guard signals again, an incomprehensible flashing, and this time a figure begins to emerge out of the darkness. A small vague individual moving quickly along the walk—perhaps a dwarf, Jacob thinks, because even though he's never seen a dwarf in these precincts you never know; the Nazis have an interest in oddities of all kinds—until the searchlights reveal him at last. It's Chaim.

Max

WE FORM A STRANGE KIND OF fellowship, those of us unlucky enough to have been in the camps but lucky enough to have gotten out. I suppose we ought to have meetings, like the AA. Coffee and cigarettes and no last names.

"I'm Max, and I survived Auschwitz."

But who'd attend? Nobody. Nobody wants to talk about that stuff anymore. Nobody who went through it, at least. Nobody who knew anybody else who went through it. Your mind recoils. Your whole body recoils. It's bad enough if you happen to see another survivor's serial number by accident, in a coffee shop or on line at the grocery store or wherever. Imagine the memories that come back, the things that you remember and the things that you picture. I wear long sleeves regardless of the weather, and it's not to keep the paint off.

Soon we'll all be dead, and we won't be able to frighten each other anymore.

The young girl I mentioned—that intern or assistant, the one from Washington—she has a couple of tattoos that you can't help but notice. I'll bet she has more that you can't see, too. Private stuff. It just slays me, the idea of disfiguring yourself like that. What are people thinking?

They're not thinking about the world I've seen, that's for sure. And the world I've seen is just people, when you get down to it. Just people doing the things that people do. The same things that people have always done and the same things that they'll do again if you let them get away with it. I say why disfigure yourself in advance, when if you wait long enough someone will come along and do it for you?

I'd tell her, if I thought she'd listen. I'd roll up my sleeve and show her my own tattoo, my serial number, my stigma. But what would that prove? You can't communicate anything that way. It's just wobbly ink on an old man's arm.

So I keep it to myself. And I paint.

Eleven

JACOB MAKES CERTAIN THAT HE GETS in the first word. "Chaim!" he says. "Why did they send for me? Do you suppose I've disappointed someone?"

Count on the boy to climb aboard any deception whatsoever, without so much as a moment's pause to gather his wits. "No, no, no," he says. "It's got nothing to do with you. It's one of the junior officers. Beck. He's lost a wager, and it's about to cost him a shaved head."

The guard laughs. Perhaps he knows this Beck. Perhaps he thinks he has it coming.

Chaim goes on. "The water's boiling and the razor's sharp. I hope your hands are steady."

"As always." Jacob holds his right hand out before him to demonstrate, the arm stiff and angled up a few degrees. There's a parodical hint of the fascist salute about it, which escapes no one but does no harm, not now that the pressure is off and the guard understands his connections and is ready to let him pass.

"They won't wait," says Chaim, and off they go together, into deeper darkness.

Once out of earshot, Jacob asks, "What on earth are you doing here?"

"I was about to ask you the same thing."

"You go first."

"The usual," says Chaim. "Plus saving your ass."

"Fair enough," says Jacob.

"And you?"

"I have to see Vollmer."

"You're in luck. He's one of the few of them who can still stand up." Ahead of them, crossing back and forth in general darkness punctuated here and there by lamps in doorways and lamps in windows and lamps hung high on blank walls, another guard paces, the one who'd signaled back to the Hungarian with his flashlight. They slow before reaching him, just a little bit, and Chaim asks, "How come you want to see *Vollmer?*"

"Because you've been right all along," says Jacob, not above employing a little cunning of his own.

"I can't wait to find out how," says the boy, taking Jacob by the hand and dragging him toward the guard at a half trot and then dragging him right on past, not stopping and not even looking up. When they're in the clear he says, "All right, tell me. What is it I've been right about?"

"That I should explain to him about Eidel," he says.

"Of course! It's about time!"

"You see, then? You were correct from the beginning."

"Take my word," says the boy. "As long as you play your cards right, there'll be something in it for you too."

"I hope so."

"But why now?" says Chaim, for he's not above suspecting a little cunning either, not even from Jacob. "Couldn't it wait until tomorrow?"

"It's Max."

"What about him?"

Quickly, Jacob explains. The accident. The broken and bleeding leg. The death watch at the hospital, which is closer to punishment than to anything else.

"Aha," says Chaim. "So you've already considered how you might profit from this arrangement."

"How Max might profit," says Jacob.

"Of course," says the boy.

Over the door to the Officers' Club hangs a gas lamp, burning white. There's no guard posted, because everyone in this part of the compound is either on the same side or so outnumbered as to be utterly overwhelmed. The door hangs open a crack and music trickles through—a jolly number played on the piano, all runs and trills and booming bass notes in rapid alternation, some old folk lullaby speeded up and retooled and accompanied by the fierce and merry pounding of boots and fists—and upon this tide of sound a prisoner bursts through, carrying a carton of empty bottles in his arms.

"Beg your pardon," he says, pure reflex.

Chaim ducks under the carton and Jacob ducks around it and to-gether they go in, down a little hallway with more gas lamps mounted on the walls, and along past a low and dimly lit room where the piano player entertains a mixed audience of SS officers and young women from the auxiliary. There are tables with tablecloths and candles and there's a jammed dance floor down at the far end, but they don't look closely. They just scurry past. Some singing starts up behind them, the chorus of that folk song with everyone raising up his voice on cue, and the surprising assault of it makes them jump. One of the officers laughs to spy their terror. "Afraid of a little singing?" he calls, as amused as if he'd shot them himself. "I'm not surprised," he hollers. "It's a German number, after all." They pretend not to hear, and he barks another laugh and returns to his music.

The card room is at the end of the hall. It's a little quieter than the music room but no more inviting, humming with low argument, dense with an air of gaiety lost and recrimination begun. A gray pall of tobacco smoke covers everything, mingling with the smells of alcohol and desperate men. Jacob knows these individuals, he knows their lowered faces and he knows the backs of their necks, but he's never seen them like this. He's never seen them exposed this way, vulnerable to one another, more like animals than ever. He pauses at the door, reluctant to set foot among them, but Chaim goes first and drags him in.

A swinging door on the opposite wall opens at the same time, and two prisoners emerge with steins and glasses and crystal goblets on round trays. They raise them up to shoulder level like old professionals, although Jacob is acquainted with both of them and knows that never in their lives were they waiters before now. One was an optometrist, the other a college professor. He doesn't know whether to admire them for having elevated their present roles as far as they can or to pity them for needing to.

The officers look up for a variety of reasons: the arrival of the waiters with fresh drinks, the light spilling through the open kitchen door, the chance to catch an opportunistic glimpse at some opponent's carelessly tilted hand. Not one of them looks toward Jacob and Chaim. Not even Vollmer, who's shooing off a waiter and shielding his cards low against the table and trying hard not to look as if he's counting the money stacked in front of him. But he's counting it all right, and he's counting the hands he's won and he's doing the math and he's realizing that even this early in the evening someone has shorted him. Probably the commandant himself, and there's no fixing that. Leave it to the old sot to pull off a stunt like that even though he's already a few sheets to the wind. He'll have to be more careful.

Chaim leaves Jacob standing just inside the door and approaches Vollmer alone. The deputy looks up from his winnings and sees the boy coming his way like a telegram bearing bad news. Not that the child is unexpected; he's here all the time, forever underfoot at the Officers'

Club and in the dining room and the devil knows where else. He's a re-
curring bad dream, that child, and from the way Vollmer presses his eyes
shut against the thick smoke in the air you would think he's hoping he'll
dematerialize. But Chaim comes on, and he takes up a position at the
corner of the table between Vollmer and Liebehenschel—between God
and His Right Hand, for all purposes—and he lifts his little voice above
the din of the arguing men and the clanging of the glassware and the
rhythmic pounding of the music from down the hall.

Vollmer's every instinct tells him to raise a hand and press it across
his mouth to stifle whatever words are about to come out, but he'd
rather not touch him. Thus the unpunishable child gets away with anything. "The barber has something important to tell you," Chaim says,
and for the first time Vollmer notices Jacob, standing there just inside
the door. He waves him over and the boy moves aside, just a step toward
Liebehenschel, and the commandant drapes an arm over his shoulder.
His breath stinking of tobacco and schnapps, the grizzled old *capo di
tutti* whispers something in the boy's ear and the boy laughs, willfully or
otherwise. Who can tell anymore.

Vollmer places his cards facedown on the table and looks up at the
barber. "What is it?" he says, glad to have Jacob situated between himself
and the boy, his mood improving already. He's about to ask if perhaps
haircuts have been rescheduled this week, but Jacob speaks up.

"It's about your painting," he says.

"The painting? The painting of the girl?"

"Yes, sir," says Jacob. "That painting and the other one—the one you
want of your family."

"The portrait."

"Yes. The portrait."

"What of it?"

"Begging your pardon, *sturmbannführer*—but I have found your artist."

"Not that landscape fellow." Vollmer half turns away, sliding his hand toward his cards.

"No, sir. Not the landscape fellow."

"Good. You're learning." He turns up the near corners of his cards, distracted. "I suppose you've located some talented fellow prisoner."

Jacob can't answer outright.

"Someone looking to curry favor."

Jacob's heart sinks for an instant. "I've found the artist who painted the girl," he says.

"The girl? Impossible."

"So you would think."

"Whoever painted the girl is in Paris. Holland, perhaps."

"No, sir. The painter is right here."

"Here in Poland?"

"Here in Auschwitz."

"Impossible."

"Not impossible. Right here in the camp."

"No."

"Yes."

"The same painter?"

"Yes."

"You're certain."

"I am."

"How do you know?"

"Because I watched her paint it to begin with."

Vollmer puts down the cards. He sits for a moment dumbstruck.

"She's my wife, *sturmbannführer.*" Jacob can hardly speak. His mouth is dry and the breath is caught within his chest, trapped nearly beyond summoning. He fears that he will strangle himself right here, right on these very words. "She's my wife," he says again. "The painter."

If Vollmer weren't suspicious before, he certainly is now. "And thus," he sighs, "is revealed the favor that you wish to ask. No doubt your dear one has been assigned some painful duty that you'd like to see lightened. So you hope to arrange for a few days' luxury in the *sturmbannführer's* apartment, doodling and sketching and fooling everyone until her charade is found out and she's sent on her way."

"No, sir. That's not it."

But Vollmer isn't listening. "You're a cunning figure, Rosen. I'll grant you that. I don't know why it surprises me."

"I'm not all that cunning, sir."

"Cunning enough."

"Maybe a little," says Jacob. "You see, it's not my wife who needs a favor. It's my son."

"First your wife, and now your son? It's as I always say. There is no host in the world more hospitable than the SS. We insist on bringing families together."

Chaim laughs, a little hysterical shriek which relieves Jacob of the need to answer. "It's my son," he says again to Vollmer. "His leg is badly broken. He's in the hospital block with that French doctor, and one way or another I believe he's doomed."

"It must be very bad."

"It is. I've been afraid to tell you about my wife, but now I'm more afraid for the boy."

"And you think that if I get my family portrait made, then—"

"Exactly. If you'd be so kind."

Alongside them the commandant stops a waiter and takes a glass from his tray and downs its contents in a single pull, his adam's apple valving. He puts the glass down hard on the tray and pushes the waiter off with the sole of his boot and reaches out the other hand to pinch Chaim's cheek, reddening it to something approximating the alcohol-infused color of his own.

Vollmer's curiosity is up. "What if your wife isn't the painter you say she is?"

"She is. Rest assured."

"Let's say you're correct. What happens if I don't like her work anyhow?"

"I imagine you'll have us killed."

"I imagine I will."

"All three of us."

Vollmer nods. "And you'd risk that?"

"I believe I already have."

Vollmer looks from the barber to the boy, from the boy to the smiling commandant, and then back to the barber. "You'd do this for your son," he says.

"Without a moment's hesitation."

"Then so be it," says Vollmer. "I'll send word to the hospital."

*

In the morning Jacob will smile more broadly than ever at the fleeting vision of his wife on the step outside the kitchen. She will see his teeth and they will remind her of the skull beneath his skin.

*

Pity poor Eidel: Rolak says she has a surprise in store. Such a thing is rarely good news and the capo knows it, so in order to draw out the suffering she lets her spend the rest of the day imagining just what the surprise might be. Not even after supper, when the women of the commando have finished restoring the kitchen to what passes for cleanliness and they've lined up to proceed back to the block for roll call, does she let on. She only gives Eidel a slow look, a gravid look of sorrow and shared anticipation, and leaves it at that. Poor Eidel can only speculate. Marching back she decides that the capo has discovered why she ducks outside at seven-thirty every Friday morning, and that she's reassigning her to some other work crew so as to take away this small joy. Standing in the yard she imagines that the capo has learned not that but something worse—that some terrible thing has happened to Jacob or to Max or to both of them—and that she's waiting to tell her at a moment when the effect will be the most crushing. Counting off she imagines the only thing worse yet: that whatever has befallen her loved ones is somehow her fault, that she's committed some unknown sin and that Auschwitz itself, in its infinite and evenhanded cruelty, has caused the punishment to fall upon her husband and her son.

Yes, she decides. *That must be it.* So when the count is over and Rolak stops her to explain that tomorrow morning at nine o'clock she will be excused from the kitchen and must report directly to the apartment of the deputy commandant, in a certain building on the main street of the town, she very nearly faints.

"That's it?" she asks.

"That's it. Tomorrow morning and every Saturday morning after that. Nine o'clock sharp."

"The deputy commandant's apartment."

"You heard me."

"What will I do there?"

"You'll mind your manners," says the capo, "if you have any sense. Beyond that, I can't say." She could say, of course—she could very easily say, since it's her business to know everything about the women under her command—but why spoil the fun? Nine o'clock in the morning will come regardless. Let her wonder.

Eidel sleeps less than usual, and not only because of the anxiety that's overcome her. The night turns bitter cold and even the choking proximity of the other women's bodies doesn't help. A breeze bearing a few flakes of snow comes in through a crack in the wall and the chill of it drifts down along her neck . She shivers. They all shiver, the same chill passing from one to the next like some contagion. If she still had her silk handkerchief she would tuck it into her collar to help keep out the cold, but it's long gone and Zofia who took it is long gone as well. The memory of it reminds her of Lydia but doesn't keep her warm.

The cold is worse and the dawn is breaking somewhere behind heavy clouds when the three alarm bells ring. The capo rousts Eidel and Gretel and the rest of the cooking commando and with a curse she sends them off to begin their work, the little flock of them emerging together from the dark block into the dark yard with steam rising up from their bodies like wasted prayers. Something precious given up that they can ill afford.

They enter the kitchen and switch on the lights and with straws broken from a witch's broom they draw lots to see who gets the pleasure of lighting the coal stoves. Once upon a time—back before Eidel arrived, back somewhere in their collective memory and in the collective memory of all such prisoners, who sooner or later come to believe that they have been here forever and that those who came before and died and have been replaced are but themselves seen from a different perspective, perhaps that of the eternal and omniscient Almighty *blessed be He*—once upon a time they took turns lighting the stove in cold weather, setting up a rotation and following it faithfully, until there were too many sicknesses and too many exceptional circumstances and altogether too many deaths to make order sustainable. Hence the broom, hence the straws, hence the falling back on the comfort of randomness.

This morning Eidel wins, and she takes her victory as an omen: surely the chance to warm herself before the fire will be the only good thing that happens today. But omen or otherwise she accepts what she is given and takes advantage of it, building a little pyramid of kindling and lighting it with the one match she's permitted and coaxing the coal fire to life with what seems like the last substantial breaths she may ever take.

The work and the fire bring her back to life, but before long the time comes. She hurries across the yard and down along the fence toward the main entrance, realizing that this is the way she sees her Jacob go each week, wondering what he would think if only he knew where she is headed. Out of the camp, of all things. Through the gate and past the guard towers and beyond the barbed wire, into an actual town with actual people living in it. Some of them will be monsters and some of them will be the wives of monsters and the children of monsters, but not everyone. Not everyone. It's not possible. Someone, perhaps some old grandmother, will see her and take pity upon her at least in her heart. Someone will see her and see written upon her face the infinite wrongs being done in the camp. Someone.

Failing that, Eidel herself will see some sign of normal life proceeding in her absence, and in that sign she will remind herself to find comfort instead of envy, reassurance instead of disgust. She will do her best on that account.

In the end, once past the guards and down the lane and exposed to life in the town, she keeps her eyes averted and doesn't see anything at all. She's like some superstitious child afraid to step on a crack in a walkway, daring to look in no direction but down. What's become of her? she wonders. What's become of the certainty with which she once met the world? What's become of the unstoppable urge she once felt to see everything, to capture everything, to make from the rough raw materials of the universe some new and shining creation of her own? She despairs to realize that this private thing has been taken away from her along with everything else, and she keeps her gaze cast downward.

Vollmer's building is heated with steam, and even in the entryway, just behind the glass door that keeps out the weather but lets in the light, the welcoming warmth feels like a miracle. To think that people could live like this. To think that she herself once did, and not that long ago, if time still means anything. She climbs the stairs to the second floor—the stairs themselves a marvel, with a blue woolen runner straight up the middle and black walnut wainscoting on either side and a hand railing that gleams like glass—and stands outside the numbered door. There are voices inside. The high happy sounds of children, no telling how many, perhaps two, perhaps three, and the soft murmur of a woman's speech below their laughter. Vollmer's wife and children. She tries to picture them but she cannot. She tries to imagine a happy family, but the vision will not materialize. And so she steels herself and knocks.

Max

YOU HEAR STORIES. An awful lot of them concern what happened in 1945, when the Red Army finally showed up. That tells you something about human nature. We like to think that the world turns on a moment of heroism, even though it usually just turns.

I guess nothing beats a happy ending.

Maybe my own perspective is different because I got out earlier, and my story isn't like the stories that end with the Russian tanks rolling in and the fences collapsing and the SS trying to cover the whole thing up, as if they'd had us there at some kind of spa. They demolished the crematorium, I understand. Dynamited it and burned it down. Everything always had to end in fire for those men. They had a hammer and the whole world was a nail.

One story sticks with me, though. One story as vivid as if I'd seen it myself or maybe even lived through it.

This fellow was on the train out. The car was crowded, jammed tight, people stacked everywhere just the same way they'd come. The crowding might well have been worse for all I know, but there was an end in sight so people tolerated it. They were all stacked up like freight. And this fellow I'm talking about, he's got a little packet of cigarettes. The Russians gave it to him, I guess. I don't know. He's got a little packet of cigarettes anyhow. He's got cigarettes but he's got nowhere to lie down. Nowhere even to sit, and he's as tired and weak as you'd imagine he'd be. Another fellow sees him standing there pressed up against the wall and this other fellow is on the floor in the corner, a nice little space he's got all to himself, and he hollers over that he'll let him borrow his spot for an hour in trade for a cigarette. He's got a German accent, this second fellow. He's been a prisoner like the first one, but he's German. Maybe he was a German Jew, I can't say. Maybe he was some kind of political prisoner. Maybe he just looked at somebody cockeyed one day and that was that. It doesn't matter. He makes this offer in that German accent of his and the fellow with the cigarettes presses through the crowd to take him up on it. Gives him a smoke. Lights it for him. Then he lies down and goes to sleep like a baby. An hour later the German comes back and wants his place again, so the fellow gives it to him. Lets him lie back down. At which point he sits down on his chest and puts his hands around his throat and chokes him to death in front of everybody. Just because he had a German accent.

This fellow, I don't remember his name, he told me the story maybe twenty years ago. Straight out of the blue at a fancy dinner party. He said if he ever had the chance, he'd do it again.

I said I wouldn't stop him.

Twelve

THE GUARDS AND THE SS MEN are laughing when they arrive at the hospital. They come on a truck with an open bed, two officers in the front and six guards in the back, seated on benches around the perimeter like people on their way to a picnic in the country. They're wearing heavy winter coats and their bellies are full and their laughter rises in a cloud of warm breath and cigarette smoke. The driver draws up to the door and stops, ratcheting the parking brake, and they all climb out. Another truck, this one closed, follows and parks nearer to the door. The driver sits inside fogging his own windows, the engine idling, a sour look on his face. A line of prisoners runs past, dressed in rags and driven by a capo who flails at their heels with a horsewhip, and each one of them looks up at the driver in his warm cabin with a look of hopeless envy. The driver doesn't even lower himself to snarl back.

The French doctor is on duty. Perhaps he's always on duty. Perhaps he's an incarnation of that famous cursed ferryman of legend, doomed to pole back and forth across the same haunted river until he can deceive another man into taking his place. He's alone on duty, and since there was no selection yesterday the hospital is full. Under ordinary circumstances in an ordinary hospital this would be untenable. There would be too much to do. Too many patients. Too little staff. But not here. Here additional staff would just mean more eyes to witness the unmitigated and irreducible suffering of the patients. It would represent a kind of cruelty that even the Nazis haven't thought of yet, or if they have thought of it they have rejected it as too subtle for their purposes.

The doctor has blood on his hands, and he's at the iron sink scrubbing them under a trickle of cold water when the men storm through the door. He's just finished changing a bandage. It's not part of his usual routine, and it hasn't been for as long as he's been here. He hasn't so much as seen an ordinary gauze bandage until yesterday, much less a bottle of iodine and a spool of adhesive tape, and yet here they are. He'd given up asking for such things months ago. But yesterday morning he'd requisitioned these and other supplies in the name of the *sturmbannführer*, and within an hour they were in his hands. Not everything he'd asked for but enough to get started, with a suggestion that there might be more to come at a future date. Everyone has orders, he supposes. His orders yesterday morning had been to bind up the boy's wounds and make him fit again for work, and he'd said he needed certain materials, and certain materials had appeared. Like magic.

There's been a general scrambling among the hospital beds ever since the trucks began rolling up outside. Men who can't walk running for the latrine. Men who can't crawl tearing open their thin mattresses and climbing inside. Men who can't sit up scrambling under the nearest bunk to conceal themselves behind junk and old rags and dirty laundry. Anything to avoid being seen by the SS and put through the selection. It's all hopeless.

The first officer through the door—an old man composed of nothing but bones, a ghastly gray spectre of death bearing upon his hollow chest a death's-head insignia—laughs and blows smoke as if something inside of him has caught fire. "Tell me, *Herr Doktor*," he says, "who is the better physician now? Do you see how the men rise up to greet me?"

The selection process doesn't take long. Two prisoners are in the latrine, one of them jammed up between the ceiling joists like a spider and the other huddled down behind some broken masonry, and although these two are clearly in fair enough condition to resume work they're loaded into the closed truck as punishment for their daring. The men who've torn open their mattresses are taken out alongside the building and shot for a lesson in destroying the property of the Reich, and the two under the beds are given another day of rest before they'll be returned to their commandos. All of the others, with the sole exception of Max, are marched or chased or hauled into the waiting truck and from there to the gas. The hospital is nearly empty again.

"There will be more patients to keep us company later on today," says the doctor. "Rest assured of that."

Max doesn't answer. His pain is too great. Nor does either of the other men make any reply, the first because he's busy coughing blood onto the floor and the other because the panic of this near miss has left him curled shivering in a fetal position, cradling a stomach wound. The doctor can do nothing for the man with the cough, but the other might have a chance if only he dared use some of the iodine and gauze reserved for Max. He thinks about it, standing in the open door and watching the trucks pull away. Watching a little snow begin to drift down from the gray sky, watching a little white smoke begin to rise up from the mouths of the tall stacks.

It wouldn't take much. The infection might yield easily. He might actually practice a little medicine again. He'd like that.

On the other hand, it would most certainly be suicide.

*

Saturday is the housekeeper's day off, so it's Vollmer's wife who answers. She's smiling when she opens the door, and she keeps on smiling when she sees Eidel. "You're the artist," she says in Eidel's own Polish, and the word comes as a surprise. Not even a surprise. It comes to her as a word from some foreign language, a word describing something unknown and perhaps unknowable here. Something like magic or fairies or kindness. She doesn't yet understand that she's here to paint, and even if she had expected it, even if she had come here with the understanding that she was to pick up a brush upon arrival, she could never have made the connection between this moment and the weekly transit that Jacob has been making for months now. Yet the beginning of the idea sinks in, *You're the artist,* and she realizes that someone must have told someone. It makes her suspicious, for suspicion is always in the air. She wonders who has been watching her, who has been learning things about her life that she herself has all but forgotten.

Vollmer's wife moves back into the entryway and on through another door, leading the way, the voices of the children still coming from elsewhere. The kitchen or the parlor. They enter the bright dining room and pass the big mirror hung squarely on the wall and she looks away from it, aghast at the vision of herself reflected there. A pale and shaven revenant in striped burlap, ears and nose reddened from the cold, not even a ghost but the lifeless husk that a ghost has left behind. She keeps her eyes on the floor and imagines the woman of the house gazing into that same mirror by the hour, experimenting with the tilt of her head, adjusting the set of her smile. There is a chair for Eidel against the wall near the fireplace, a narrow wooden chair much abused and rocking on uneven legs and altogether very little better than firewood, a negative image of the eight padded chairs set evenly around the table. She sits in it without looking up, and thus she doesn't see her own painting where it hangs only a little distance away.

Vollmer's wife goes to one of the east windows and opens it a crack to thin the smell that has come in with Eidel. She puts her back to it and folds her arms around herself and moves away, shivering. She is still smiling but something about the curve of her lips has turned suspicious. "I had hoped you would recognize your work," she says.

Eidel has no answer. Her mind blanks completely for an instant and then fills up all over again, charged this time with visions of every possible kind of deceit and treachery, every unhappy ending known to man and some unknown as of yet, unimagined even in this camp at the end of the world. She decides that she's been brought here merely as an amusement for this woman, that she must have taken a misstep somewhere along the line and not been called to account for it until now, until this very moment when Frau Vollmer requires a victim upon whom to exercise an appetite for cruelty that is as yet untapped and unfathomable.

But then again, maybe not. For at this instant the woman of the house gives something away after all, and it's not entirely inhumane. Her eyes flash for a moment toward the place over Eidel's head, the wall over the fireplace, and Eidel dares follow their direction and look there herself. To see the portrait. No. Not even the portrait. To see Lydia. Her own daughter, brought back. The flesh of her flesh, lifted up into a rightful place of honor even in this den of savages. She very nearly faints. She certainly doesn't think. She clutches the rough burlap of her uniform around her neck and rises to her feet and cries out, "My daughter, my daughter, my daughter." The tears beginning, the tears that she's caused herself to hold back all these months. "Lydia," she says, torn between reaching out to touch the image of the girl and stepping away so as to see her more clearly. "Lydia."

"*Your daughter?*" says Frau Vollmer. Her smile has collapsed in on itself.

Eidel can't answer. She can hardly breathe.

"Your daughter, you say?" Coming a little closer, around the table.

Eidel lifts a shoulder to dry her face on the rough fabric of her uniform. *Yes,* she nods, biting her lips and struggling to compose herself. *Yes.*

"Then it's true," says the woman of the house. "You are who they say you are. An excellent development." Turning on her heel as she speaks, and vanishing through a swinging door into the deeper realms of the apartment.

When she returns, she has the children with her. A boy and a girl, Karl and Luzi. She has given no thought as to what this lowly Jewish prisoner ought to call the two of them, but it seems ridiculous that they should go by anything other than their Christian names, so that will have to do. Karl says he is seven and Luzi says she is five, each of them speaking as if having reached such ages and expecting to continue into the future stacking year upon year without foreseeable end is the most ordinary thing. Eidel dries her eyes and keeps looking from them to the portrait of her daughter and back again. She fears that she'll seem distracted, but she can't help herself.

The woman of the house, by her own declaration not *Frau* but *Madam,* pulls a chair free and gathers Luzi onto her lap and calls Karl to her side. She explains that Eidel is here to paint their family portrait. The three of them and her husband, *sturmbannführer* Vollmer himself. Eidel knows of Vollmer, doesn't she?

Yes, yes, she does. Of course. Dabbing at her nose with her tattooed forearm. The low fire in the fireplace is warm against her back. It feels like summer. To be entirely truthful it feels like summer in Zakopane, with the yellow sunlight streaming in through the blue windows of her attic studio. She half wonders if what she feels is emanating in some mystical way from the painting, as if the image of her daughter has the power to open a doorway otherwise inaccessible. It's a ridiculous idea but a disorienting one, particularly in her extreme state of hunger and anxiety and exhaustion—a dream state in this nightmare place where anything at all could prove to be true—and before she knows what's happening she has collapsed to the floor, very nearly into the fireplace but not quite.

She awakens stretched out on the carpet, her head throbbing, the boy Karl looking down at her with the dull curiosity of a hungry animal. His round face swims in and out of focus. "She's awake," he says, satisfied, and then he disappears and things go black.

Vollmer is there when she opens her eyes again. He has a mug of tea in one hand and a sliced apple on a small plate in the other and he's speaking her name in a voice neither commanding nor tender. Just saying her name. The mug of tea and the sliced apple are not for her but the name is, her name and not her number, and she takes the use of it for the kindness it's meant to represent. Embarrassed at her fall, she props herself up on her elbows and comes slowly to her feet and apologizes.

"Very well," he says through a mouthful of apple. "We had hoped to let you make some sketches today, to see if you were the artist you've been reputed to be, but I understand that such a step won't be necessary."

"No, sir," she says. "I suppose not."

He indicates a pad of paper and a pencil on the table. "Then write down whatever supplies you'll need—brushes, paints, solvents, and so forth—and we'll begin next week."

She looks lost. It's been so long.

"You *can* write, can't you?"

"Oh, yes sir," she says. "I can write." She's tempted to ask him whether he would prefer she make the list in German or in Polish, but she bites her tongue.

"Very well, then. Proceed."

She steps toward the table and writes out the list while he watches from the corner. It takes a few minutes, since she's afraid of forgetting something. It's been so long. In the end she makes two columns side by side—one in German and the other in Polish—and she would add a third if she dared, a third column in perfect schoolbook French, this ignorant slave brought in to raise up devils by means of the highest art.

*

After an anxious day has passed, Wenzel tells Jacob that he may visit his son in the hospital. The capo smiles broadly as he says it—as magnanimous as if he has arranged this kindness himself—but the lie implicit in his large-heartedness stands because who is Jacob to protest and what difference would it make if he did. At the close of the day, in the minutes between returning from Canada and standing in the freezing wind for roll call, he sets out, wishing only that it were Friday morning already and he could pass by Eidel's kitchen door and suggest to her by the width of his smile and the joy on his face that some impossible transformation has taken place. That they—husband and wife, father and mother—have together engineered the resurrection of their son from a fate that she hasn't even suspected.

There's a little coal stove in the hospital to help keep the suffering men from freezing, but it's more punishment by suggestion than anything else. The prisoners are huddled in corners, huddled in cots, huddled together in great heaps like cats or corpses. Among them only Max is alert. This would be remarkable enough—it's the first time his father has seen him awake since before the accident—but the plaster cast on his leg is an astonishment of an entirely different order. An undiluted act of God. The doctor points it out the way he'd point out any other miracle: blood seeping from a carved crucifix, the likeness of a saint materialized upon a rock face. As time goes by the boy's special treatment will draw various responses from various other prisoners; some will be envious and others will take it as a sign of hope and still others will look upon Max himself with a kind of superstitious reverence, making of him a living embodiment of some transcendent mystery, of some reality deeper and more forgiving than this one, and angling for a cot closer to his upon which to spend their last nights on earth.

Just yet, Max himself doesn't understand. "Why me?" he asks his father, and the doctor answers first. "Why anyone?" Jacob looks the doctor's way and nods and waits, *why anyone, indeed,* but the doctor is at his desk sorting papers, his glasses slipping down his nose, not the least bit interested in continuing this conversation or pursuing this line of reasoning anywhere but within his own mind, if there. It's settled.

Jacob kneels by the cot and explains everything. How he persuaded Vollmer to intervene. How it was his idea although only part of it was his doing—braving the *sturmbannführer* in the Officers' Club to ask a favor and make a deal—because his mother had actually been the one to save the day by going straight into the lion's den unwitting and unprepared. Imagine the terror she must have felt, being called into the deputy commandant's apartment for who knew what reason. And yet she had borne up. She must have borne up, she must have faced the entire Vollmer family and agreed to paint their portrait, perhaps without even knowing why she had been called to do so—she must have endured the sight of Lydia's portrait hanging on the wall of that monsters' den—or else neither one of them would be here in the hospital now. Max would have been taken out with the first selection. The medical supplies would never have come.

The Nazis have sent plaster of Paris, for God's sake. Manna from heaven.

"That's *why you*," he says, tapping lightly on the boy's great white cast and preparing to shove off for roll call. "Because there are still people in this world who love you."

Max

YOU'D THINK IT WOULD HAVE BEEN every man for himself in the camps, but it was worse than that. A situation becomes every man for himself only among those who've lost every last shred of human decency, and that was never the object. The Nazis never wanted you to part with the last scrap of your decency. Hanging onto it served their purposes, because something like that could always be used against you.

I had my father and my mother to consider, but even in the absence of family a person will make connections. The smallest kindness will get it started. A hand up out of a ditch, or a look with some compassion in it when the capos are doing their worst. Little insignificant things that become significant. The next thing you know there's a line running between you and another person, a line that you hope the guards and the capos won't notice, because if they do their minds will start grinding away, thinking of ways to leverage that little bit of human connection against you.

It's economics, really. When two people care about each other, a pistol shot to the temple will destroy two men for the price of one bullet.

That was the risk that was developing around my little family. Somehow, everybody in the camp knew there were three of us now instead of just two, and that wasn't necessarily good. There would be that many more angles to work, that much more complexity. But everybody also knew what had happened. That my father had made a deal with Vollmer and that Vollmer was protecting us for his own purposes. It made us untouchable for as long as it lasted. But it couldn't last forever.

Nothing does. Not even Auschwitz.

Thirteen

THE DAY DAWNS WET AND RAW, and the kitchen door is shut against the weather when Jacob passes on his way to the administration building. He hunches forward against the cold and jams his hands beneath his armpits and lets a million thoughts race through his mind, most of them having to do with what might have gone wrong over in the women's camp. It's the first Friday morning that she hasn't been watching for him since the day she broke the bowl, and pelting sleet or no he persuades himself that there's some deeper and uglier reason behind her absence.

He would die of a broken heart if something happened to her, and Max would be doomed all over again. That's how tenuous this arrangement is. Nonetheless, he must go forward. He must report for duty in his warm corner of the officers' kitchen and cut the hair of a score of terrible men and try to distract himself with the concrete fact that he's manipulating various cutting implements in the vicinity of individuals who would kill him for the slightest transgression. One nick and who knows. Especially if Eidel is gone and the structure he's built to support his family has collapsed without his knowing.

"You're a bit off today," Chaim says as they sit at the bench over their regal luncheon. Blood sausage and rolls with butter and spaetzel in gravy, and for dessert a pie made with molasses and raisins.

"You," says Jacob, "are a sharp observer of human nature."

"It pays," says the boy. "And let me give you a little advice in that department: You're not doing yourself any favors by wearing that long face around these fellows." Chewing away at a roll dipped in gravy, indicating with a tilt of his head a couple of officers walking past the kitchen door.

"What long face? How could anyone seated at a banquet like this have a long face?"

"Nice try," says the boy. "But you still look miserable." He mops at the gravy and stuffs the roll into his mouth.

"Fine. I'm worried about my wife."

"Don't be."

"That's easy for you to say."

"Really," the boy says, dabbing a napkin at his lips. "Don't be."

"I'm worried something's happened to her."

"Quit it."

"I can't. I'm worried."

"How come?"

"Signs."

"*Signs*," he says. "That's great. That's just great."

Jacob leans across the table, speaking rapidly and low. "This morning, you see, she wasn't where she usually is. She wasn't waiting to see me pass by."

"So? Something came up."

"Something came up."

"Things come up."

"The kitchen door was shut. The whole place was sealed like a tomb."

"So? The weather's lousy."

"You're right," says Jacob, sitting back on the bench. "You're right about everything. I know."

"Of course I am."

183

"But what if—"

"To hell with *what if,*" says the child. "*What if* will drive you mad. *What if* will make you careless. *What if* will draw attention to you and that long face you're walking around with."

Jacob's face only gets longer.

"Here's what you do. When we get to the apartment, you ask Vollmer if he's looking forward to sitting for her tomorrow. If there's any problem, you'll know it right away. Just by looking at him. No matter what he might say."

"All right," says Jacob. "I'll do that."

But in the end, he doesn't have to.

It's the housekeeper who lets him know that he has nothing to worry about, taking him aside in the entryway to say how much the family is anticipating his wife's visit. Despite the differences in their station—he a poor doomed Polish Jew, she a German relocated to this country only until the work of extermination is done—she speaks to him for this private moment with a warmth and a confidentiality from which he can conclude only one thing: having a contented Frau Vollmer around the apartment is a change for which the woman has been praying without letup, and therefore he's become her savior, witting or otherwise.

The woman of the house, she says, has taken her children to the nicest shops in town and outfitted them with new clothes for the portrait. Traditional German outfits easier to find here in Poland than they once were: a dirndl for Luzi, bundhosen for Karl, all finished with the finest embroidery money can buy. The shopping alone got her out of the apartment for two entire mornings. She advises him to have his wife remark on how marvelous they look. Such a compliment will make Frau Vollmer happy, even coming from one whose opinion doesn't matter in the least.

But no, he says, he can't communicate with his wife. It's not possible. They're in a prison camp, after all. A death camp. Men are kept apart from women, even husbands from wives. Especially husbands from wives. As he says it he wonders if it's possible that she's forgotten the horrors living in her own back yard.

"Be that as it may," she says, opening the door and letting Chaim run in ahead, "it would make my life easier if she could put in a word."

The dining room curtains are drawn against the cold, and even if they were wide open the gray skies and the pelting rain would admit only the weakest and dreariest of light, so the electric chandelier hanging is lit and a couple of gas lamps are burning and together with a slight chill in the air they give the room a gloomy quality. It feels like a cave at the end of the world, Chaim briskly setting out the tools and then scurrying off to the safety of his dim corner like some creature accustomed to dark places. A secretive rodent. Jacob shakes off the strangeness as best he can and unfolds the white cotton drape beneath which he'll conceal every sign of Vollmer's allegiance and rank, that snowy drape the only thing that lets him pretend that the *sturmbannführer* is an ordinary man or even a man at all and not something far worse. But the light makes him ill at ease regardless of how he busies himself, and the sounds of Vollmer moving through the depths of the apartment are the sounds of a spirit prowling, and as happy as he is to have learned that all is most likely well with Eidel he begins to doubt all over again that he's done the right thing by letting her be sent here. Perhaps tomorrow the weather will improve. Yes. Things will be brighter.

He looks up from his work as Vollmer's hand falls upon the knob, and rather than be seen casting his eyes upon the *sturmbannführer* as he enters he looks respectfully away, across the room toward the fireplace, where the absence of the painting arrests him. His daughter is gone. His heart sinks as if he has lost her all over again. Vollmer comes through the door and sees what Jacob sees and doesn't so much as acknowledge it. It was just a painting, after all.

Watching from his dim corner, Chaim perceives that Jacob not only can't endure the painting's absence but can't even risk asking about it. He, on the other hand, has nothing to lose. His standing with Vollmer slipped down to zero or thereabouts a long time ago, and in the meantime he's cultivated plenty of partisans other than the *sturmbannführer*, so he uses up a little of his remaining capital and asks outright. "What happened to the girl?"

"The girl?" says Vollmer, settling himself in the chair, not even glancing in Chaim's direction. It's as if he's talking to a disembodied spirit. "The girl?"

"Yes, *sturmbannführer*. The girl."

"I had her removed," says Vollmer. "We have enough Jews infesting the place, without singling one out for a position of honor."

Jacob holds his breath and settles the drape around Vollmer's shoulders, but Vollmer makes no more comment. He's through talking about the painting, he's certainly through talking about the girl. Whatever he may think about Jacob having concealed her identity is his secret and will stay that way because it's no business of the barber's. Jacob's hands shake, though, and he turns away and arranges his tools for a moment longer than ought to be necessary, concentrating on settling his heart. Thinking that there's only one way that Vollmer could have found out: Eidel must have let it slip. Of course. Then again, she couldn't have stopped herself.

Yet they want her back tomorrow.

He keeps that thought in his mind as he raises the scissor and comb.

It's all he has to sustain him.

*

The day's steady fall of rain has softened the ground a little, so while the other women eat their evening meal or divide it up so as to keep out a morsel or two for tomorrow's breakfast, Gretel decides that the time has come to bury her vinegar bottle. She wolfs down a scrap of bread and a tough waxy rind of cheese and slips away from the others, explaining that she's on her way to the latrine, stopping as she goes at the spot where she's hidden the bottle in the rafters over her bunk. It's as full as she can make it, and when she gets outdoors she plugs up the neck with a stone that fits pretty well and packs the rest of the opening with mud. It will have to do.

Searchlights in the yard pierce the rain and materialize out of the darkness like blades, some tracking steadily through the air and others slashing and swerving like things gone mad, all depending on the relative commitment or lassitude of the men behind them, men whose work is at best driven by certain private theories and principles that no handbook of operations could formalize. The result is a random and moving maze of hard light in darkness, which is probably as efficient a result as any. No one else is outdoors. Just wet men huddled together in windswept towers and fully saturated men standing at attention along fencelines and this one lone woman. She finishes sealing the neck and rises up from the dirt and tucks the bottle into her sleeve to keep it from reflecting light. Her instinct is to dodge and duck the moving beams, but since furtiveness can only lead to trouble she keeps her wits about her and walks slowly toward the latrine, vanishing at the last instant around the corner and back toward the place she's chosen as the burial site. The spot where rain drips from the roof and loosens the gravel and makes the clay soft.

She takes off one shoe to dig, kneeling down in the wet mud with the gravel cutting into her knees and the vinegar bottle by her side. She wonders how deep is deep enough and she decides that the answer is as deep as she can go. Every day in the camp she accomplishes more than she starts out thinking she can. The Nazis have taught her that; they've proven to her by her own example that she has more capacity for labor than she would have ever thought possible in a perfect world or at least an ordinary one. So she digs. And when the sole of her shoe cracks she puts it back on and removes the other one and digs some more. In the morning she'll regret breaking it—she'll regret it for days and weeks to come if she has days and weeks left to her—but she digs. And when she can dig no more, when the other shoe is cracked and useless too and she dares to be absent from the block for not one more minute and she thinks she might be hearing the sound of the roll call starting up, she lays the bottle into its grave like a baby, and covers it up with mud. Her testament, commended to the earth.

*

Saturday dawns bright. Eidel awakens to it with a strange good feeling welling up in her heart. She can't quite identify it, but soon the haze of sleep clears and it comes to her. Today is the day she'll see her daughter's picture again. Not only that, but it's the day she'll take up painting for the first time in perhaps a year. She wonders if she can still do it. If she can still do either one of these two things, bearing witness to her child on one hand and painting on the other. Each will take reserves that she hasn't lately called upon.

In the kitchen she refuses to join in the drawing of lots, believing that someone else ought to have the benefit of starting the fire because she'll be spending a few hours in the deputy's warm apartment. Why not share the wealth? Perhaps, she thinks, there isn't a fixed amount of good and bad in the camp after all. Perhaps by distributing her own good fortune among her sisters in the kitchen she's set in motion something positive that will go on forever. She thinks it but she doesn't dare believe it. There's a difference.

Just before she sets out for the village she grazes the heel of her hand on the red-hot stovetop, and to cool it she holds it under a stream of icy water from the tap. She's on edge, no doubt about that, and her nerves have made her careless. As she watches the water run she remembers her childhood in Warsaw, how her mother—her mother now hiding somewhere in Sweden, God bless her—had believed that butter would soothe a burn. Although Eidel herself had never seen any value in it she'd gone on to practice the same folk medicine on her own children anyhow, because where was the harm. It was just butter after all, bright yellow butter as plentiful as air. Here in the camp it's as precious as gold bullion and twice as rare, so water will have to suffice. At least there's plenty of it. And it's icy as death.

When she arrives at the apartment, the supplies that Vollmer has sent for are stacked up in the entryway, carton upon carton. The housekeeper brings a bread knife, and Eidel methodically unwraps each package, going slowly, moving as if under a spell. The things that she unwraps have extraordinary qualities both mystical and physical, and the merest touch of them takes her back to a world she's forgotten. Everything is of the highest quality, as fine as any goods she's ever laid her hands on, each bottle and tube and brush sent all the way from Berlin wrapped in a soft drawstring bag or a set of nested boxes, all of it cushioned with bale after bale of tissue paper. Vollmer has spent a fortune. Enough to feed the women of Eidel's bunk three excellent daily meals for a month or more, enough to last years at their present rate.

The housekeeper begins tidying the wreckage as Eidel picks out what she'll need for today's work, a sketch pad and a packet of soft graphite pencils and a gum eraser. She finds the sharpener and puts points on three of the pencils and sets the sharpener back down on a narrow table along the wall, between a vase and a small lacquered box. The housekeeper looks daggers at her and points to the sharpener and says that perhaps she should have asked Herr Vollmer for a supply chest rather than making a ruin of the furniture, and she sweeps it off onto the floor where it smashes to bits. More to clean up, she says with a curse.

The sound of breakage draws the boy, little Karl in his embroidered bundhosen and his starched white shirt, careening through the kitchen door and stumbling upon the various wrappings and boxes as if he's missed his own birthday. "Hey!" he says, the trussed-up little creature, red jam smeared across his chin. "What's all this?"

His mother comes for him before either of the women needs to answer. He's tearing through the castoff boxes and bags and wrapping papers like some burrowing animal seeking cover, and she opens the door again and stands watching for a moment, amused. The girl, Luzi, pokes her head out from behind, arms around her mother's knee, and peers into the tempest with round eyes. At last the woman speaks. "Now, Karl," she says, just as he turns his attention from the empty wrappings to the carefully arranged jars and bottles and brushes, "I'm sure there'll be time for you to play with those later on." Sending him a sweet smile and letting some of it spill over in the direction of the other women.

"If you please, Madam," says Eidel, "it might be best to get him his own."

The woman of the house raises a single elegantly-penciled eyebrow and holds it there like the blade of a guillotine.

Eidel goes on. "Water colors," she says. "They'll be easier for him to work with."

Slowly, slowly, the woman lowers her eyebrow.

Heedless of anything, smirking up at the prisoner who would deprive him of his due, the boy chooses one tube of paint and jams it into the pocket of his snowy white shirt. The paint is a Chinese red, almost the red of the German flag, and although Eidel hadn't requested this color in particular the supplier in Berlin must have felt it necessary. They're all critics, after all. Everyone in the world. She doesn't mind seeing it go, but because she'd still like to record a decisive victory over the boy she says to his mother, "These oils, you know—they never come out of anything." And then, rather than wait for the result, she pretends to study the fresh points of her pencils.

*

The portrait of Lydia is missing, of course, when they go into the dining room. The wall above the fireplace is bare except for the empty nail and a tiny crack that runs down from it, ramifying like a vein until it disappears at last. The fire is dead in the grate on this sunny day and the wind whistles ghostly somewhere above the top of the chimney and no one in the deputy's family seems to think that Eidel should feel anything at all regarding what they've done. They don't even look her way. Instead the boy pulls the girl's pigtails and their mother separates them bodily and their father enters through the rear door on a hot gust of bad temper. Only Luzi, situated at length on her father's lap, finally notices Eidel's frozen stance before the empty spot. She points to her with a chubby finger and says, "Father said we have plenty of Jews around. That's why he got rid of it." And when Eidel doesn't respond—when Eidel doesn't even move unless you count the shuddering of her breath and the tightening of her grip on the fistful of pencils—she takes a kind of childish pity on her and adds, "It was a good painting. We just have too many Jews."

At length she composes herself. She takes a seat on the wobbly chair and props the sketchbook in her lap and directs the family into the most pleasing composition possible. Her instinct would be to catch them as they are, that was always her method and it comes back to her now, but the business of portraiture for hire is something different. She has the boy stand behind his seated mother with a hand placed gently on her shoulder, a nice compositional curve starting at Vollmer's face and dipping down to his wife's and then up again just a touch to Karl's. But the woman doesn't want Karl hidden back there with his expensive new trousers, so she insists that she and her husband separate and place the boy in the middle. Eidel copes, adjusting her vision and trying again, leaning forward in that hard chair with her back to the groaning fireplace. Doing her best to deny the absence behind her.

Max

REMEMBER THIS: *Sentiment is the enemy of the work.*

That was old Uncle Andy's mistake from the outset.

Fine, all right, maybe not from the outset—I've never claimed to be any kind of an expert on the complete Wyeth *oeuvre;* it could be that he was more interested in formal matters in the early days, before he got started stamping out those windy fields and farmhouses like so many Christmas cookies; it could be that he took a wrong turn somewhere, started letting himself be distracted by the money or the adulation or whatever, surrendered to certain cheapening influences—but in the end, no question about it, his downfall was an excess of sentiment.

To be perfectly clear, I suppose I ought to say *sentimentality*. It's difficult to communicate these things properly. If you could get them right by just talking about them, you wouldn't waste your time painting.

People are forever telling one another how this or that work of art *makes them feel,* as if that were the point of it. As if the artist had set out with no higher goal than to affect them personally, to *touch* them, as they say, for Christ's sake. The painter as *masseur.* It gives me the willies.

It's no business of mine how you might feel about something. It's no business of mine whether or not you feel anything at all. The minute a person starts worrying about that, he's doomed. He's no better than Andrew Wyeth, backed into a corner by his own hunger for approval, rendering up that same old reliable pathos again and again. Revved-up old sterile Uncle Andy with just one uncompromised and unmediated urge left to him at the end of his life, one pure God-granted spark, up there worshipping his naked Helga in Frolic Weymouth's back bedroom, dying to let the world in on his faithless little secret because he just can't help himself anymore. He's got to make it all public. He's got to make them feel what he's been feeling. Give them that little massage that they've come to count on.

And not just his audience, but himself too.

That's the difference, you see. It's mutual, this *feeling* business. It goes in both directions, and it breaks down the integrity of the work by breaking down the integrity of the workman. By weakening him and making him needy.

Think of my mother. She could have been one of the greats, had she lived long enough. Had times been different. You'll have to take my word for that, as I believe I may have said, but it's true. My word should be sufficient. I think I've earned that. She could have been one of the greats, and even though her work was utterly and completely informed by a love for certain things and certain people—not to mention a love for beauty as if beauty were a thing itself, and a love for certain paintings and ways of painting and even ways of seeing that had gone before—although her work always sprang from love, as I was saying, it never, ever insisted that you must love it in return, or love her subjects in return, or love the artist herself in return, God forbid.

Never that. Not *Mama*.

An artist who makes that demand isn't an artist anymore, no matter what he accomplishes with paint or stone. He's a *masseuse*. And all he really wants is for you to rub his back in return.

Fourteen

IT ISN'T POSSIBLE THAT MAX has lost track. There can't be a selection this morning—the SS and the guards have been coming every second day, steady as a drumbeat, and they came again yesterday, he's certain—but the trucks are pulling up outside and the men are climbing out and the hospital door is bursting open and there they are. Everybody shrinks or runs as usual, everybody except Max and the French doctor, but something is different this time.

"Delousing," says the first of them through the door, that old skeleton of an officer. He stations himself beside the coal stove and waits grinning as his men go about their duties, some chasing prisoners who've run off into the latrine or vanished into a crawl space beneath the building, others stumbling in weighed down by machine guns, pressure tanks, and lengths of red rubber hose, gas masks dangling from leather straps around their necks. "Everyone up," says the officer, with a look toward Max that says he is excused from this as from everything else. The look also indicates that he would rip off the boy's forearm and impale him with it if he could, right through the heart, but that there will be no opportunity for such joys today. "Everyone up and out."

The door is wide open, and at a certain tilt of the officer's head his men throw open the windows as well, letting the weather pour in with a vengeance. The temperature was already perilously low, but in a heartbeat it drops another twenty or thirty degrees. "Lose your uniforms," says the skeleton, and the prisoners obey. "Blankets, everything. Mattresses. Pile it all by the door." His face bears testimony to his impatience and disgust. If only most of these men didn't have to be killed every other day, perhaps they could master the routine.

Two of them carry everything to a waiting wagon while the rest line up shivering along the walls. One or two collapse from the cold, hugging themselves with arms of bone, and one or two more are collapsed already, entirely unable to stand. These the officer directs to the waiting van, these and a handful more, chosen for reasons that no one—perhaps not even the officer himself—will ever know. They all pass through the door into the blowing weather, naked as they came into this world. They climb into the van and the van pulls away for the gas and the wagon pulls away for the laundry and the rest of the prisoners are chased outside and herded to the baths, the real baths, with real ice water instead of Zyklon-B, where they will spend the rest of the day waiting for the return of their deloused clothing. Some will die of exposure and some will simply die, and by evening the hospital will have been freshly supplied with openings for new patients, who will continue to arrive without ceasing.

Only Max stays behind as the van disappears and the guards chase the ambulatory few across the frozen ground, only Max and the French doctor, to wait outside the hospital walls while a team of men in gas masks go to work with their tanks and hoses.

*

It's like the old days, but neither Jacob nor Eidel knows. It's like the old days in Zakopane, when from time to time they would discover that a single thought had somehow settled upon both of their minds at once. It was as if they possessed only one mind between them, and one mind was enough. The thought could have been anything at all. A line of music. A desire for some favorite pastry from the *cukiernia*. A notion to bundle the children into their beds early and spend the evening together, just the two of them, either by the firelit hearth under a snowfall of blankets or out in the moonlit garden under a high canopy of stars, cradled all around, in either case, by a familiar ring of invisible mountains.

The thought that has invaded their minds now, and that links them across the gulf of time and distance and barbed wire that has come between them, is the unanswered question of Lydia's portrait. What on earth has become of it? Where in the world has it gone, if it's gone anywhere besides up the chimney? For one must of course consider the fireplace, after all. The fireplace is the first thing that a certain kind of person would think of for disposing of such an object, and they've endured exactly that kind of person for an eternity now.

Jacob tells himself that the remains of the painting weren't in the fireplace on Friday noon, but he can't be sure. Almost a week had gone by since Eidel had made whatever confession she'd made. Anything may have happened. A dozen fires had burned in the grate, the weather has been so blustery and bitter. Perhaps twice that many.

Such a quantity of ashes. So much smoke gone up the chimney. Each day, at work outdoors in Canada, he studies the gray skies as if he has missed the flight of the last bird.

Chaim has different ideas, though, and more practical ones. "She paid good money for that picture," he says. "They wouldn't have burned it."

"Then they've put it away," says Jacob. "They've stored it somewhere."

"I doubt that. I doubt that very much."

"In a crawlspace. In a cabinet in the basement. Somewhere."

"A painting of a Jew? It's bad enough that they're about to own a painting whose *artist* is a Jew, but they've gotten over that for the sake of their pride."

"Then they must have burned it," says Jacob. "They burn Jews. They certainly wouldn't flinch at burning a picture of one."

Chaim shakes his head, an old scholar with infinite wisdom to impart. "They don't burn us while we still have value," he says.

"Value." Jacob laughs out loud, right there in the open, by the side of the broad main street of the village of Auschwitz, shaven head and shivering frame and burlap uniform and all. People pause to stare. *This one has finally gone mad,* their looks say. *For months now we've permitted him to walk our streets, and in the end he's proven to be just another defective.*

Chaim lifts a quieting finger to his lips and urges Jacob along. "Value," he says. "Yes. You work, you live. That's the bargain."

*

Eidel closes the kitchen door behind her and wraps her arms around herself and hurries toward the gate, planning a second morning with the pencil and the sketch pad. She's not ready for anything further. She couldn't seem to get the composition right last week, and she'll have to try again. She's forgotten so much. She fears that she can't trust her own hands the way she once did. They've gone stiff and clumsy, thick with calluses and burned in places and incompletely healed where they've healed at all. To say nothing of the pressure that comes with this particular project. The only thing that ever depended on any of her old paintings, the paintings to which she had devoted so many hours of the life that she had before this one, was the capturing of a single moment in an endless river of moments: a window gathering light, a child at play, a sunrise. If she failed, another moment would come along soon enough.

It's no longer the case. Just one more lesson of the camp. Nothing endures.

The day is gray but slowly clearing and sleet has fallen overnight and the walks have been cleared but not perfectly. Her shoes are broken down, the heels in particular, and she must shuffle to keep from stepping out of them. She skitters rapidly but carefully across a thin scrim of ice, keeping her wits about her. Against the gray morning the windows of the shops are yellow with light that spills out thick as buttermilk, spreading across the walks but giving no warmth to an outsider.

The housekeeper greets her with a cautious enthusiasm. On the table in the entry hall is a new pencil sharpener in a box packed in wood shavings that it might have generated of its own will; perhaps this replacement has cost the housekeeper something and perhaps it hasn't, but either way she's learned that Eidel possesses some value in this equation.

She whispers that the family is already gathered in the dining room. She says they're quite eager to see what progress she might make today, giving her words a dark edge. Eidel scrapes her collapsed shoes on the mat one last time and goes in. There can be no delay. No slipping out of a coat, for she has no coat. No checking herself in the mirror, for her gray head is rimed with stubble and her poor slack face simply will not bear study.

The dining room still smells of breakfast. Grilled sausages, omelettes stuffed with cheese and peppers and onions, hot yeasty breads with butter. Each scent in the densely charged air stands out, like a pin stuck into the map of Eidel's deprivation. Even the dregs in the coffee cup that the *sturmbannführer* has just set down reach out to her. She dips her head and sits in the wobbly chair and takes up her sketch pad, daring at last to look at them. They've settled into a different arrangement this time, a tableau of their own invention that they no doubt believe

suits them better, and she decides that the time has come to stop inter-
fering and let them have their way. She might be hearing the familiar
voice of desperation, but on the other hand it might be the impulse of
her old art, making itself known through the acts of these willful monsters. Saying *leave well enough alone.* Saying *paint what there is and nothing more.* Saying *make of the world only what you can.*

The pencils have been freshly sharpened, every one of them, although by exactly whom she can't say. Perhaps it was another burden
laid upon the housekeeper. More penance if there was any penance to be
done. It doesn't matter. Her hands are frozen and her touch is all wrong
and the first point snaps the moment she touches it to the paper. A pistol shot couldn't have startled her more. She looks up at the family with
a fragile crystalline smile and sets the pencil down, rubbing her hands
together and blowing into the crevice between them.

"Perhaps some tea would warm you up," says Vollmer. "Or coffee, if
you'd like." The *sturmbannführer* himself, smiling and solicitous. Finding
himself in need, and catering to another's need as a result.

"Yes, sir. Please. That would be a great help."

"Coffee, then? Or tea?" He tilts back on his chair and steadies himself with one hand on his son's shoulder and reaches back with the other
to rap on the kitchen door, bringing the housekeeper on the run.

"Either one," she says. It's all too much.

"But you must choose," he says. There is a threat in his command,
although he might not intend it that way. There is a threat in everything.

She chooses coffee, coffee inspired by the fragrant dregs that have
called out to her since she entered. The housekeeper produces a cup of it
in no time, lighting the stove and reheating a potful that has gone cold
and would otherwise have vanished down the drain.

"Sugar?" says Vollmer. "Cream?" Holding the housekeeper in the doorway by the power of a sideways glance. Sugar. Cream. It's plain that nothing is too good for the artist. Unless he's testing her again, if he was testing her the first time. Forcing a decision.

Poor Eidel. A teaspoonful of sugar is a good deal more nourishment than she would otherwise see today, and a treat that she hasn't enjoyed since she can't remember when. Certainly long before she arrived at the camp. The very last sugar she recalls encountering was scraped from the bottom of a canister in some rented apartment in a village whose name she might as well have never heard for all she can remember, scraped up and stirred into a cup of tea for Lydia, who was catching cold. *Cream*, though. Cream is beyond imagining. She nearly goes dizzy imagining the fattiness of it, the smooth tactile embrace of its touch upon her tongue. It would be too much to endure, she decides, steadying herself in that wobbly chair with her back to the void above the fireplace, the intoxicating scent of coffee swimming in her head. She might not be able to endure the richness of cream. It might curdle in her stomach and then where would she be.

"Just a little sugar," she says. "Please. If it isn't too much trouble."

*

Two more weeks and the cast will come off. Max is restless. He wants to go home from the hospital, if you could call it home. Back to the block, anyway, and back to work or something like it. Something invisible. He feels like a living target here, loafing in the bed reading dusty German medical textbooks to the French doctor, translating everything on the fly into their mutual Polish. Every other morning the skeletal officer arrives with his wagon and his van and his squadron of brutes, and every time the selection is finished Max feels that he's narrowly escaped some particularly inhuman punishment that's building up inside the man like a head of steam inside a boiler. He wonders how long his protection will last, for it certainly can't last forever. His mother must be making some progress on that painting. She's always worked fast. If only she knew the trade that she was making—her days for his—perhaps she'd go slowly, take her time, stretch things out. Maybe even make a few false starts. But she can't know, and so she must be making good progress.

Night has come and the only light in the hospital block is a faint pulsing glow from the little coal stove. He sits in darkness listening to the man in the next bed struggling for breath—he's a crooked little gray man of indeterminate age and he's dying of something, perhaps of everything, breathing now with a sad and heroic effort as if life is a physical thing that he's chasing across a vast empty space—and against his better judgment he pictures his mother at work in the *sturmbannführer's* apartment. He imagines the terror with which she must approach each visit, the fear that surely lies behind every brushstroke, the anxiety that no doubt threatens to subvert her God-given talent at every turn. And he hates himself. He hates himself for his broken leg and his unwitting need, and he hates himself because she can't know that she's going through all this on his account. And because she would do it anyway, if she knew.

He wonders if he'll be sent straight back to work on the water project, of if some other work has materialized in the meantime. Anything will be better than staying here, out in the open ward with that skeletal officer arriving to size him up every second day. It's like being fitted for a coffin, if these people hadn't give up on coffins a long time ago.

*

Chaim has made some inquiries, put out some feelers, tugged on a few slender silken threads. People owe him favors. People actually *want* to owe him favors. And so there are men both inside and outside the camp, men of the highest rank and men of the lowest rank and men of no particular rank whatsoever, who have been keeping their eyes open for any sign of that lost painting.

Counterfeits have actually begun to appear, counterfeits and rumors of counterfeits. Childish drawings on rough paper and lithographs purloined from living room walls and images torn straight out of magazines, folded or rolled up or elaborately framed beneath window glass. Stuff found and stuff stolen and stuff made to order, and every scrap of it worthless. It's all that Chaim can do to keep up. It's all that Jacob can do to continue hearing stories that begin with such hope and end with such disappointment. He curses the Nazis for inventing Auschwitz. He curses God for permitting his family to be brought here. He curses himself for allowing the picture of Lydia to kindle in his heart some sense of hope and continuity in a world where such things are willfully murdered every day. As each week passes and Friday morning comes again and they meet in the kitchen where Chaim shrugs and frowns like a stage comedian miming disappointment, his heart sinks further, until at last there's no lower point to which it can go. The girl is gone. The picture is gone. The love with which her mother created it has been brought low and repudiated and crushed dead under the boot-heel of time and history.

But today Chaim isn't frowning. On the contrary. He's bouncing. Checking the stacked towels and adjusting the flame underneath the kettle and bouncing.

"I've got a lead," he says.

"A lead." Jacob grips the back of the makeshift barber chair.

"Two leads, really."

Jacob's shakes his head. "Perfect. A matched set of false trails. The usual dead ends, then."

"No," says the boy. "These are anything but. They point to the same thing." He has no patience with Jacob's despair. It might be infectious, and at his age he can't afford to be contaminated. He unfolds the white drape and spreads it over the back of a chair and comes around to look Jacob in the eye. "Two different sources tell me it's back in the antique shop."

"Who?"

"It doesn't matter who."

"The antique shop."

"Correct. Right where Frau Vollmer got it in the first place. Do you remember?"

"Of course I remember. So your sources have seen it there?"

"Not exactly. But people hear things. People tell people things. Word gets around."

Jacob lifts the drape and snaps it. "You'll forgive me for not getting my hopes up," he says. "People tell people lies."

"Not this time."

"People tell people what they want to hear."

"No. It's in the shop. Trust me."

"Then how do we get it?"

"*Get it?*" says Chaim. "You never said anything about getting it."

A distant door swings open and the clamor of pots and pans in the kitchen hushes at the entry of the first officer of the day.

"There's no getting it," says Chaim.

"Use your imagination," says Jacob, his words the only sound in the kitchen other than the whistling of steam and the officer's footsteps approaching across the tile floor. "You're the one with the ideas, with the connections. Prove to me that the world isn't the terrible place I think it is. That there's one small spot of light left within it."

Chaim bows his head. He has the look of an individual who's been attempting to do just that. He brightens though, eagerly and reflexively, altogether pathetic in his instant enthusiasm, when the SS officer steps into their little corner for his haircut.

*

Eidel has stretched and prepared the canvas and begun to apply paint. She works roughly at first, laying down great deep pools of color, a churning blue-black mass from which it seems nothing particular could ever possibly emerge. It's the fierce dead darkness at the edge of the universe.

After a while Karl and Luzi break away from their parents and come to see what she's been doing. The looks on their faces give away their consternation. The boy squints. The girl picks up a page from the sketchbook and turns it this way and that, trying to reconcile the outlines drawn upon it with what she sees on the easel.

"Oh-ho," says their father, rising up and straightening the crease in his pantlegs and coming near. "Unless I miss my guess, the two of you are in for an art lesson." He hasn't been smiling before, perhaps because Eidel is a long way from painting his face and perhaps because he plans not to let the least bit of kindness soften his image for all eternity, but he's definitely smiling now, at the children and at their befuddlement. "This is called *underpainting*," he tells them. "It's all about building up the oils in layers. They'll ultimately take on great depth and mystery—just like real life. Things behind other things. Hints of the invisible."

If the prisoner standing six inches away from him with the loaded brush in her hand has anything to add, she doesn't say. He goes on at length, boring the children and the painter alike, now and then begging her to *go on, proceed, don't let me stop you* even though the quality of the light in the corner where the family had arranged themselves has changed utterly without his presence and the children's. Now it's just Madame Vollmer and a thick blue-green curtain the color of an angry sea, along with a bright gilded chair only one arm of which will appear in the final portrait. Eidel can't go on. She can't conjure a real world out of an imagined one, but she smiles and nods and pushes some paint around as if she can.

A strong wind kicks up outside and rattles the shutters and Madame Vollmer moves the curtain aside to look out. As she does so a burst of light streams in through the window, and all is lost. Eidel would beg her to please let go of the curtain, but it's already too late. The woman has spoiled everything. They've all spoiled everything. Even after the *sturmbannführer* and his children have returned to their places, Eidel can still see that burst of unbidden light, can still imagine it boiling behind the thick folds of the sea-green curtain, a thing unseen behind things seen. Something in her mind wants to scrape the canvas raw, take it back down to nothing, and begin again with this other knowledge, with the intrusion of the bright white day behind the blue-green shadow, but she can't do that either. The brightness behind everything is gone. It's just an illusion. Worse. It's the memory of an illusion. And her fate is to move forward in the world as it is.

She resolves to rough in the shapes of her four subjects, but it's difficult. Referring to the sketchpad doesn't help. It's as if she can't quite see these people, even though they're seated only ten feet away. The harder she tries the harder it is, and she wonders if something has gone wrong in her brain, if this is a sign of some failure of the optic nerve brought about by malnutrition or overwork or exhaustion. She shakes her head and rubs her eyes with the back of her hand, but that doesn't help. So she stalls, turning away and mixing paint. And then she loads her brush with a thick greenish black and chooses a fold in the curtain above Vollmer's head and paints the smooth subtle drape of it in a single sinuous stroke that has about it the power of conjury. Reality on the canvas. So it's not her vision after all, and it's not her brain. It's something else.

All she can do is fall back on technique, trusting that the details will emerge from the process if not from the intent. And so she proceeds, choosing colors mechanically, ignoring the treacherous light that pulses behind the curtain and ignoring her own inability to see Vollmer and his wife and their children with any kind of clarity. Just working.

The wind is still pounding on the house when she's done all she can for the morning, and after she's packed away her things and made her way to the entry hall Madame Vollmer approaches. She opens a closet door and pushes aside more coats than a family of four could possibly wear in a lifetime and emerges with a short jacket of light gray wool. "Why don't you take this old thing?" she says.

"Oh, Madame Vollmer," says Eidel. "You're far too kind."

The woman holds up the jacket. It's of an elegant cut and barely worn, and although there was a time when it would have fit Eidel perfectly—she can see now that she and the lady of the house are similarly built—at this point it will wrap around her twice. That, she decides, will make it warmer.

Max

FAILURE TO EXPAND YOUR HORIZONS is a terrible thing, in an artist or in anybody. It's the closest thing there is to death, I think. It might even be worse than death. It's death in life.

And if anybody knows something about death in life, it's me.

I say listen to Ezra Pound: *Make it new.* Don't worry. I'm not going to start talking about poetry. I've got enough to keep me busy in my own back yard. Too much, if I want to stay on track. You want an example? All right, here you go: *Don't get me started on Jackson Pollock.* Just don't get me started. Honestly. When a man can put on his workboots and walk all over a wet canvas and then convince people that that's art, there's something wrong with him and there's something bigger wrong with the people who buy what he's selling. That doesn't even need to be said.

People disagree as to whether I've always followed my own advice. As to whether I've always worked at making things new. Isn't that a kick in the head? People are out there judging the things you've done by the standards you've set and they can't even agree on the outcome. These are the same people who paid big money for Jackson Pollock's footprints, remember. The very same people. So don't take them too seriously.

That tattooed girl from the National Gallery, though? Her head's screwed on pretty straight in that particular department. I gave her a little test one time. I showed her some of my pictures on cards—all mixed up and out of order, some of them from when I'd just gotten to the states and nobody knew who I was and some of them from the last six months and some of them from in between—and she surprised me. She put them pretty much in order, no sweat, even a few that almost nobody'd ever seen.

In other words, I must have been keeping it new all these years. I must have been going through some kind of traceable evolution.

I wonder one thing, though. I wonder where she'd have slotted the paintings I keep down in the locker.

Fifteen

EIDEL REPORTS BACK TO WORK, wearing that light woolen jacket. Saturday is a day like any other here in the kitchen—she marks the Sabbath only by her visit to Vollmer's apartment—and the women are working like coal miners over the little bit of food that they've been given to prepare. Making it go around, even to the poor extent that it does, is heroic work. Beans and ashy flour and an onion or two will stretch only so far. Passing through the door as she does on these occasions, when the air is warmed by the heat of the stoves and the counters have been scoured clean of every trace of breakfast and the work of preparing the next meal is well under way, the place seems to her more like a factory than a kitchen. She could swear in these moments that the food coming from it isn't merely prepared by these broken individuals but actually created by them, created out of nothing, out of the sheer power of their will, out their very sacrificed bodies.

Rolak is standing inside the door, leaning on her poker, picking her teeth with a long sliver of wood. "You're late," she says.

"I'm sorry," says Eidel, bowing her head. Atonement is a reflex by now, complete and instant, although she does keep an eye on the poker.

"So where were you?" says Rolak.

So that's it, Eidel thinks. *She's forgotten it's Saturday.* "I was with the *sturmbannführer,*" she says. Some other woman in some other place might speak these words like the incantation that they ought to be, but Eidel knows better. Every capo is doomed to bring herself low sooner or later, it's a law of nature, and angering Vollmer by murdering his portrait artist with a fireplace poker could easily be the fate that lies in store for Rolak. So she says the words softly, without hubris or even pride, without the slightest indication that they should form not merely an explanation but something on the order of a pardon. They are hardly words at all.

Rolak shifts her weight on the poker, but she doesn't raise it. Beyond Eidel's field of vision the long damp sliver of wood comes from between the capo's teeth to pelt her shoulder and fall to the floor, but nothing else happens. Eidel lifts her eyes slowly and sees Rolak propped sagging on the poker, her weight her burden. No wonder she doesn't use a cane made of wood. She'd need a table leg.

"I know all about the *sturmbannführer,*" Rolak says as their eyes meet. The other women in the kitchen go about their business, frail little Gretel included, as if nothing whatsoever is happening. As if by ignoring whatever may be about to unfold they may save themselves from being caught up in it. As if Eidel's fate is a whirlpool in which they fear being drowned.

"Yes," says Eidel, looking at the floor again. "Of course you do."

"So where have you been since?" The tip of the poker lifts from the floor and hovers in the air. It must take great effort on the capo's part.

"Nowhere. I came straight here."

"You came straight here." The tip lowers again, bumping the floor, perhaps an inch closer and perhaps not.

"Yes. As fast as I could."

"Then you need to come faster."

"Yes, capo. Yes. I will."

"You will."

"I give you my word," says Eidel.

"I don't want your word." The tip of the poker rises again and this time it most definitely swings forward, the capo taking a step behind it.

Eidel has no answer for her. She can only wait.

The poker swings like a pendulum and the capo takes one more step, the poker now close enough that Eidel could lean on it herself. If she were to collapse from anxiety or panic or a heart attack she would fall straight down upon it to no good end. For whether the poker strikes the woman or the woman strikes the poker, the result will always be the same. "Do you hear me?" says the capo.

"Yes. I hear you."

"Good," says the capo. "I don't want your word. What I want is your coat."

"Of course," says Eidel, unwrapping it and slipping it off. The kitchen already feels colder.

The jacket, with its soft gray wool and its narrow cut, drapes over Rolak's broad shoulders like a prayer shawl. Owning it pleases her, that much is plain—Eidel can imagine her in the storeroom, posing before her reflection in some shiny surface that might distort her figure into something that passes for a human being—and the capo stumps off down the hall with her poker, satisfied. Calling over her shoulder that Eidel should bring her something else next Saturday. Surely the *sturmbannführer's* apartment is crammed with riches.

*

Gretel has finally gotten her hands on another bottle. It's a jar, actually, with a wide round mouth and a slab of old wood worn into a rough circle that fits the opening more or less. The jar was empty when she found it except for a little dirt and some bits of straw and the partial shell of a plover egg. It could have been a collection that some child was keeping or it could have been the remains of a nest, but either way—whether it signifies a life cut short or a life begun or both—it's hers now and she begins putting it to use.

Eidel has given her a fresh pencil and some little scraps of paper stolen from the supply in the *sturmbannführer's* apartment, a tiny cache of untellable worth. The paper she tears into smaller pieces rather than risk growing careless in the face of such wealth. The pencil is so precious that she gnaws a notch into the middle of it with her front teeth and breaks it in half; that way if she loses it she won't have lost everything. She keeps one half in her pocket and the other half in a crevice in the wall, packed in behind a makeshift masonry of sawdust and spit that she checks and renews every night if she has the strength. Such rituals preserve life and hope, if life and hope can be preserved at all.

The jar fills up quickly. She remembers that she hasn't written down Eidel's story yet, the story of how the Nazis took from her both her family and her art, and she regrets that the narrative has grown more complex while she's delayed getting it down. If she plans to make a full account now, she'll have to include the subversion of the poor woman's skills to the heartless vanity of that wicked Vollmer. This is the way it always goes. Complication folds in upon complication, tragedy unfurls from tragedy. A great collapse and a great blooming forth, all in one perpetual instant. She can never hope to keep up.

Haunted, she awakens in the middle of the night. Sleep is always elusive, and prisoners who manage to capture it for any length of time do so knowing that they may never wake up at all. It's a risk, for the boundaries are thin between one state of consciousness and another, between life and death, between dream and doom. But on this particular occasion she's been sleeping soundly—without any particular dreams that she can recall—when she's roused up with infinite slowness by the sound of scratching. It's furtive and faint, and it's not a noise made by any rat or mouse. Rats and mice are rare here in the camp, especially in the cold months, for their status as scavenging omnivores has been co-opted by far more desperate creatures higher up the food chain.

No. It's the sound of a pencil point on wood. She's certain of it. She doesn't worry that it might be her own pencil, fallen somehow into other hands—she doesn't worry because she can feel one half of hers grinding into her hip against the hard bunk, and she can see from the corner of one eye that the sawdust concealing the other half is still intact—but it's a pencil for sure. She lies still listening for a while, not willfully but because movement is nearly impossible in the tightly packed bunk, and as long as she listens the sound keeps up, one scratch after another. Long strokes with long intervals between them and shorter strokes coming in rapid little flurries. It isn't the sound of writing. After a while she's sure of that. Cursive writing would be steadier, more even. Lettering would be more staccato. So it's neither. She decides instead that she's listening to someone who's drawing a picture.

A different woman might be able to push her bunkmates aside and roll over, but Gretel is too small and too weak. She's wedged in tight, lying on one side where she takes up the minimum amount of space, and the sound of the scratching is coming from behind her and above. She stretches her neck until the bones threaten to snap, but the farthest she can see is the patch of wall where she's hidden her pencil. The scratching goes on. Light comes in through cracks—the familiar darting of search-lights, known but not entirely predictable, a photonic equivalent of the cruelty that's everywhere. She begins to edge herself around, the friction of her body against the bodies to the left and the right enormous, her fear that any noise she makes will cause the user of the pencil to abandon her work, but her need to witness overcoming everything nonetheless.

She already knows who the artist will be. She knows who would have access to a pencil and who would be working away on a drawing here in the middle of the night. It can only be Eidel. Eidel, whose art until now has been to her nothing but a rumor, a fairy tale, a secondhand memory. Eidel, whose talent she'll finally have the opportunity to see for herself, provided she's quiet enough.

She wonders what she's drawing on the low ceiling of the bunk. Her daughter, perhaps. Yes, of course. Lydia. That's it. She's bringing the child back to life. How deep her love must be, to possess such power! How great her gift must be, to carry such a burden! Gretel marvels, straining every muscle and edging herself another fraction of an inch closer to seeing the miracle for herself. The beam of a searchlight rakes the darkness, nearly blinding her for a heartbeat, coursing past and blinking out for a fraction of a fraction of a second as the artist's up-thrust arm severs it for an instant and then blinking back on and then disappearing. She's close now.

It's an effort like giving birth, and no doubt with a similar outcome. She'll see the child, Eidel's beloved, restored to the world.

One more push and she's there. She tilts her head back and to the side and focuses her eyes as the fragmentary beams of the searchlights slash the darkness, but when the image above grows clear it's not the child after all. There are four creatures up there, heavy creatures arranged in a tableau, their ragged outlines hatched by way of shading. Black graphite on black wood. In some places the outlines have been drawn so ferociously that the pencil lead has cut into the wood and left behind more white than black.

Gretel can't make out many specifics. The drawing is still just a sketch, hastily and furiously done, but the fierce vitality of the lines has already brought it to a kind of ghastly life. Studying it she thinks of the golem of Prague, raised up from mud in defense of the Jews. She thinks of how Rabbi Judah Loew ben Bezalel set the terrifying thing on their attackers, and how its murderous rage grew beyond all proportion, and how the Emperor himself finally begged to be granted mercy. And she remembers how the rabbi accomplished that one final miracle by rubbing out a single letter on the creature's forehead, turning the word "Reality" into the word "Death."

They say that the lifeless husk of the golem is stored to this day in the attic of the synagogue, ready to be brought to life again by a single penstroke.

And this, Gretel decides, is what Eidel is doing. She's creating a family of golems to replace her own family, raising up monsters to avenge her loss. At least she still believes in something. It's difficult, though, to draw a clear line between belief and insanity. At least here in the camp.

*

Weeks go by and Max grows comfortable with a crutch, but the French doctor won't let him leave the hospital. He's filed his reports and that's the answer he's received. Another week goes by and the cast comes off and the doctor still won't release him. "I've been told to take no chances," he says. "You must build up your strength. You must exercise."

Max is without doubt the only Jew in the world whose health the Reich actually cares about at this moment. At least it means his mother is still at work for the *sturmbannführer,* which means she's still enjoying a few hours each week in a warm and comfortable apartment building, which means—at the very bottom of it all—that she's still among the living. That alone is reason enough for him to rejoice.

Another week goes by and the doctor files another report, and this time he receives authorization to let him go. At first Max fears that some terrible fate has befallen his mother, but on hobbling back to the block and joining his father in the line for rations he learns otherwise. Her work goes on. Jacob has actually seen the painting with his own eyes, and it's a thing of great power, and she seems to be in no hurry whatsoever to finish it.

Wenzel comes down the line with a rare and menacing sort of off-handedness in his manner, sauntering along with his hands jammed into the pockets of his trousers, heading in Max's direction. He walks as if he's here by chance, but he's never in all his life been anywhere by chance. Jacob sees him coming and whispers to his son *enough about your mother*, and Max understands. He breaks off and heads for the back of the line, jolting along on the crutch as if his leg hurts more than it does, as if a person could excuse his having forgotten the rituals of the block after an absence of such length. He'll learn, his departure says. He'll fit in once again.

But the capo keeps coming. When Wenzel's hand claps down on his shoulder Max tenses and spins on the crutch, the leg hurting every bit as much as he's been pretending it does, and under the assault of the pain he very nearly collapses. It's as if Wenzel's hand weighs a thousand pounds and he seeks to crush him with it. "Forgive me," Max says, wincing and putting one hand to the place above his knee where the bone went through. "I didn't mean to break into the line."

"Think nothing of it!" says Wenzel. "I was going to bring you forward myself!"

Max looks at him the way he'd look at a talking chimpanzee. He can't help himself.

But the capo doesn't notice. "Come along," he says, his hand sliding down from shoulder to elbow. "No need to put off your recuperation!"

So Wenzel has gotten the message too. Max wonders how. A direct order, the grapevine, no one can say. He might not even know the specifics—how it all has to do with Max's mother—for if he did, wouldn't he be just as solicitous of Jacob? Wouldn't he? God only knows.

The capo walks him along as if the two of them are going up the aisle. Endlessly patient, uttering a word of encouragement now and then, keeping his voice low. As they draw nearer to Jacob he indicates him with his free hand and whispers to Max, "Perhaps you've heard that your assignment has been changed. You've been given a position in Canada. That's right. Canada, with your father. Side by side. It will be like a family business."

Good news. More good news. So much good news that as Wenzel sweeps aside the last few men and hands him a bowl and personally selects with his own fingers the largest and leanest scrap of fatty pork in the pot, Max doesn't notice how the other men are assessing him. How ravenous they are.

*

They're walking to Canada on the first day, and Chaim appears out of nowhere. His short legs ordinarily work double-time to keep up with Jacob, but today Max's crutch and the rutted ground have brought their pace to a crawl.

"The painting," says Chaim.

"What about it?"

"It's definitely in the antique shop."

"You're sure."

"I spoke to someone who knows for sure. Frau Vollmer returned it herself."

"So it hasn't been destroyed."

"No."

Max gives his father a hopeful look, but his father doesn't return it.

"As far as we're concerned," Jacob says to both of them, "it may as well be."

"But I had another idea," says Chaim.

"And that would be?"

"Buy it. Buy it fair and square."

Jacob coughs and spits on the icy ground. "In case you haven't noticed," he says, "we're not exactly rich men."

"People owe me this and that," says Chaim. "You know."

"I'd rather not owe you as well," says Jacob.

"Never mind that," says Chaim. "Nobody owes me quite enough, as it turns out. You see, now that your painting has hung in Vollmer's apartment, the price has gone sky high."

"But Vollmer didn't want it."

"That doesn't matter."

"Vollmer *hated* it."

"Who cares? Provenance is everything."

"Provenance. You pick up the most curious information."

"I pick up what I can pick up," says Chaim. "You never know when something's going to be useful."

They've neared the corner where they'll need to separate, Jacob and Max keeping on for Canada and Chaim turning off. Guards stand to the left and the right but they're occupied with the tricky business of lighting cigarettes in a cold wind, so the three pause for just a moment. Jacob frowns and chews his lip and studies the sky. Max slumps, only the crutch holding him up. Jacob says he's learned to live without the paint-ing before. He supposes he can learn to live without it again.

Chaim shakes his head. "You shouldn't have to do anything of the sort," he says. "Maybe we can figure out a way to steal it, instead."

*

Eidel works slowly, not for any selfish reason but because she must. Her pace is a product of her uncertainty, but as the weeks go by the figures of the Vollmer family do begin to emerge from the depths of that blue cur-tain, resolving into a kind of life that she'd never thought she'd manage. By and by the weather beyond the window turns brighter and a little springlike, but the thick curtain excludes any such change from the twin sealed universes of the painting and the dining room. When she enters each Saturday morning, stepping into that little hallway redolent of cin-namon and sausage, she goes straight to the dining room to draw the curtain tight against the day. She pauses sometimes to look out the win-dow, out over certain low buildings and fences and underbrush, into the middle distance where the camp lies like some treacherous thing sleep-ing. Only the smoke from the crematoria moves in the bright air, heav-enward if there were a heaven. She watches the change of the seasons and she fears that by taking so much time she's captured something false in the painting. It's taken her too long. Things are different. The girl Luzi is taller than when they started. The boy Karl is heavier, more filled out, although he was plenty filled out before. The result of too much sausage, she thinks. Karl is practically made of sausage. Overstuffed and slow, lazy in his movements.

If there were any consistency in the judgment of the Reich, someone would send him off to the gas as unsuited for work.

The painting itself, though. Sometimes she hates herself for granting this family of monsters a thing so fine, whatever the reason. Even with a gun to her head. They should have been satisfied with the picture of Lydia. As she nears the end of each morning's session and as the sun creeps around the building and begins to illuminate the family from over her shoulder, she thinks she understands what Vollmer saw in that painting. Not its evocation of a time and a place. Not its attempt to capture the sweet and hopeful soul of a young girl. But the resemblance that Lydia, with those caramel highlights on her sunshot hair, bore to his own daughter.

Each time her mind begins to travel down that path she knows that the time has come to leave off for the day. Stopping is the only way she can go on. So she purses her lips and squints at the paint on the easel and pushes some last little dab of it around, sighing and saying that although she would like to get more done this morning, the pigment must have its way.

It's the only power she has.

*

"This is not a game," says Jacob to Chaim. They're alone in the corner of the kitchen, late on a Friday morning, in between customers. "You talk about taking the painting as if it were something we could actually accomplish. As if we'd know what to do it with it if we had it."

"The war won't last forever."

"That's a comfort," Jacob says, passing the blade of a straight razor over a rough leather strop. "I won't last forever, either."

Chaim is pushing a broom, and he stops to look up at the barber. He's grown some in the last few months as well. He's noticeably taller but he's no more filled out—or at least not much. Jacob wonders how long a child like Chaim will be able to work his magic in this place, once he's a child no more.

"Don't worry," says the boy. "We'll find someplace to keep it. That's the least of our troubles."

"We'll find someplace like where?"

"Like the attic over the Officers' Club. The waiters keep things up there you could never imagine. Bottles of schnapps. Big wheels of cheese from Switzerland. Champagne, even. Real live French Champagne."

"Champagne."

"I'm telling you the truth. I've seen it with my own eyes."

"How do they get such things?"

"The same way we'll get your painting. They steal them."

"And the officers don't notice?"

"The officers have been known to look the other way. It's either that or train new waiters. Waiters who might turn out to be even bigger thieves than the ones they already have."

The idea strikes Jacob like a blow. Here he is with a straight razor in his hand, paralyzed in the manner of old dead Schuler, yearning to take the sharp edge of it to the neck of some high-ranking officer but stayed by the enormity of the consequences. For Schuler's understanding was true: the murder of one such as Liebehenschel or Vollmer, or of some lesser functionary like Drexler or even that ridiculous officer with the bicycle, would take a thousand men and women in its wake. Ten thousand, if the SS could manage to kill that many that fast. They're already doing their best, and it's hard work with certain intractable realities about it—the irreducible physicality of bodies to be disposed of, for example, a business that takes time and fuel no matter how you approach it. So Jacob is dizzied, at least for a moment, by the notion that he and the rest of the prisoners may be actually holding the Nazis in a kind of reciprocal but unequal stasis. Why find another barber, when you already have the deferential Jacob Rosen? Why not offer a special kindness to Max, when it keeps his mother content behind her easel?

"We could store it there, you think?" he says.

"Until the war's over," says Chaim. "Or until somebody comes to tear this place down."

"The Messiah, I suppose."

"Sure," says the boy. "The Messiah. Or else the Russians."

Later, after they've trimmed every neck in the Administration Building and proceeded into the town and made their way to the commandant's villa down the road and found him too drunk to sit up straight in his chair (the housekeeper, deaf as the rumors always promised she was, seemed unaware of the man's condition in spite of the volume at which the old songs—*Ab in den Süden, Fuerstenfeld, Skandal im Sperrbezirk*—rang out from his study), after they've stolen a choice morsel of roast beef from beneath the nose of the squint-eyed U-boat cook who's too busy having a cigar out in the ruined kitchen garden to notice, they return to Canada.

Jacob finds his son without his crutch, leaning against a table, sorting children's clothes. Max has a tear in his eye but it's not for the pain in his leg and it's not even for his own lost sister. It's for every lost child there is. Children not much younger than he but smaller and therefore less fortunate, should you consider an early exit from this place under whatever terms unfortunate. He's beginning to wonder. Jacob gets a curt nod from Jankowski, out patrolling the margins of this place like some slow engine of destruction, and he goes to help the boy.

"What's happened to your crutch?" he says.

Max keeps his mouth shut and tilts his head toward the fire that burns in the middle of the yard. Gray smoke rises in the afternoon air and collects like a thunderhead beneath the partial roof.

"Who did this?"

Max tilts his head toward the capo, who's just now vanishing through the door.

"Doesn't he know? Doesn't he know you have a protector?"

"Maybe he knows, maybe he doesn't. Maybe he resents it like the rest of them, Papa."

"Let them resent you. Resentment doesn't matter." Jacob picks up a pair of trousers suited to a child of no more than four or five years old, shakes them out, and folds them tenderly before putting them in the pile.

"It matters if I don't have a protector after all," says Max.

"Your mother is still painting."

"It's been three weeks since I left the hospital, Papa. Three or four."

"She's still painting."

"Maybe Vollmer has forgotten about me. Maybe he forgot about me the minute I left the hospital. Maybe there's nothing to this *protector* business."

"I'd prefer to believe that there is."

"We'll see, Papa. We'll see."

Max

I GAVE UP ON GOD, as did so many.

It was easier for me than it was for a lot of them. I'd never been especially religious. I'd never been all that attached to the synagogue. I was just a boy, remember, and in the years before the camp I'd been more of an outdoor type than a religious scholar. I guess I was an Animist by nature if I was anything at all, which meant that while I was in the death camp I missed the Carpathians more than I missed the Almighty.

Blessed be He.

Old habits die hard, you see, but they're just habits. Just habits, in the end.

I remember men who would cry out in the night, though, hammering at the wood of their bunks and hammering at their own chests, struggling to understand how their God had forsaken them. They'd have torn at their clothes if they'd been dressed in anything other than rags already and if a man couldn't have been shot for destroying the property of the Reich. The racket was all around me some nights, lamentation on an ancient and biblical scale, and all it did was keep me awake.

I don't remember my father going through it. I don't think he thought about God much. He was too busy worrying about my mother and me.

Sixteen

GRETEL HOLDS OFF ON TELLING Eidel's story until she's gotten a good look at the picture she's inscribing into the ceiling of the bunk. So she works on other things whenever she has a spare moment. Writing down the stories other women have told her, and searching for a likely place to hide the new jar that she's nearly filled up already. The secret place behind the block where the water drains from the roof has proven to be a problem. She passed it last week and caught from the corner of her eye a glint of the old vinegar bottle, which apparently wasn't buried deeply enough. Snowmelt had washed away gravel and undermined some of the earth beneath it and left a bit of glass exposed. She must get to that, too. She must cover the bottle again, before it's discovered and dug out and emptied and all of her work comes to nothing. Her testimony scattered, reduced to a thing no more credible or lasting than birdsong.

One morning she awakens long before the three alarm bells, flat on her back, Eidel asleep beside her. It's dark, darker than midnight, since the beams of the searchlights move more lackadaisically at this early hour of the morning. Even the guards are weary. She lets her eyes adjust, listening to the breathing of the women around her and listening to Rolak beginning to stir in her compartment and knowing that the day will begin soon. And in the few minutes that she has, she manages to get a good look at the drawing overhead. At the thing that has been occupying Eidel for the last weeks.

The figures aren't human after all, or not entirely. They're strange and terrifying and highly particular, creatures called up from a very specific nightmare. Two larger and two smaller, the larger pair alongside one another and one of the smaller ones fitted in between them and the other one seated on a lap. The largest of them is some kind of demon, perhaps a demon whose function is to torment lesser demons, perhaps even Satan himself, his curved teeth arrayed in a great gaping grin, his twisted horns thrust up and out like the horns of a ram, his enormous wings unfurled into black curtains. Beside him sits his bride, for this one is without question a bride, clothed in a wedding dress whose ironic whiteness would be a triumph of technique if only Gretel knew how to perceive it. The face beneath her cunningly invoked veil is a mask of bottomless hunger, and her hands where they jut from the lace of her sleeves are a pair of bony talons, bloody and made for grasping. One clutches a child, a girl, the most human of these creatures and therefore the most horrifying. She has an unfinished look about her, the look of something brought from the womb too hastily and for the wrong reasons. Gretel can't look at her too closely. Besides, her attention is drawn to the figure in the middle, the figure that to judge by his bundhosen and his stiff white shirt must represent a boy. This one is neither a monster like its father nor a revenant like its dam nor an ill-formed atrocity like its misshapen little sister. This one is a pig. Plain and simple. It's a young German boy incarnated as both the unthinkable and the untouchable. *Trefe.* And he, even more than the rest of his family, looks deeply proud of what he's become.

Gretel has seen enough, and for a change the dawnshattering shriek of the alarm bells comes as a relief.

*

So this is how Eidel maintains her sanity: painting one truth by day, and drawing a different one by night. The truth of technique on one hand

and the truth of the heart on the other, neither one of which she can hope to alter in the least.

In the apartment, Vollmer only encourages her. He slips around behind the easel at the close of each session and studies her work while she cleans up, admiring the day's progress and praising what she's accomplished. Over time he seems almost to forget that she's a prisoner exactly, and to see her instead as a kind of vessel or passageway or conduit for something else, something greater than either one of them. Call it art or call it the will of God.

His daughter presses him on the point one day, just after he's swept an indicating hand along the curve of a particular line, asking him how it is that a Jew might create something that he would praise so highly. She asks with the simplicity and innocence of any child, and with the directness that comes from knowing that the person before whom she's asking the question doesn't qualify as a person at all.

The answer is obvious, her father says: "God, not man, is the creator. God works in mysterious ways, and quite often He selects the least of us to perform His greatest miracles. Witness this beautiful painting. Witness this lowly Jew."

Eidel dares to watch him from beneath her eyebrows. There's nothing kind in what he says, nothing humane, beyond how it permits her to very nearly vanish from her own story. In the camp, invisibility may be the greatest gift of all.

Vollmer bends to tousle his daughter's yellow hair. "Remember this lesson," he says, "should you ever doubt the power of the Almighty."

*

"The problem," says Max, "isn't just getting out. It's getting back in again."

"They're *both* problems."

The two are in the lineup for roll call, waiting while Wenzel flips through some papers on his clipboard. The instant he looks up they'll have to stop whispering, but the look of consternation on his downcast face suggests that they have a moment. Other men talk, too, and Wenzel doesn't mind. He's the only capo in the camp who wouldn't, no doubt about that. He tolerates a little fraternization, as he calls it, as long as the prisoners observe limits. As long as they snap to attention when the time comes.

Some of the prisoners maintain that this studied laxity of Wenzel's is going to get him shot one day—probably sooner rather than later—but as long as the work keeps getting done he remains untouched if not untouchable. No one is untouchable.

"Right," says Max. "They're both problems. Getting in and getting out. That's what's got me thinking."

"Thinking what?"

"That you and Chaim should do it together."

Jacob can't help but raise his voice a little. "And send two men instead of one? And double the difficulties? Double the risk?"

"On a Friday, I mean, when you're already in the town."

"I see. You'd like us to go on a little shopping trip, then? While we're at liberty."

"Keep an open mind," says Max. "The next time the commandant's drunk, see, you don't go straight to Vollmer's. You take advantage of the change in schedule, and you go to the shop instead."

"And we tell the antique dealer what, exactly?"

"I don't know. Chaim will think of something."

"Fine. I'll leave it to Chaim. But then we just snatch the painting right out from under the man's nose? Is that what you have in mind?"

"It's only an idea," says Max. "It needs refinement."

"You're right about that," says his father.

*

There are ginger cookies and hot tea on the dining room table, and fat little Kurt can't seem to get enough. He keeps leaving his place in the family tableau and dashing to the table and snatching up another sweet, returning with his mouth full. His father orders him to stop, but his mother intervenes. He's just a growing boy who needs his strength, she says, although Eidel can see that those bundhosen of his are fitting much more closely now than they did back in the wintertime.

Frau Vollmer sips tea and leans over to replace the cup on the table, asking Eidel what has become of her coat. She hasn't seen it hanging in the entryway for a long while now.

"With all respect," Eidel says, frowning down at her palette, "I was able to pass it on to someone more needy."

"More needy?" laughs the woman of the house.

"I hope you don't mind."

Kurt pipes up, his mouth full of crumbs. "I know about this," he says. "I'll bet she traded it for food."

"Now, Kurt. Don't be ridiculous. A beautiful coat like that."

Eidel mixes paint.

"There's a whole black market," says Kurt, swallowing and giving his head a vehement shake. "Isn't that so, Papa?"

Vollmer doesn't move. He may as well be posing for a photograph as for a painting, his chin horizontal, his eyes fixed straight ahead, the faintest suggestion upon his lips of a smile withheld. "There *is* a black market," he says. "No question. I don't suppose I need to add that it's strictly against regulations."

Eidel adjusts herself in her chair.

Frau Vollmer leans forward. "You wouldn't have traded that beautiful coat of mine for something as fleeting as food, would you?"

"Of course not, Madam," says Eidel. "Never."

"I believe you," says the woman of the house.

"Thank you, Madam. It's the truth. I received nothing for it."

There are still cookies on the plate when the session is over, and the instant she's alone Eidel takes two of them. The first she eats right off while she puts her things away, keeping her back to the room in case someone should return. The cookie is soft and thick and dusted with crystalline sugar that she licks away first, trying to pace herself but fearing to be caught. Small bites lead to larger, panic and hunger getting the best of her good intentions, and soon it's gone. The sugar makes her lightheaded and raises her heart rate a little, and she can feel it pumping through her veins like a drug as she hides the other cookie in the pocket of her uniform. The housekeeper returns for the dishes and makes no remark, but Eidel's heart doesn't slow. The cookies are loaded with butter, fragile as dreams, and as she leaves the apartment and makes her way back to the camp she goes carefully lest the one in her pocket crumble to dust.

The delivery commando's wagon is pulled up near the kitchen, and the two men—the little junkman from Witnica and Blackbeard himself, the mender of pots—are hauling a dead woman down the steps. Her legs trail behind, one shoe having come off on the doorsill, her heel scraping against the concrete and leaving a trail of blood. They grunt and toss the corpse onto the wagon—which is loaded up with coal today and not flour, thank God—and then they tip their caps in Eidel's direction, smiling their toothless joy.

She ducks her head and goes in. The door is propped open and the room smells of fire and burned meat, and a woman unknown to Eidel is scraping the top of the stove with a blackened spatula. Whatever she is working at is stubborn as death. Standing at the table nearby is Gretel, looking smaller and more pale than usual. She grits her teeth and draws one shallow breath after another, a little tremor in her jaw, her arms and hands nearly too weak to knead the dough before her.

Eidel comes to the table and reaches into her pocket. The cookie is still nearly intact. She describes it to Gretel, whispers that she's stolen it to appease Rolak, but perhaps—

"The capo is in a rage," says Gretel, barely loud enough to be heard over the scraping of the other woman's spatula. "Don't go wasting it on me."

"Half, then," whispers Eidel. "Just half."

"Rolak would know. You'd be next. Or I would."

"But you need it."

"We all need it." Gretel turns a few degrees, putting her shoulder toward Eidel, a stance that shuns any act of kindness. Through the open door they can see the deliverymen climbing back into their seats, and Gretel tilts her chin to indicate the body on the wagon bed. The face blackened on one side, the uptilted palms worse if anything could be worse. "Go on and give it to the capo," she says. "You must."

Max

THAT TATTOOED GIRL KEEPS ME up to date on how the retrospective is coming along. Just the logistics of it are incredible. Day after day, paintings show up from all over the world. The truth is they've visited places I've never been myself. Venice, for example. I'd love to see Venice, but for some reason I've never made it there and I guess it's probably too late now. Venice was where they built the first ghetto. I wonder how many people know that. How many people, even good Jews, know that the word *ghetto* comes straight from Italy.

Italy of all places. You'd think Germany. Poland.

At any rate there's a gallery over there with two or three things of mine in it. If they hadn't been kind enough to loan one of them to the National Gallery, I don't suppose I'd have ever seen it again. That's the way it is. You paint something and it means the whole world to you while you're painting it and then it's gone.

By God, this thing is turning into a big family reunion. A family reunion without a family, but still. Everything I've ever done is coming home to roost, thanks to that tattooed girl. The one who now spends half of her time here in New York, keeping an eye on me.

I'll bet the Venice picture looks different over there than it will look in Washington. I say *the Venice picture* even though it doesn't have anything to do with Venice other than that it's been on a wall over there for thirty-five or forty years. I wonder if that famous Venetian light has transformed it in some way. I wonder if I'll have trouble recognizing it.

Light, though. As a painter you think about light all the time. You think about light the way a swimmer thinks about water. Light affects everything. It changes everything. By some measure, it *is* everything.

I made a few trips to the basement and brought up some old things from the locker. Paintings I hadn't looked at in the longest time. The light in my studio apartment isn't exactly the misty light of Venice, but it's served me well enough. It's the light I need. That's how it is. You don't just find the subjects that suit you, you find the light that suits you too. Mine comes in a third-floor window in Brooklyn. Willowtown, they call my neighborhood, although there isn't a willow tree in sight. There are plenty of sycamores, though, and they soften the light just enough. In the winter months they don't soften it at all, and that's fine too. Hard light and darkness. That's a lot of what I do.

I had the paintings set out on the couch and on the pass-through to the kitchen and on every functioning easel I could locate, on the windowsills and the counters and the toilet tank, and they were still out when the buzzer sounded. I've hated the sound of an alarm ever since my year in the camp, where three of them in a row would go off to wake you up, and I must admit I jumped.

It was the tattooed girl. Now you tell me what I was supposed to do.

Seventeen

THE JUNKMAN'S WORK IS NEVER DONE. During the interval between evening rations and the second roll call Gretel spies him talking with Rolak, and his presence is the distraction she needs. While he and the capo are haggling over something, the pair of them huddled secretive and confidential as thieves, she slips out the door with a scrap of paper and the stub of her pencil and conceals herself in plain sight at the mouth of an alley between the block and the latrine. The shadows are deep there, but there's just enough light to work on Eidel's story. The Nazis' theft of her family and her art. Vollmer's insistence upon her painting the portrait. The horrifying vision she's created to balance out that painting, for this is what Gretel has decided the drawing in the bunk it is, a leveling-out of things. One more case of the camp's insistence upon keeping good and evil in an immutable ratio.

For every beautiful work of art, an equal and opposite atrocity.

She puts down the story in as much detail as she can. The pencil is hardly as long as a single joint of her finger, and it's almost intractably blunt. To sharpen it would be to waste it, perhaps even to surrender it up as lost, and yet to go on using a blunt pencil is to write too large and waste space. There will never be enough paper to go around, there will never be enough pencil lead to wear away, there will never be enough bottles to store it all up, and yet she soldiers on. By the time she's done, the story has taken up both sides of the paper, marking the first time since beginning her project that she's devoted this much space to a single prisoner's tale. But Eidel has been particularly kind to her after all, so she uses the space she needs without too much in the way of regret, and then she folds the scrap over twice which is all the folding it will stand, and at last with both the paper and the pencil concealed in her tiny fist she comes to her feet and begins drifting back toward the block, keeping close to the wall.

Some object passes between Rolak and the junkman as they part. Something small, but everything that changes hands is small. A cigarette, maybe. A bit of chocolate or cheese. She wonders what power the capo has over the junkman that lets her bid him to do this or that, for as often as she has seen these two exchanging something the transaction has only gone in that same direction. The junkman surely has a capo of his own to report to. Perhaps he fears a bad report from Rolak, manufactured or otherwise. Perhaps he fears a bad report from every single capo at every single stop he makes. Perhaps this avatar of the free and easy life at Auschwitz, making his way from place to place without active oversight, is as penned in as the rest of them after all. Perhaps more so. Perhaps he has learned that the entire camp is a spiderweb rigged to catch him in the slightest transgression, and he only pretends to make the most of it.

Everyone has his own woes. Everyone has a lens through which he must understand the world of the camp. Gretel herself, for example, having seen the transaction between the two of them, reflects only for a moment on the poor junkman before she begins to wonder what fate might lie in store for the scrap of unburned cigarette paper or bit of foil that will remain when Rolak is done with whatever he's given her. She vows to keep an eye out, already adding this potential treasure to the storehouse of material that she keeps for her project. So it is that riches trickle down, even here.

*

They lie in the bunk back to front, Max with Jacob behind him, listening to the noises of the sleeping and the sick. It's hard to fall asleep with the racket and the stench raised by so many collapsing lives—the gasping and the coughing, the scrambling of some individual to the edge of the bunk where he can spill the little contents of his digestive tract onto the floor from one uncontrollable orifice or another—but the alternative is worse, for silence is death.

Jacob steadies his breath and whispers into his son's ear, thinking he's read somewhere that those thoughts reinforced as sleep approaches are best remembered and most deeply understood. "The next time there's a special burial detail," he says, "you must volunteer."

"I can't," says Max. "Wenzel knows my leg won't take much weight."

"Wenzel is in the habit of going easy on you. He'll accommodate your desire to volunteer."

"What if he doesn't?"

"We'll think of something else."

"What if he does?"

"If he does, the leg works to our advantage. A man with a bad leg can't dig a grave very rapidly. So you slip away while the other fellow digs, you get the painting from the town—it's five or six minutes, even for you, the shopkeeper hides the key in the gas lamp beside the door— and then you slip back."

"And the painting?"

"You bury it with the dead man."

"What about the attic over the Officers' Club?"

"There isn't time. We'll move it another day."

"And what if I'm caught?"

"If you're caught they'll kill us all, but they'll kill us all sooner or later. At least we'll have accomplished something. Now go to sleep."

*

It will be the last snowfall of a long season and it comes up out of nowhere, blowing in across the distant hilltops and settling on the camp like something vengeful. Yet Auschwitz endures. The officers gather the collars of their coats around their necks and the Red Cross vans of Zyklon-B career down the treacherous gravel road and the smoke goes up the chimneys.

Gretel has filled up her jar, and although she probably ought to hold off burying it until the weather improves, she can't. Done is done. So after the evening roll call, when she's soaked to the bone anyhow and couldn't possibly get any colder, she retrieves it from its hiding place among the rafters and goes out. The red-brown clay of the yard is still almost impenetrable, and where it's covered over with snow she's reluctant to disturb it. Yet there's one place she knows, a place hidden by little drifts that have collected against the wall of the latrine, and she gravitates in that direction. Other women huddle and mill in the falling snow. The place she's looking for is a weak spot where one of the foundation stones was loose and when she reaches the latrine she sets out to find it, edging along, keeping her back to the wall and kicking with her heel. Snow fills what remains of her shoes, but she doesn't care. Why should she care? The storm keeps up and the wind gusts and she clutches the jar with all her strength. The glass is difficult to grip.

At last one heelstroke finds its target. The loose stone gives way, either sliding a good distance back or perhaps even falling into whatever crawlspace lies beneath the building. Either way it's gone, and Gretel curses her luck. With the stone missing, how can she block the hole? Clay will never do. Someone would notice it.

She lowers herself onto her knees to make certain, pinning the jar against her ribs with one arm and pushing the fingers of her free hand into the hole. Nothing. Nothing but snow and dirt and spiderwebs. It's hopeless. Gretel begins to cry, squatting there with the jar clutched tight and the snow assailing her cheeks and the searchlights slashing the early dark, and when Rolak materializes from nowhere she springs to her feet, gasping.

The jar drops to the hard clay and breaks open, releasing a little storm of paper that takes flight within the bigger storm of snow.

"What's this?" says Rolak.

"Nothing," says Gretel. And then, "I'm sorry."

The wind and wet have pasted some of Gretel's handiwork to the wall, and the capo peels two or three pieces away. She holds one up to what light there is and squints at the smeared letters as the searchlights rake the storm. She can't read more than a hundred words under the best of conditions, but she can read well enough.

*

"That Rosen," she says to the junkman when he comes around the next morning.

"Rosen?" he says, leaning on the shovel and tipping his head toward the kitchen door. "Your Rosen? What of her?"

The capo frowns. "She's been living in the lap of luxury, that one."

"Orders from the top," he says with a shrug.

"*Orders from the top* is right. And what have I gotten for my cooperation? What have I earned from my kindness? A thin wool coat and a bit of ginger cookie, that's what."

*

It's one small shock, but it reverberates throughout the system. By morning the news of Eidel's perfidy has reached all the way to Vollmer, who pushes back from his desk and straightens his perfect tie and dismisses the captain whose secret pleasure it has been to pass the word along to him. This captain, one Heissmeyer, got it from a certain first lieutenant who got it from a certain second lieutenant who got it from a certain sergeant major who got it from only God himself knows who. The trail has gone cold, but by now everyone short of the commandant himself knows about the drawing carved into the bunk in the women's block. Along its upstream course the report has borne with it a cloud of relief and retribution and barely concealed glee, traveling as it has along a dual gradient—from those at the bottom who've resented Eidel's special treatment, to those toward the top who've resented Vollmer's freedom to use her talents as he sees fit. Turning her in will ensure that the parties on both ends of the bargain get what they deserve. That the world of the camp will return to normal. That no one will benefit too much from any advantage, no matter how great.

He walks to the block in question. The sun is out and the ground is soft from last night's snowfall. The change in the weather indicates that spring is here at last. Vollmer's boots get muddy, but he doesn't care. An orderly will polish them. He could have had himself driven here, he could have taken a car, but this is something that he needs to see quietly and alone. He wants no fuss.

Past the kitchen he goes, and when Rolak sticks her head out the door he beckons her with one raised finger, not stopping or even turning his head her way. Doglike she comes along behind. They pass along the fenceline that Jacob walks every Friday morning, a commando of prisoners wrestling creosoted railroad ties beyond the barbed wire and the French doctor standing in the dark door of the hospital with his hands folded behind his back and his face pulled down into a frown as a van pulls away in a spray of mud. The sun warms everything.

The block is empty. Vollmer steps inside and orders Rolak to bring him to the bunk in question.

"*You* found this," he says. "No?"

"Yes," she says, permitting herself a little smile. "I found it, *sturmbannführer.*"

He bends to look at the ceiling of the bunk but it isn't easy. Every surface is filthier than every other surface and he's reluctant to touch anything but touch it all he must, getting down on his knees and leaning in and craning his neck to look up at the drawing. He doesn't need to see much. When he regains his feet his face is red, but it could be from the exertion.

Rolak smiles at him, utterly satisfied with everything. "Just as I said, no?"

Vollmer doesn't acknowledge the question. "Have you a box of matches?" he says.

"What would I light?" Showing him her yellow teeth.

"Don't press me," says Vollmer. She unlocks the door to her little cell and goes in. She keeps a box under the mattress with twelve or fifteen matches in it, and she tips out all but three rather than let Vollmer have them.

He's waiting in the doorway when she turns back, idly toying with the padlock. "All of them," he says. "Just in case."

She returns and gathers the rest and gives him a sheepish look as she hands them over.

"Now kerosene," he says. "That lamp on your table."

"Yes sir," she says, unscrewing the tank. "This is just what we need to burn away that thing. Shall we take the entire bunk outdoors? Burn it in the yard? I'm sure whichever way you choose will be the best."

"We'll be doing nothing of the kind," says Vollmer. "Stop trying to use your head."

She smiles brightly through those yellow teeth. "Yes, sir," she says, as he closes the door with her inside and slips the padlock through the clasp.

"Leave it to me," he says through the door. He holds the tank up into the light and frowns at it, for there's not nearly enough kerosene there to do the job. So he puts it down and walks without the slightest haste to the next block over, where he locates a tin container holding the better part of a gallon. Then he returns at a steady pace, holding the container away from his leg so as not to soil his trousers, not hurrying, not even actually hearing Rolak's cries as they rise from the locked compartment. She's hammering on the door with something large and heavy, either the table or the chair that the SS has wasted on her, but there's hammering everywhere in the camp. Once back inside he empties the little tank first, using all of it on the offending bunk. Then he opens the larger container and splashes kerosene on the floor and on the rest of the bunks and on anything flammable upon which his eye lands. A blanket. A urine-soaked mattress. A single forlorn shoe.

When the container is empty he goes out and sets it in the yard, and then he returns and stands in the doorway. "Capo?" he calls. And when her pounding and crying doesn't stop he waits. "Capo?" he calls again, when she's paused for breath.

Silence answers.

"Had you seen to your duties properly," he says, selecting a match from his pocket, "this would not have been necessary."

*

The rumors are everywhere, numberless and varied as birds, as if the warm weather has brought them. Some indicate that one of the prisoners set the fire in a failed suicide attempt that has landed her in the hospital *en route* to a slightly delayed doom. Others say the capo is responsible, big fat Rolak temporarily absent from duty, smoking in her bed during working hours. Some say that every woman in the block survived and some say that all of them died and most of these latter envy them for it. Still others report that the women weren't present at all, although some of them were called back from their stations to fight the blaze when the fire brigade failed to appear, that band of worthless layabouts busy lolling around the rooftop water tank they're widely known to use for a swimming pool in warmer weather. Reliable reports suggest they have a diving board, although no one has ever seen it.

Never mind the diving board. Never mind the fire brigade. Jacob asks and asks and asks again, asks everyone he knows and many he doesn't, hoping that a pattern of reliable information will eventually emerge. He asks all afternoon and he asks all evening and he asks all night, and in the end the only thing he knows for certain—since he's seen it with his own eyes—is that Eidel's block has been burned utterly to the ground. Not a stick remains. Perhaps, as those who speak up in defense of the fire brigade maintain, it's true that some member of the SS kept them at bay and oversaw the destruction personally and utterly. Vollmer, some say. The commandant, say others. And a wild-eyed few maintain that it was Satan himself, although why the devil would want to inflict any damage upon the facilities at Auschwitz is a mystery beyond knowing. Perhaps he too works in mysterious ways.

There's additional information making the rounds in Canada the next day, but none of it is necessarily more credible than anything he's already heard. Vollmer's name comes up again and again. But it always comes up. Prisoners can be counted on to discuss the highest ranks of the camp's management with the kind of certainty and devotion that men under other circumstances would reserve for the discussion of gods.

Even little Chaim, happening by Canada on his way to who knows where, doesn't know for certain. "Somebody died," he says. "That's all I know. But somebody always dies."

Friday comes again before Jacob can get any kind of satisfaction. He'd rush through the morning's haircuts if there were anything to be achieved by it, if he could speed up the turning of the world or alter the fixed routine of the camp by the work of his own hands, but the stream of officers moves on its own schedule and there's nothing he can do to change it. The day drags. Even lunch at that rough plank table, a sumptuous feast of chicken and apples and root vegetables all roasted together and smelling like a holiday, tastes like ashes.

Chaim snaps him out of his revery with a word and the flash of a napkin that he's filched from somewhere. "Save that leg for Max, why don't you?" The cook is gone for a moment and he holds up the white linen like a toreador. "You'll know about her soon enough. Regardless of what's happened, Max needs to eat."

Even the commandant is sober today, sober and entertaining a group of visitors from Berlin who keep him occupied before his haircut and distracted during it and whose presence generally slows things down in any number of frustrating ways. Jacob would kill Liebehenschel if he could. He would kill them all, if the consequences of such a thing weren't already determined. Standing there armed while the commandant pontificates on some point of military law, his foamy jowls flapping and his already low brow knitted like the most devoted Torah scholar, Jacob vows that he will do just that—he will murder him—if Eidel has been killed in the fire.

What could he and Max live for with her gone?

His mind races as the razor drips. Should his wife be lost, everything will be possible. All strictures will be removed. And he knows exactly what he will do. He'll persuade Chaim to feign illness, and in the boy's place he'll arrange to use Max as his assistant. For just one day. One day is all they'll need. The two of them, father and son, will murder Liebehenschel together, locking the door to keep the cook and the housekeeper out and tying him to his chair with the linen drape and letting his blood paint the walls and soak the carpets and run down between the floorboards. Then out the window they'll go. Out the window to freedom or whatever else might be waiting.

An entirely different dream comes true, though, when they reach Vollmer's apartment.

They find the dining room the same as ever, although the windows are open to permit the breeze to begin scouring away the stale air of winter. Eidel's materials are neatly arranged in a corner as usual, the painting hidden beneath its white sheet. The easel faces out into the room, and with a kind of urgency that he's never quite felt before—an urgency driven by fear that she may have set her brush to this panel for the last time—Jacob dares to step over and lift the sheet and see what lies beneath it.

Every bit of oxygen leaves his body. He doesn't care that the painting shows Vollmer and his family. He doesn't even *register* that it shows Vollmer and his family. To him they may as well be a bowl of fruit, a sunset, for to him the painting shows Eidel in every stroke, Eidel his one beloved, Eidel and Eidel alone. He stands enraptured before it—before *her*—when Vollmer enters, his usual self, dour, stiff as a hairbrush, and he's too absorbed to release the drapery and get to work, too dumbstruck to invent some fawning remark as to how handsome the family looks in their portrait, too uplifted to note that he's been caught transgressing at all.

So Vollmer leads the way instead, taking up another corner of the white drapery and studying the painting with his head tilted at an angle and saying, "One more session, maybe two, and she will be finished."

"Then she's still alive," says Jacob. Saying it without daring to say it. The words just coming out. "After the fire."

"Oh, yes. She's very much alive."

And thus the spell is broken. He can go on.

*

Who else but the junkman? Count on that little itinerant opportunist from the country to gather up such tags and scraps of information as sift down among the dregs of this world and assemble them into something of meaning, if not exactly worth. Count on him to reach, in his own way, the bottom of everything.

"You're still here!" he says to Jacob as Blackbeard pulls the old horse to a stop alongside the outdoor sorting tables of Canada. With the change of the seasons the work here is perhaps a little better than before, but the scale is always relative.

"Oh, yes," says Jacob. "I'm still here. My pardon hasn't come through."

"What a kidder," says the junkman. "If you're still here, it's only because your wife hasn't finished the painting."

"The *sturmbannführer* said she has another session or two." He says it like a person who enjoys consulting with the *sturmbannführer* on a routine basis.

"Today's Sunday," says the junkman, lifting his hat to scratch underneath it. "So that's one down. One to go."

"One what?"

"One more session before it's over. You heard about the picture, didn't you?"

"Heard about it? I've seen it with my own eyes. Right there in Vollmer's dining room. It's a masterpiece."

"No. Not *that* picture." The junkman cranes his neck to be sure that Jankowski isn't observing them. "I mean the *other* picture. The one she drew in her bunk. The one that Vollmer burned down the block to get rid of."

"I don't know about any such picture."

"According to what I hear," says the junkman, "it was't especially flattering." And then Blackbeard clicks his tongue and the horse begins to draw away and the junkman tips his hat, raising it with a slowness that gives this farewell a quality of absolute valediction.

*

Jacob finds himself praying that someone will die soon, and he doesn't care who it might be as long as it's someone who deserves one of Wenzel's special burial details. There hasn't been any pattern to these things that Jacob can discern, any connection to the dead man's nationality or reputation or duties, any link to the weather or the time, but that just makes his prayer all the more fervent. He doesn't even know whom he's praying to, exactly—the God of Abraham or some other god, lesser or greater—but pray he does and with a vengeance.

A special burial detail will be Max's opportunity to escape. Never mind the painting of poor lost Lydia. Never mind rescuing it and never mind preserving it. It's gone and Lydia is gone and very soon Eidel and Jacob himself will be gone too. The time has come to accept all that.

Max, though.

Max, he can save.

So he tells him there's been a change in plans. He's to forget the pipedream of salvaging Lydia's picture. He's to escape, simple as that. He's to go out on a burial detail and never return.

"I won't go without you," says the boy. For he's still a boy, regardless. A boy to whom his father cannot and will not explain everything.

They're in the bunk again, back to front, the father dripping lies into the son's ear like poison or its antidote. "They won't," he says. "Your mother is still in an enviable position. They won't harm us, not while Vollmer needs her. And if you go now, while she still has a good bit of work left, they'll forget about you altogether."

"They never forget."

"They do. They will."

"No."

"Yes. In this case. Vollmer's pride will make him forget."

Max stiffens.

His father presses himself closer, whispering. "That painting of your mother's will save us all if you let it. But you'll have to be the one to go first. You must have faith." It's an impossible request, but he makes it.

Max breathes. "What about you?"

"We'll come along later. We'll find a way. I promise."

*

The days pass slowly. Men die. One by one and two by two and a dozen at a time they go off to be buried or burned by the *Sonderkommando*, but not once does a special burial detail materialize. Day follows day, bringing death but not enough of it. Jacob waits and watches and wonders what sort of creature he's become.

Wednesday crawls past with Jacob propped against his table in Canada, leaning forward and then back as he works, unconsciously recapitulating the motion of old men at prayer. Thus do the ancient forms come back, invoked by the flesh if not by the spirit. Jankowski is in a jolly mood today, perhaps his first on record, and life in Canada is placid, so Jacob's intense concentration goes unnoticed and unremarked. As he works he watches the yard for the appearance of anyone from his block—they're at work extending a bit of railroad track on the other side of the camp, and the labor is brutal and the footing is treacherous in the spring mud and from time to time an injured or dead prisoner will return either on foot or in a wheelbarrow. Losses have been high. He watches and hopes and he lets two dreams mingle in his mind, one of Max making his escape tonight, and the other of himself committing murder tomorrow—with no possibility of retribution beyond the two deaths that are already fated. This time, though, it's Vollmer, not Liebe-henschel, who goes under his razor.

But Friday morning comes all the same. Max breaks off for Canada and Jacob breaks off to meet Chaim by the fence, but not before telling his son to keep an eye out. Keep his fingers crossed. Perhaps tonight will be the night when their good fortune strikes.

Max says there's no hurry, and his father doesn't disagree.

At the administration building, though, word awaits that neither

Vollmer nor Liebehenschel will require the barber's services today. The clerk tells Chaim that they've been called to Berlin, but Jacob doesn't believe her. Something is afoot. Perhaps the painting is already complete and Eidel is dead—the kitchen door was closed again today, so who knows?—and Vollmer has given orders that Jacob is to go straight to the ovens when his morning's work is finished. But how could that be? Wouldn't Vollmer have done the thing right away, if Eidel had finished the painting last Saturday? Wouldn't Jacob have felt something, some deep and unmistakable burst of woe within his heart, if she were already under the ground?

And yet the day passes. He cuts hair and he shaves necks and he believes that each mustache he trims will be his last. Noon comes and the cook sets out a meal according to her custom, but Jacob doesn't have any appetite. He watches Chaim eat, settling his stomach with sips of water and putting a little something in his pocket for Max, thinking that this morsel will see one of two very different fates. Either the entire Rosen family will be wiped out tomorrow and this will have been his son's last proper meal, or else Max will get away tonight without having had the opportunity to eat it—leaving it to be found instead in Jacob's own pocket when they go through his clothes.

*

The good news, unveiled when they return to Canada, is that there's been a catastrophe on the rail project and scores of men have died. Some were buried alive in an instant, and some were hauled away for burial or burning elsewhere, and the rest were merely covered up where they fell. The luck of the draw. There were hundreds of injuries as well, more than the hospital can possibly hold, and broken men lie scattered about the yard as if felled by some military encounter. The French doctor paces among them, his hands folded behind his back.

The deaths keep up all afternoon and into the evening, wrecked bodies giving up the ghost one after another. Everything falls apart. A van comes to the block and takes away some of the bodies. Two guards from the fenceline stroll over like a pair of bored gunslingers and put an end to the suffering of a few more, but because it seems a waste of ammunition when they're so close to death already they cease fire and advise Wenzel to have them loaded up as they are, dead or otherwise. What's the difference. But the capo doesn't report to them, so he keeps on.

When roll call comes, it's impossible. Every man, alive or dead, seems to be propping up another man in the gathering darkness. Sometimes a pair of them breathe their last at the same time, as if nothing but mutuality has been holding them up, and together they collapse, inward and downward, sliding onto the clay. Wenzel's trusted clipboard and his businesslike intentions are of no use now, not in the face of so much onrushing random death. He sends word that he needs another van, but no van comes.

"*Now,*" whispers Jacob to his son. "Find some other strong young fellow. Tell Wenzel he can rely on you to bury a couple of corpses, out beyond the fence."

Max has a different idea. He steps forward and volunteers all right, but not with some other young man from the block. Not at all. Instead he volunteers himself and his father. Together. As a team. The proposal comes from his lips as if he's been planning it this way for a while, and he has. At least since this new torrent of death has begun. Why not? Deprived of his usual sense of order, Wenzel might never miss them. He might assume that they've been killed too, hauled off in one of the vans perhaps, their serial numbers unnoted in the rush. It's possible.

Except Wenzel still has some of his wits about him. "You go," he says to Max. "And you as well," pointing to another prisoner altogether. "This isn't some family outing."

Max

DID I UNDERSTAND THAT I WAS leaving them to die? I suppose I did. It was a long time ago, and what I remember most is the weight of the moment, the pressure and the opportunity, with death all around and my father telling me it was time to go and Wenzel giving me the order. What else could I do? Regardless of the year I'd spent in Auschwitz, I was still a child.

My mother would have wanted it as much as my father did. They'd had enough of dread. We'd all had enough. And if they couldn't save Lydia, at least they could save me.

So I did as I was told. Until I got beyond the fence, anyhow.

The key to the antique shop was exactly where Chaim had said it would be. The painting was in a bin, rolled up with some others. I wrapped it up in brown paper and tied it with string, and I helped myself to a heavy coat that was hanging on a peg behind the counter, and I pocketed every coin that was in the cashbox. And then I set out toward what I hoped was France.

I traveled by night, keeping to the margins of anything like civilization—if you could call what was happening in Poland and Germany at that time *civilization*. I lived like an animal, furtive and shy of human contact and very nearly starving, which was nothing new. The whole world terrified me.

I had no sense of myself, really. The whole way to England and beyond, I didn't have any more sense of who I was than a rat has. It had been wrung right out of me. I can't say when I recovered it, or if I ever really did. Maybe not entirely.

Back in the sixties, people spent a lot of time talking about alienation—in those days you couldn't swing a cat without hitting somebody who was talking about alienation, not in the art world anyhow—and it always seemed to me that I could give them all lessons on the subject. You don't know what alienation is, until you've been alienated from yourself. Those people in my paintings, with their backs turned and their eyes averted? They're not just uninterested in *you;* they're uninterested in *themselves.* They don't even recognize themselves. They've lost track of who they are, they count for so little in the world.

But nobody asked me about all that. Everyone was too busy explaining their theories to everyone else. Not that I would have told them, even if I'd been asked straight out. It's only in a moment of weakness that I'd ever consider explaining anything, and moments of weakness always pass.

The only thing that occupied my mind on my long trek across Europe was my mother's painting. You could picture the two of us as an Olympian and his flaming torch, as long as you didn't imagine anything too heroic. I was just a broken boy with a badly-healed leg and an empty belly and a stolen past, making his way toward a future that he couldn't imagine. But I did have the painting. It led me on, drawing me away from one thing and pulling me toward something else. In that way, I believe it saved my life all over again.

*

Call it a moment of weakness, then, when the tattooed girl from the National Gallery rang my bell and I let her up without putting everything away first. But how could I have done otherwise? She was in the lobby, and I'd have had to get to the basement, and it was impossible.

The painting was right there in the middle of the couch. My mother's painting. There's certainly no mistaking it for one of mine, and particular evidence to that effect was everywhere, on windowsills and on easels and on every stick of furniture I own. Failed attempt after failed attempt. I kid myself, you see. I'm pathetically hopeful. I bring them up now and then and I look at them in all kinds of light—two or three at a time, a dozen at a time—but the truth is that they never get any better.

You can't paint someone else's painting, even though I've tried.

The tattooed girl dropped her briefcase as if she'd never seen paint on canvas before. She didn't ask where I'd been keeping these pictures or why, even though she'd asked a million times if I had anything else tucked away somewhere. Something I hadn't shown anyone. She didn't criticize me for misleading her. And she didn't say a word about Wyeth and his goddamned Helga, thank God.

The truth is that she was dumbstruck, and she stood there in front of the couch with her mouth open for a while before she thought to ask me anything at all. I told her a little. Just enough. How the girl in the painting was my sister, how she'd been murdered on our first day in the camp, and how my mother had painted this picture back when we'd lived in Zakopane. Back before the war, when all of us were children. I didn't say how this one painting was all I had left, but anyone could have seen that.

And now it's on its way to the National Gallery. My mother's painting along with a few of my lousy copies by way of contrast, all of them crated up like the treasures of King Tut and loaded into an armored van. Such caution, so much security, for a painting that I carried rolled up in butcher paper over better than a thousand miles' worth of occupied Europe. A painting I used for a walking stick when I could barely stand on my own.

According to the tattooed girl, it's exactly what she's been yearning for all along. That was her word. *Yearning.* She said something about devoting one modest gallery to *contexts* and *influences* and so on, the way they do, and using my mother's painting as the centerpiece. I believe that's what she said. I wasn't paying attention. I was busy watching them box it up for the trip. I was hoping that they'd light it properly down in Washington, although I suppose I shouldn't worry too much about that. The light coming in through that attic window, with my mother behind the canvas and my father working downstairs and my sister dreaming away at her table, will be enough.

* * *

Notes and Acknowledgments

My last novel, *Kings of the Earth,* was in many ways a memorial to central New Yorkers of my parents' generation—country people whose voices are dying out and whose stories are on the verge of vanishing forever. In *The Thief of Auschwitz,* I hope to have created a second memorial to that same generation, this time honoring those on my wife's side of the family of man—the Jewish side—whose stories are likewise in danger of being lost.

Reading and rereading the first-person accounts of Wiesel and Frankl and Nyiszli over a period of a year or two, I had no plan to write a book. But along the way I discovered something within myself that disturbed me to no end: the more closely I studied the raw materials, the more repellent they became and the more difficulty I had in maintaining my focus on them. It was as if the facts themselves, horrible and numberless as they were, were conspiring to drive me away again and again, preventing me from connecting with the people behind them as fully as I needed to.

Supposing that other readers might face the same difficulty, and intent on the preservation of these voices and these stories, I wondered if fiction might provide an answer. I hope that it has, at least a little, by way of this book.

As always, I owe a great debt to my first readers, Wendy and Emily and David and Robbie, whose guidance and patience and support are so terribly important to me. Thanks are due as well to my far-flung internet correspondents—Amy, Danielle, Elizabeth, Jessica, Karen, Keith, Lauren,

Renee, Sachin, and Tasha—who have provided me with so much wise counsel and so much encouragement for so very long. And last, I mustn't sign off without a tip of the hat to Sam Winston, who went on ahead.

Jon Clinch — The Green Mountains, 2012

*

Also by Jon Clinch:

> *Finn*
> *Kings of the Earth*
> *What Came After* (writing as Sam Winston)

*

Jon Clinch is on the web:

> *Web site:* jonclinch.com
> *Twitter:* @jonclinch
> *Facebook:* facebook.com/JonClinchBooks
> Visit jonclinch.com to download a Reading Group Guide.